The Devil
Who Tamed Her

Also by Johanna Lindsey

Captive of My Desires
Marriage Most Scandalous
A Loving Scoundrel
A Man to Call My Own

JOHANNA LINDSEY

The Devil Who Tamed Her

POCKET BOOKS

NEW YORK LONDON TORONTO SYDNEY

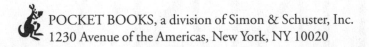 POCKET BOOKS, a division of Simon & Schuster, Inc.
1230 Avenue of the Americas, New York, NY 10020

This Pocket Books hardcover edition June 2007

ISBN-13: 978-1-4165-3730-4
ISBN-10:   1-4165-3730-9

10   9   8   7   6   5   4   3   2   1

POCKET and colophon are registered trademarks of
Simon & Schuster, Inc.

Manufactured in the United States of America

For information regarding special discounts for bulk purchases,
please contact Simon & Schuster Special Sales at
1-800-456-6798 or business@simonandschuster.com

*For Sharon and Douglas, who made
sneakers and mashed potatoes a recipe for memories.
Thanks for so many years of laughter.*

The Devil
Who Tamed Her

Chapter One

I<small>T WAS QUITE A DISTINCTION</small> to be the most beautiful and desirable debutante to join the marriage mart in a century, and also be the most hated woman in England. Oddly enough, Ophelia Reid had strived for that distinction, on both counts. It was her bane to be so beautiful that people behaved like utter fools around her.

The people gathered at Summers Glade, the Marquis of Birmingdale's country estate, were no different. Ophelia stopped at the top of the grand staircase. She'd hoped the foyer would be empty, but no such luck. It appeared that many of the people who had come for her wedding to the marquis's heir were gathered below, some who were, apparently, already aware that the wedding had been called off and were preparing to leave. Others appeared confused and were talking excitedly. But the moment she appeared, all eyes turned to her, and as usual the whispering began.

It might appear to the people below that she was making a grand entrance. She was rather fond of doing so and was quite practiced at it. But not this time. A grand exit was more like it, though not by her choice. She had *hoped* to leave unnoticed.

"When are you going to tell me what happened?" asked her maid, Sadie O'Donald, who was beside her.

"I'm not," Ophelia said stiffly.

"But you were supposed to get married today."

As if Ophelia could have overlooked that appalling fact. But now wasn't the time to discuss it. "Hush, we have an audience if you hadn't noticed."

Sadie said no more as she followed Ophelia down the stairs. The whispering grew louder. Ophelia even caught a few bits and pieces of conversations.

"First they're engaged, then they're not, then they are again, and now they've changed their minds yet again. She's too fickle, if you ask me."

"The groom said it was a mutual decision to cancel the wedding."

"I doubt it, she's just hard to please, but I would be too if I looked like her."

"I agree. It's a sin to be that beautiful."

"Careful, dear, your jealousy is showing."

"—spoiled rotten if you ask me."

"Shh, she'll hear you. She has a viper's tongue, you know. You don't want her turning it on you."

"Good God, she's beautiful. An angel, a—"

"—back on the marriage block. Don't mind saying how delighted I am. Gives me a second chance."

"I thought she turned you down before the Season even began."

"Me and countless others, but we didn't know she was already engaged to MacTavish."

"Don't waste your time. Your title isn't grand enough for her. She could have a king if she set her cap for one."

"Surprised her parents didn't aspire to that. They're appalling social climbers, you know."

"And she isn't?"

"She just turned down the marquis's heir, what does that tell you?"

"That her parents are going to be furious with her, as they were when—"

"Now Locke there might stand a chance as the next Duke of Norford. Surprised to see him back in England."

"He's not interested in getting married, or did you never hear that he left England just to get away from all those marriage-minded—"

Ophelia pretended that she hadn't heard any of those whispers, but the mention of Raphael Locke, Viscount Lynnfield, made her look at him. She'd known he was there in the foyer bidding some of his acquaintances good-bye, or possibly leaving as well. He was the first person she'd noticed when she reached the stairs. But then a man as handsome as the Norford heir had drawn her notice from the moment she'd first glanced at him.

She'd even considered him briefly for a husband, before she'd gotten reengaged to Duncan MacTavish. But Locke had obviously gone over to the enemy camp, the camp that thought the worst of her. What had he called her? A "spiteful rumormonger." He'd even threatened to ruin her if she told anyone she thought that he'd been bedding Sabrina Lambert.

She *had* thought it was true. Why else was he paying so much attention to that little wren Sabrina? But he could have just told her she was mistaken, instead of insulting her. And she wished it had been *anyone* but him who'd caught her crying upstairs.

"How are we getting home?" Sadie whispered when they reached the bottom of the stairs.

"In my coach, of course," Ophelia replied.

"Your coach doesn't have a driver. The blasted man hasn't returned yet."

Ophelia had forgotten about that. Her father's man hadn't wanted to bring her back to Yorkshire in the first place, and once they'd arrived here after much persuasion on her part, he had insisted he'd lose his job if he didn't return to London posthaste to let her parents know where she had run off to. As if she hadn't intended to send off a note to them herself. In due time. When she stopped being so furious about that slap her father had given her after Duncan had broken their first engagement and they'd all been ousted from Summers Glade.

"We'll just have to borrow one of the marquis's footmen, I suppose. That fellow bringing down my trunks will do. You can inform him while I wait in the parlor."

She would have preferred to wait outside, away from the marquis's remaining guests, but while she'd already donned her traveling coat, it was designed to flatter her figure, not to provide warmth, and in the heart of winter it was simply too cold to stand outside for any length of time. But since it appeared that most of the guests were in the foyer waiting for their own coaches to be brought around, she hoped the parlor would be empty.

She moved into that room. It wasn't empty. The occupant was the one person she'd hoped never to see again, Mavis Newbolt, her onetime best friend, now her worst enemy. And it was too late to find a different place to wait. Mavis had noticed her.

"Running away with your tail between your legs?" Mavis smirked.

Oh, God, not again. Hadn't her former friend said enough when she'd arrived to prevent what everyone involved considered a tragic marriage? Apparently not.

"Hardly," Ophelia replied, her emotions well in hand now. Her old friend was *not* going to make her cry again. "How galling it must have been for you to do me that favor today, so I wouldn't have to marry the Scotsman."

"I told you I didn't do it for you. You're the last person I'd ever help."

"Yes, yes, I know, you were playing the heroine just for Duncan's sake. But you still saved me from having to marry him. I suppose I should thank you."

"Don't!" Mavis snarled, the curls on her head shaking. "No more pretenses, Pheli. We both hate each other—"

"Stop it!" Ophelia cut in sharply before the wound opened again. "You don't have your audience now to revile me in front of, so the truth if you please. You were the only real friend I ever had and you know it. I loved you! If I didn't, I wouldn't have tried to protect you from Lawrence by showing you the truth about him. But you preferred to blame me for his perfidy. And, how did you put it? That the only reason you continued to abide my presence is you were waiting all this time to witness my downfall? And you called *me* spiteful?"

"I told you I barely recognize myself anymore," Mavis said defensively. "But that's your fault. You made me so bitter that I don't even like myself."

"No, I didn't, *he* did. Your precious Lawrence, who used you to get close to me. There, I've finally said it. I tried to spare you that too. He was begging me to marry him all the while he was courting you, but I'm done protecting you from the truth, Mavis."

"You're such a liar! And yet you branded me one in front of our friends."

"Oh, so now they're 'friends' again, those two leeches? When you pointed out today that Jane and Edith are no friends of mine? As if I don't know that? And you provoked me that day I called you a liar. You know you did. How long did you think I'd continue to put up with your catty, snide remarks without retaliating? You know better than anyone how little patience I have. But I reserved it for you. I certainly have none left for Jane and Edith, who we both know only come around because it's fashionable to be seen at my side. But you failed to mention that today, didn't you, when you were reviling me for all my faults. You claimed I use them?" Ophelia snorted. "You know very well it's just the opposite, that every one of my so-called friends use me and my popularity to further their own ends. Good God, you used to point that out yourself, when *you* were my friend."

"I knew you'd come up with excuses," Mavis said stiffly.

"The truth isn't an excuse," Ophelia countered. "I know all my own faults, and my temper is the worst of them. But who usually sets off my temper?"

"What has that to do with how spiteful you are?"

"You're the one who brought it up, Mavis. You claimed that Jane and Edith spent all their time with me trying to soothe my ruffled feathers so I wouldn't turn my spite on them. That was quite an allegation. Would you care to discuss it now that we don't have an audience for you to impress with your vindictiveness?"

Mavis gasped. "I'm not the vindictive one, Pheli, you are. And it was the absolute truth. You've turned on them in the past, yet you had the gall to try to deny it today."

"Because you were making more of it than it was. Of course I've lost my temper with them, many times, but you failed to mention I did so, because they're sycophants. All of my so-called friends are. And it's their toadying and insincere flattery that usually make me lose my temper in the first place."

Mavis shook her head. "I don't know why I bothered to point out how mean you are. You'll never change. You'll always be caught up in yourself, causing others misery."

"Oh, come now, we both know exactly why you said everything you did today. You even admitted you only continued to pretend to be my friend so you'd be around to witness my downfall. Well, have I fallen down, my dear? I don't think so. I'll return to London and marry one of those idiots who profess to love me, but what about you? Are you happy, now that you've spilled all of your bitterness at my feet? Oh, wait, you didn't exactly get the revenge you really wanted, did you? I've merely been saved from a disastrous marriage—by you. And thank you very much. I mean that sincerely."

"Go to the devil!" Mavis snapped, and marched out of the room.

Ophelia closed her eyes, fighting back more tears. She should have just walked out of the room when she saw Mavis there. She shouldn't have rehashed that horrible scene she'd had with her old friend earlier.

"Should I applaud? And here I'd thought you two had finished the performance earlier."

Ophelia stiffened. *Him*. God, she couldn't believe she'd cried on *his* shoulder today. But she'd overcome that appalling weakness and was in control now.

She turned around and raised a brow at him. "Hardly a performance when we *thought* we were alone. Eavesdropping, Lord Locke? How shamefully boorish of you."

He grinned unrepentantly. "Couldn't help m'self, when your transformation is so fascinating. How fleeting was the damsel in distress. But I see the imperious ice queen is in true form again."

"Go to the devil!" she shot back, borrowing Mavis's parting line. And as her former friend had done, she marched out of the room as well.

Chapter Two

"WHAT WAS SHE TALKING ABOUT?"

"Why do I feel insulted?"

"She must have overheard you talking about her. I *told* you not to talk so loud."

"I don't gossip," said a female voice with a humph.

"You were doing just that. But don't worry about it. A pretty gel like that will always inspire gossip."

Raphael was chuckling softly to himself as he listened to the indignant huffing in the foyer. The ice queen, the name he had given to Ophelia Reid, his friend's ex-fiancée, hadn't just taken her annoyance out on him for his remarks that caused her to storm off. She'd also said to the large group in the foyer, "Don't mind me, I'm just passing through. You can get back to gossiping about me in a moment," before she disappeared back upstairs.

The tongues had returned to wagging, just louder this time, now that they were assured Ophelia wasn't as close as the next room. What a fascinating creature she was, much more complex than he'd first thought, when all he'd known about her was her capacity for starting and spreading nasty rumors.

Raphael hadn't expected to make new friends in this small corner of Yorkshire. Being the Duke of Norford's firstborn and in line for the title, he'd never lacked for friends, real or otherwise, but had lost touch with most of his chums when he'd gone abroad several years ago. He was surprised at how quickly he'd taken to Duncan MacTavish though, possibly because the Scot was so testy when they'd first met and was so easy to rile up, which he'd found quite amusing.

They were of a similar age, Raphael in his midtwenties, Duncan a bit younger. Both were tall, strapping young men, athletically built, quite handsome, though they otherwise looked nothing alike. Duncan's hair was an unfashionable dark red, his eyes dark blue, while Raphael was blessed with blond locks and blue eyes of a lighter shade. And their positions were identical in that they were both at the top of the list of the most sought-after bachelors to show up in the same Season, both in line to inherit esteemed titles.

Raphael wasn't looking for a wife though and wouldn't be doing so for a good number of years yet. But Duncan had two grandfathers who agreed that he couldn't get started soon enough on producing their next heir, which was why so many young debutantes had been invited to Summers Glade, and why for once, Raphael wasn't the object of their pursuit. The ton knew that Duncan wanted a wife, and that Raphael didn't.

Oddly enough, the one female that Duncan had shown the most interest in hadn't been invited to the gathering, Sabrina Lambert, his charming neighbor. Such an adorable chit, no beauty, but priceless nonetheless with her wonderful sense of humor that could cheer even the dourest disposition. Raphael had only been half-joking when he'd asked her to marry him himself! But he'd quickly become friends with Sabrina—how could anyone not—and had even dabbled at matchmaking, something he'd never done before, to get her and Duncan to realize they were made for each other.

"What's all the jabbering aboot?" Duncan said when he joined Raphael in the entrance hall.

"Do you really need to ask?" Raphael replied with a grin, and motioned for them to move into the parlor where they wouldn't be overheard. "Ophelia caught your guests gossiping about her and actually remarked on it."

"She hasna left yet?"

"Just waiting for her coach I believe. But you'll never guess what happened after the Newbolt chit was done reviling Ophelia. I'm still a bit dazed by it m'self."

Raphael had listened to most of Mavis's earlier allegations when she'd arrived to save the day, spilling a good deal of bile that pretty much explained why she was Ophelia's enemy. Some of it he'd just heard repeated in the parlor between them, though Mavis hadn't seemed nearly as vitriolic when she'd thought she and Ophelia were alone. She'd actually seemed a bit defensive, leading him to wonder if any of them had really heard the whole of it.

However earlier, he hadn't felt that Ophelia was quite contrite enough for all the trouble she'd caused, and he'd intended to castigate her some himself. He certainly hadn't expected what had occurred when he'd caught her alone upstairs.

He didn't keep Duncan in suspense any longer. "Ophelia Reid was in my arms, crying her heart out. It was a most amazing experience!"

Duncan wasn't amazed, in fact his snort was quite loud. "So you dinna ken the difference 'tween fake tears and real ones?"

"On the contrary, they were quite real. Look here at my shoulder. My coat is still a little damp."

"A little spit, nae doubt," Duncan scoffed, barely glancing at Raphael's coat.

Raphael laughed, but then Duncan hadn't been present to see the tears running down Ophelia's pretty face. "By God, they're real, aren't they?" he'd said to Ophelia when he set her back from him after she'd collided with him in the upstairs hall. He'd even touched her wet cheek with his finger before he'd added, "And you thought to not share them with anyone? I'm impressed."

"Leave . . . me be," she'd barely managed to choke out.

He didn't. Awkwardly, and utterly amazed by his own impulse, he had drawn her back to him and let her make use of his shoulder. Appalling shortcoming of his, to be a sucker for tears, real ones, that is, but there it was, and he was bloody well likely to regret it in this instance.

He'd sighed inwardly, but there was no help for it. Ophelia's narrow body was trembling with emotion, and it was incredible just how much emotion was pouring out on his shoulder. Not that he thought the ice inside her was melting. No indeed. Never would he think that. The Lockes did not raise fools.

But to Duncan he said now, "What a skeptic you are, old man, but I *do* happen to know the difference. Fake tears have no effect on me, none whatsoever, but real ones manage to wrench my gut every bloody time. It's my gut that tells me what's real or not. My sister's tears, for instance, my gut tells me they're *always* fake."

"Tears from Ophelia would imply she was hurt by that verbal lashing Mavis gave her, but I've proof tae the contrary," Duncan said.

"What proof?"

"When I was thinking I'd be stuck wi' the lass, I feared it would be impossible for her tae change, that she was tae far gone in her self-absorption. I was sure it was a lost cause. So I confronted her. I told her that I dinna like her ways, dinna like the spite she was capable of, dinna like the way she treated people, as if nae one matters but herself. But I was desperate, so I told her we could live in peace only if she could change. D'you think she agreed tae try?"

"If you really did say all that to her, she probably got defensive," Raphael guessed.

Duncan shook his head. "Nae, she merely stated what she truly believes. She said there is nothing wrong wi' the way she behaves, and she even stressed the *nothing*. And there's your proof. That shrewish beauty will ne'er change her ways. I'd be staking my life on it."

"I wouldn't want your life in the pot, but I'm always game for a friendly bet. Fifty pounds says you're wrong. Anyone is capable of changing, even her."

Duncan chuckled. "Make it a hundred pounds. I love a sure bet. But she'll be returning tae London now tae cause trouble there, and I'm hoping I ne'er lay eyes on her again, so how will we be settling this bet?"

"I'll be returning to London as well, or—hmmm . . ."

The thought that occurred to Raphael was so surprising, it shocked even him, so he certainly wasn't going to voice it aloud. He needed to dissect it carefully and consider the ramifications.

"What?" Duncan asked impatiently.

Raphael shrugged nonchalantly to put his friend off. "Just a thought that needs further examination, old chap."

"Well, now that I've been saved from a fate worse than death—having tae marry that shrew!—I'm just glad I'll be seeing the last o' her. I'll be asking the right woman tae marry me now, the one I love."

Raphael knew his friend was referring to Sabrina Lambert, and he took it for granted that her answer would be yes. From Duncan's grin, he could see his friend did too. Sabrina might have professed they were only friends, but it was obvious that she was in love with Duncan. "I'm not sure yet where I'll be staying, so send the wedding invitation to Norford Hall. They'll know where to find me."

Duncan nodded and went off to find his grandfathers to give them the good news. Alone in the parlor, Raphael considered the amazing idea that had occurred to him, but he only had a few minutes to decide whether to act on it or to discard it as ridiculous. Ophelia's coach would be outside soon, which left him no time for a thorough deliberation. He either had to act immediately or not at all.

Chapter Three

Ophelia stared out the window of the coach at the harsh winter countryside as she and Sadie traveled south through Yorkshire on the way home to London. The grass was all brown, the trees mostly barren, though a few still held on to their brown leaves. It was a scene as bleak as her own thoughts.

Had she really thought it would be different, her actual come-out? That the men she met wouldn't be dazzled by her mere glance? That there wouldn't be another hundred proposals to add to the countless ones she'd received before she had even reached a marriageable age. And why did they do it? Did even one of them love her? Of course they didn't. They didn't even know her!

Her so-called friends were no different, liars the lot of them. God, how she despised such leeches. Not one of them was a real friend and never had been. They only flocked to her because of her popularity, which was merely because of her beauty. The fools! Did they really think she didn't know why they called themselves her dearest friends? She knew why. She'd always known it. If she didn't look the way she did, they wouldn't keep coming back to receive the brunt of her bitterness.

She despised the way she looked, and yet she took it for granted that no other woman could compare to her, and that pleased her. But two such opposite feelings had never sat well with her, had always pulled her one way or the other, causing her discomfort.

Mirrors were her enemies. She loved them and hated them because they showed her what everyone else saw when they looked at her. Light blond hair with no dark streaks to mar its perfection, ivory skin without a blemish, arched brows that were ideal with a little plucking, blue eyes that weren't remarkable except that they were set in a face with exquisite features. Everything about her face, the narrow, straight nose, the high cheekbones, lips that weren't too lush, but not too thin, the firm, little chin that only jutted stubbornly when she was being stubborn—very well, that was most of the time, but it still completed the package that had dazzled every person she'd ever met, with the exception of two, but she wasn't going to think about *them* anymore.

Ophelia glanced at her maid sitting across from her in the coach. It was her personal coach, not a large one such as her father's, which had the crest of the Earl of Durwich emblazoned on its doors, but big enough to carry her two large trunks of clothes and Sadie's portmanteau on top of it, and seat four comfortably. It suited her well enough, with its velvet, cushioned seats, which she'd cajoled her father into having added, and a brazier to provide warmth. Sadie kept a lap robe over her short legs, but then she didn't wear as many petticoats as Ophelia did, and it was quite chilly outside, deep into winter as it was.

"Are you ready to tell me what happened back there?" Sadie asked.

"No," Ophelia replied adamantly.

Sadie tsked and said knowingly, "Of course you will, dear, you always do."

Such impertinence! But Ophelia didn't say this aloud. Even her maids had fallen under the spell of her beauty, afraid to touch her exquisite blond hair, afraid to run her bath in case it was not to her liking, afraid to lay out her clothes in case they wrinkled them, afraid even to speak! She had dismissed them, one after the other. The count had risen to a dozen when this one applied for the job.

Sadie O'Donald wasn't the least bit in awe of or intimidated by Ophelia. She scoffed at a sharp tone, she laughed at a severe look. She'd raised six daughters of her own, so there wasn't much that could disturb her in the way of theatrics, as she called most of Ophelia's displays of temper. Middle-aged and plump, with black hair and dark brown eyes, Sadie was frank, brutally so sometimes. She wasn't actually Irish as her name implied. She'd once confessed that her grandfather had merely borrowed the name when he'd wanted to change his own.

For once, Ophelia didn't react to Sadie's silence as she usually did, by telling all. Most people who knew her knew she'd get right to the point if they stopped asking questions. She detested this appalling flaw of hers, but then, she detested all her flaws.

But without the answer forthcoming, Sadie's curiosity got the better of her. After all, there was supposed to have been a wedding this morning, Ophelia's, yet Ophelia had found Sadie and told her to have them both packed and ready to leave Summers Glade in no less than five minutes, because they were going home to London immediately. It had taken twenty minutes to pack, but that was still probably the fastest Sadie had ever thrown clothes into a trunk.

"Leaving him at the altar then, are we?" Sadie pressed.

"No," Ophelia said stiffly. "And I really don't want to talk about it."

"But you said you'd have to marry the Scotsman, that there was no getting out of it after Mavis caught the two of you in your bedroom alone. I know that pleased you well enough when it happened since you wanted him back, if only to end the gossip that occurred when he ended your first engagement. Then you changed your mind and wanted no part of him—"

"You know why!" Ophelia cut in sharply. "He and his grand-father were going to turn me into a country bumpkin. The very idea! No entertaining, no time for socializing. Just work, work, work! Me!"

"You were resigned to it, dear. What—?"

Ophelia interrupted again, snapping, "Did I have a choice, when Mavis was going to ruin me if I didn't marry that rude bar-barian?"

"I thought you agreed that he wasn't really a barbarian? You were the one who started the rumor before you had even met him, just so your parents would hear of it and break off the en-gagement for you."

Ophelia glared at her maid. "What has that to do with any-thing? That was before, not now. And it didn't even work! They still dragged me to Summers Glade to meet him. And look how that turned out. One little thoughtless remark on my part and he's so insulted *he* breaks off the engagement. But I didn't intend to insult him, you know. It wasn't my fault that he shocked me when he came into the room wearing a kilt. As if I'd ever seen a man wearing a kilt before," Ophelia ended with a huff.

"As if you wouldn't have said exactly what you did if you *had* thought about it," Sadie countered, knowing her too well.

Ophelia almost grinned. "Well, probably. But only because I was desperate by then. They said he'd lived his whole life in the

Highlands. You know I feared he really would be a barbarian, or I never would have gotten the idea to brand him one in the gossip mills."

"But you finally agreed he'd do very well as a husband."

"Honestly, Sadie, you aren't usually this obtuse," Ophelia said with a sigh. "Yes, he suited me just fine until his grandfather outlined the long list of duties they expected of me. All I ever wanted was to be a social matriarch, to give the grandest parties London has ever seen. My balls would be the only balls worth attending. That's what I want out of my marriage, not to rusticate out in the country, which is what Neville Thackeray had planned for me."

"So you're running away?" Sadie finally guessed.

Ophelia rolled her eyes. She would have thrown up her hands in disgust too if they weren't so toasty warm in her white fur muff.

To shut Sadie up, she said, "If you *must* know, Mavis arrived to save me from that horrid marriage, so we're merely going home."

She said no more, didn't even want to think about it anymore, but unfortunately, Sadie knew very well that Mavis wouldn't do her any favors, that Ophelia's onetime best friend despised her now. The maid knew all of Ophelia's friends quite well from the countless times they'd all gathered at Ophelia's house. She didn't judge. If anything, she was probably the only person who really understood Ophelia and accepted her, faults and all.

But Ophelia really didn't want to talk about it and so she tried to change the subject. "I'll be so glad to be back in London, but I suppose my father isn't going to be pleased when he finds out, for the second time, that he isn't going to have a marquis for a son-in-law."

"That's putting it mildly, dear. He was the happiest man in England when Lord Thackeray contacted him about the match. They probably heard him crowing about it down the block."

Ophelia wasn't surprised by the derision she heard in that remark. Sadie didn't like the earl very much. But then neither did Ophelia. Yet she winced, remembering how furious he'd been when they had all been kicked out of Summers Glade, the precious engagement he'd been so delighted with quite broken. He'd actually slapped her, blaming it all on her.

"If he'd just listened to me from the start, or even paid attention to the rumors I started and pulled me out of that match himself, then all of that unpleasantness could have been avoided. He didn't need to snatch up the first offer that suited him. I would have done just fine finding a prominent son-in-law for him, one that was *my* choice, but he never gave me a chance to."

"I hate to say it, dear, but you know why he was so sure you'd never make a choice in the matter of husbands."

"Yes," Ophelia said bitterly. "Because for three years he's been trotting men, young and old, before me, showing me off like the bauble he thinks I am. Good God, I was still in the schoolroom, much too young to think about marriage yet, but he wanted me to show a preference in men I wasn't the least bit interested in."

"Impatience runs in your family, I think."

Ophelia stared at Sadie blankly for a moment, then laughed. "Do you really think I get that from him?"

"Well, it certainly didn't come from your mum. Lady Mary, bless her, would take a year to make up her mind about something if someone wasn't prodding her along."

Ophelia sighed. She loved her mother, even though Mary had never been able to stand up to the earl about *anything,* least of all anything to do with their only daughter. But she should have known it wouldn't do any good, talking to either of her parents, but her father especially. She was merely an ornament to him, a useful tool to advance his social position. Her feelings didn't matter to him one bit.

"He probably doesn't even know yet that I was reengaged to Duncan," Ophelia remarked in speculation. "That cowardly driver of his only went home to tell him that I was back in Yorkshire visiting the Lamberts, which was the case before I was invited back to Summers Glade."

"You didn't send him word about it, but surely Lord Thackeray did."

"Yes, but I doubt he would even open a letter from the marquis, as angry as he was over being kicked out of Summers Glade."

"You're thinking our homecoming will be quiet, without all the yelling this time?"

"At least until my father hears about it—actually, I think I'll tell him myself if he doesn't know."

"Why?"

"Because if he'd just listened to me in the first place, none of this would have happened."

"I don't think I'd be risking another slap just to tell him, 'I told you so.' "

"But I would."

Sadie shook her head and glanced out the window at the late-afternoon sun peeking through a bank of dark clouds. Ophelia was sure she'd successfully avoided the subject she *didn't* want to discuss and settled back in the seat determined to put every part of the disastrous experience at Summers Glade behind her. But she should have known better. Sadie could be quite tenacious.

As if they hadn't even just been discussing something else,

Sadie remarked, "Mavis wouldn't be that generous, to help you. I warned you long ago to stop letting her come around. She's too bitter these days and especially after you finally let it be known that she's a liar."

"She provoked that," Ophelia said quietly. "I never would have mentioned it if her snide cattiness didn't snap my temper that day."

"You don't need to explain, dear. I know very well how she is. I'm the one who told you that the bad feelings she harbored for you would spill out and burn you eventually. You suffered her bile far too long just for the sake of the friendship you once had with her."

Ophelia's voice got even softer with emotion choking her again when she said, "She was the only real, honest friend I ever had. I'd so hoped she'd forgive me eventually for the wrong she thought I did her, when all I tried to do was protect her."

"I know," Sadie said, and leaned forward to pat the fur muff covering Ophelia's slim hands. "That man she fancied was a philandering fool, the worst sort of blackguard, just to use her to get close to you. You tried to warn her repeatedly. She wouldn't listen. I probably would have done exactly as you did under the circumstances. She needed the proof set before her eyes. You gave it to her."

"And lost her friendship for it."

"But she came to her senses today? Is that why she saved you?"

"Oh, no," Ophelia replied, her tone turning bitter now. "She only did it for Duncan's sake, but not before she reviled me in front of him and Sabrina and Raphael Locke. She said there's nothing but blackened, bone-chilling ice beneath my pretty surface."

Sadie gasped just as Ophelia had done when she'd heard it.

"And that wasn't even the worst of it," Ophelia added, and repeated most of that horrible encounter for her maid, the painful memory still so fresh in her mind.

After Mavis had finished lambasting Ophelia the first time and assuring her that she didn't have a friend in the world, as if she didn't already know that, Ophelia had slipped away unnoticed, unable to contain her emotions any longer. And having just repeated most of that to Sadie, she felt that self-pity welling in her chest again and trounced it soundly. She'd cried. How appalling to let *those* emotions get out of control like that. It had never happened before—well, not since she was a child, but she would *not* think about that. She'd strived her whole life to make sure she'd never be hurt again and she'd succeeded—until today.

But Sadie, dear Sadie, she understood too well. She'd listened without interrupting, and now she merely opened her arms wide. And that cracked the dam again.

Chapter Four

Raphael snapped the reins to get a little more speed from the horses pulling the fancy coach he was driving. He was enjoying the experience, it being a new one. Carriages, in good weather, with a single horse, he was quite used to driving about town, but he'd never tried to drive a large coach before. He usually traveled nice and warm inside them, as the occupants of this coach were doing.

It was cold. The wind whipped his blond hair about his shoulders and into his face, reminding him that he needed a haircut. He wouldn't get one where he was going.

He wasn't sure if he'd come up with a brilliant plan to win the bet with Duncan, or the most stupid idea imaginable, but he'd acted on it nonetheless and could only hope now that he wouldn't live to regret it. There was still time to change his mind. Ophelia was so absorbed in her self-pity that she didn't even know yet that she and her maid weren't on their way to London or that he was driving her coach. But the truth was, he didn't want to change his mind.

He'd been intrigued by her reaction to receiving her comeuppance at Summers Glade. Tears from the ice queen made that monicker a misnomer. Had she been hurt by what was said? And if so, why? Or had her tears been no more than an expression of self-pity? And then that amazing transformation in her when she spoke with Mavis in the parlor, where she was self-contained and imperious again, showing no trace of resemblance to the woman who'd cried in his arms. He'd assumed the worst about her. They all did. Yet what he'd heard in that second conversation implied there might be more to it than what he'd thought. He didn't like being wrong, so he wanted to find out the answers for himself.

But that was just one of several reasons why he'd impulsively acted on his idea. There were benefits other than just winning the bet with Duncan, if he succeeded in his plan. Performing a miracle and turning Ophelia Reid into a likable woman would be doing everyone who knew her a favor. He rather liked that notion. Playing the hero, as it were.

But it wasn't even just that that motivated him. If he could believe everything her ex-friend Mavis had said about her, and he had no reason not to believe it, then Ophelia, despite her beauty, was despised by one and all, aside from the besotted fools who didn't really know her, and those idiots didn't count. Oddly enough, that made her the underdog. And it wouldn't be the first time Raphael had championed the underdog.

Of course, there was also his desire to win the bet, and Duncan had been right, Raphael wasn't going to convince Ophelia to change her ways in London. He could follow her around to every party she attended, but to what purpose? She knew he didn't like her. He'd made that clear more than once. So he couldn't very well pretend an interest in her now. She wouldn't believe it. He wouldn't be able to pull it off anyway. Pretense of that sort was beyond him. Besides, if he even looked at a woman twice, the London gossip mills somehow had them engaged. He'd been unable to enjoy his first foray into the London social whirl because of that. In fact, that was why he'd gone abroad. So he'd as soon not be "seen" with Ophelia.

He had enough reasons now to settle it in his mind. For good or bad, he was going to make his best effort to help Ophelia see the error of her ways and change for the better, and then even she could make a good match and find happiness eventually. Quite the challenge, but then Raphael loved a good challenge. And if he succeeded, everyone would be happy, even her.

It was growing late, the sun beginning to set. Her coach wasn't designed for night travel, at least not out in the country where no lampposts lit the way. Raphael debated whether to take a chance and find an inn for the night, or to continue on and hope he could find Alder's Nest in the dark.

It was one of the many properties he'd inherited from his grandfather, one so remote that he'd only been there a few times over the years. A retreat, the old man had called it, while Raphael's father had scoffed that a cottage would have done well enough for a mere "retreat," that his father didn't need a bloody manor out in the middle of nowhere. The previous duke had merely laughed and said, "Me? In a cottage? Preposterous!"

So he'd built his large retreat out in the wilds of Northumberland, and he'd even enjoyed his solitude there quite frequently. None of the other Lockes ever did. The consensus of the family was that Alder's Nest was too far from *anything*. But the Nest was still hours away. And the occupants of the coach Raphael was driving were no doubt getting as hungry as he was. Nor had they even crossed into Northumberland county yet; he was sure they were still riding through Durham. But inns were few and far between, even in Durham, and the farther north they went, there'd be even fewer.

He'd stayed at his aunt's house the last time he'd come this way. Esmerelda was the oldest of his father's many sisters. She'd married a Scotsman, but had insisted they live in England. Her husband had agreed, but only if it was a short jaunt back to Scotland, and in fact he'd wanted to live right on the border! They'd settled on Durham, one county farther south, but still a long way from London. Esmerelda could have moved back closer to the family when she became a widow, but she'd lived long enough in Durham to come to love it there. And Raphael was a dunce for not thinking of her sooner.

Her house was only a few more miles down the road if he wasn't mistaken, at least the side road leading to it was. If he hadn't passed it already. He'd go back, though, if he had passed it. Ophelia wouldn't be hearing from anyone there that they were in Durham, north of Yorkshire, rather than halfway to London down south as she assumed. Come to think of it, his aunt would make a much better chaperone for Ophelia than Ophelia's maid would, and he didn't doubt his aunt would be pleased to join them at Alder's Nest for a while. He did need to assure that no scandal whatsoever resulted from his impulsive plan, after all.

Fortunately, he'd already taken care of the only obstacle that he had foreseen. Ophelia's parents. He'd jotted off a brief note to them when he'd made his decision and had pulled aside the footman that had been enlisted to drive her, to have him deliver it posthaste. Two birds with one stone, as it were, since he assured the man that he'd find someone else to drive Ophelia.

Her parents were far too impressed with titles more lofty than their own. That they had arranged her marriage to the marquis's heir against Ophelia's wishes proved it. So he had no doubt at all that they would give their wholehearted approval to her sojourn with his family. He'd implied he'd taken her under his wing. If they assumed that meant he had an interest in her himself, he could hardly be blamed for such an errant notion.

It was five miles farther on the main road and another thirty minutes down that side road to his Aunt Esme's house. It was full night, by then, but light flooded out of the front of the house from a long bank of windows off the parlor, enough for Ophelia to see that it was no inn they were stopping at for the night.

Raphael braced himself for an unpleasant scene when he opened the door to the coach and offered his hand for the lady to step down. She took it without even glancing at him. A footman, as she assumed he was, would be beneath her notice, after all.

But he caught himself staring at her as she alighted and he sighed mentally. Even rumpled from the ride, and drowsy by the look of it, or maybe her eyes were just puffy from so many tears, her exquisite beauty still took his breath away. He'd been bowled over when he'd first clapped eyes on her at Summers Glade. Fortunately, he'd been across the room from her, so by the time he actually stood next to her when she'd joined Sabrina and him for introductions—*intruded* was more like it—he'd had his amazement well in hand.

She turned back now to say something to her maid and gasped when her eyes passed over Raphael then abruptly returned to him. "What the deuce are *you* doing here?" she demanded. "Following me back to London?"

"Not at all. You took it for granted that one of the marquis's footmen would drive you all the way to London, but as it happens, they would have only driven you as far as Oxbow to find a driver there. They aren't paid to be away from Summers Glade for days, unless the marquis himself sends them off. So I'm doing you a favor, dear girl, since we happen to be going in the same direction."

"*You're* driving us?"

"Amazing, ain't it?"

She huffed, possibly because of his jaunty grin. "Don't expect any thanks, since I didn't ask you to do this."

He didn't usually lie. Couldn't tolerate people who did. But the alternative would have been to tell Ophelia he was absconding with her, and that wouldn't have gone over too well, he was sure. She still had no idea that they weren't traveling toward London, and he'd just as soon reach their destination tomorrow before she figured that out.

With a huff she walked toward the front door, but her step slowed and then stopped completely when she finally realized they were at someone's residence, not a hostelry as she'd assumed.

She glanced over her shoulder. "Where are we?" Her tone was merely curious now.

He helped her maid down from the coach before he strolled past Ophelia and rapped on the door. Keeping her waiting for an answer wasn't intentional. He didn't yet know how impatient she was. He just wanted to be careful for the time being with every word he said to her. So when he turned, he was rather taken aback to find her glaring at him. It took him a moment to recover and assume his usual jaunty air.

"Erm, I have a *large* family spread across the breadth of England. Makes it quite convenient, for me anyway, when traveling. My aunt Esmerelda lives here. Esme, she prefers to be called. We'll be staying the night. Much softer beds than an inn could supply, I do assure you."

The door opened before he finished. Old William stood there, squinting at them through his narrow spectacles. As blind as Esmerelda was deaf, William was the butler she'd stolen from her father when she'd left home to marry all those years ago. At least that was how the previous duke told it.

"Who's there?" William asked.

The spectacles obviously didn't help the old butler much anymore. He knew Raphael well. Perhaps if there was daylight, he would have recognized him. Then again, perhaps not. Esmeralda was getting up in years herself, and William, quite her senior, must be eighty by now.

"It's Rafe, old chap. Just stopping by for a little hospitality before we continue on in the morning. We'll need three rooms, and some food would be nice. Is my aunt still about, or has she retired for the night?"

"She's up, in the parlor, attempting to burn the house down she's got so many logs crackling in the fireplace."

Raphael grinned at the complaint. Esmerelda took chill easily in the winter. His grandmother was the same way. Most of the family dreaded visiting Agatha Locke because she kept her suite of rooms in Norford Hall so warm. But William would never admit that he needed that extra warmth at his age, as much as Esmerelda did.

"I'll let her know I'm—," Raphael began, only to be rudely interrupted.

"I'd like to be shown to my room, thank you," Ophelia said as she marched into the entryway. "And I'll take my meal there as well."

"Certainly, my lady," William replied promptly by habit. With his bad eyes he couldn't probably see the finery she was draped in to know she was a lady, but her imperious tone must have been sufficient indication that she was an aristocrat.

Raphael shook his head, watching Ophelia climb the stairs. She'd taken it for granted that William would be following her to show her to a room. Not likely at his age, and in fact he rushed off to find the housekeeper. Apparently, she'd also dismissed Raphael from her mind and didn't intend to say another word to him. He wasn't used to being ignored. While her disdain was helpful in that it kept him from having to lie again if she asked how much longer it would take to reach London, her complete dismissal of him actually annoyed him.

"Apparently I'll see you in the morning, then," Raphael said to her back.

"Early," she replied without turning to look at him. "I don't want to spend another entire day on the road."

He disappeared into the parlor before she finished. He *hoped* she'd turn around and see that, but she probably wouldn't. Damned haughty chit.

Chapter Five

"WHAT D'YOU MEAN, YOU'VE KIDNAPPED her? Speak up, boy. I must have misheard you."

Raphael patted his aunt's hand. He wasn't going to shout. He didn't need to because he was sitting next to her on her left side and her left ear was still in moderately good working order. But she currently had her neck *and* ears bundled in a scarf. A thick shawl was about her shoulders too. He was surprised she wasn't wearing gloves as well.

Good God, the parlor was hot. He loosened the neck of his shirt. He'd been nigh frozen after driving the coach all day, but not two minutes in the room and he'd had to remove his jacket.

"You didn't mishear me. But it's not what you're thinking. In a few days I'll have her parents' full approval to keep her as long as I like."

"They're selling her to you?"

"No, no, nothing of the sort. They're just going to think that I have matrimony in mind, and I do, just not for me. The chit is the veriest shrew, rude, mean-spirited by all accounts. She spreads lies without the least care that someone might be hurt by them."

"And half of London doesn't?" Esmeralda remarked with a snort.

Raphael laughed. "At least they think they're spreading the truth when they pass a rumor around. Ophelia knows full well the rumors she starts are lies."

"Then what the deuce are you doing with her?"

"I've taken it upon myself to turn her about. Her beauty is unparalleled. Imagine if she were just as beautiful on the inside."

"Then she'd be good enough for you?"

"Don't turn your matchmaking tendencies on me, Aunt Esme. When you meet her, you won't like her a'tall, I do assure you."

"But you're going to be turning her about, so I'll ignore first impressions."

He shook his head. "Why is it women always look on the bright side?"

"Because you men are such pessimists that you never do. Well, I'll allow you might be the exception, since you seem to think you can change this gel for the better."

"It's a hope, certainly not a foregone conclusion. But if it does happen, I'll sponsor her m'self in London, to assure she makes a good marriage. It won't be with me, though. I have quite a few more years of grand debauchery to enjoy before I even think of settling down."

"Then why even do this?"

"If you must know, it's a bet. A friend of mine is convinced that Ophelia Reid is a lost cause. I'm not so sure. So we bet on it."

"I should have known," Esmeralda said in disapproval.

"That's a bad habit you have, m'boy, of taking up the challenge so easily. And why does it sound like you'll be cheating in this case?"

"Me?" He grinned. "Never say so. I'd merely call it an edge. But someone needed to take up the gauntlet. The chit isn't going to give over her bad habits without some assistance, not when she doesn't think she *has* any bad habits. By the by, I do intend this to be on the up-and-up, so what would you say to joining us at Alder's Nest? You'd make a splendid chaperone for her."

"Why don't you just stay here?"

He gave that a moment's thought, but then shook his head. "Your home isn't remote enough. You have neighbors too close by."

"So?"

"So I don't intend to keep her under lock and key. But I do want to assure that she won't be walking away from this little sojourn in the country. Can't very well help her if she flies the coop, as it were."

"As you wish," she said with a shrug, then admitted, "I *have* always been curious about my father's folly, as my sisters and I called it. Never been to Alder's Nest m'self. He didn't exactly invite the family along when he went there to get away from all the noise we created at Norford Hall."

"Never say so. You? A rambunctious child?"

"I said no such thing," she huffed, but her brown eyes twinkled. "It was always my sisters Julie and Corinthia who did the screaming—well, the loudest anyway. But your father was the instigator, you know. A day wouldn't go by that he wasn't teasing one of us, or chasing us around the house, or pulling his pranks on us. At least he finally outgrew those terrible tendencies."

Raphael wondered if *he* ever would. That was one habit he'd picked up from his father that he still enjoyed. He loved teasing his sister, Amanda. But then the darling was so gullible that he simply couldn't help himself.

"We'll leave early in the morning," he said as he rolled up his shirtsleeves and wiped his brow. "And don't let on to Ophelia where we're going. She still thinks we're on our way back to London." Then he finally had to ask as he glanced at the fireplace that was still roaring, "Are you really so cold, Aunt Esme?"

"No, I just want William to feel useful," she admitted in a whisper, in case the old man was eavesdropping. "He was talking about retiring. I'd miss the old boy too much if he did. We get so few visitors up here, so he doesn't man the front door like he used to. But he does pile on the logs for me."

Raphael laughed. "Mind if I open a window for a few minutes?"

She grinned at him. "Please do."

Chapter Six

I T HAD SNOWED DURING THE night, not enough for it to stay on the ground for long, though. But for a little while, it would be lovely. Which was another of Ophelia's contrary opinions. She loved the snow, but she couldn't tolerate the aftermath when it began to melt and became quite dirty. Of course, she was only used to seeing it in London after heavy traffic turned it to sludge. Hyde Park was usually especially pretty after a snowfall, but that never lasted long either, with so much soot in the city. But she'd surely be able to enjoy the snow this morning at least, before it began to melt.

Her driver—it still amused her to think of the Locke heir as that—was waiting in the foyer for her. She'd donned her prettiest traveling ensemble just for him, the same one she'd worn for Duncan MacTavish when she'd tried to patch things up with him at that inn in Oxbow. With a white fur cap about her blond head and a powder-blue velvet long coat with a short cape trimmed in the same white fur, she knew she looked her best. The mirror upstairs said so.

She'd dazzled Duncan in this outfit, though not enough to soften him up. The insult she'd dealt him by calling him a barbarian had cut too deep apparently. Such a tricky situation that had been, and one of her finer performances, if she did say so herself. She had wanted him to forgive her so they could get reengaged to put an end to the gossip, then end their engagement amicably, as they should have done with their original engagement. But she'd also wanted to assure that he didn't revise his negative opinion of her too much and fancy himself in love with her like all the other men who met her. That wouldn't do a'tall.

She'd carefully balanced her contrition with his already bad opinion of her, and he'd offered her the perfect solution—her own conceit. His last remark had been "I dinna think I'd care tae be competing wi' m'wife for her own attention."

That had annoyed her at the time, though she found it rather amusing now that she'd been extricated from that horrid match and could find amusement in things again. For instance, it was amusing that the handsome, wealthy Lord Locke was acting as her driver. It *was* rather nice of him, she supposed, or at least she'd briefly considered it so. But after she'd given it some thought last night, she'd wondered why the man would take on such an arduous task when he didn't even like her.

He'd made that abundantly clear in the few conversations they'd had at Summers Glade. As for his driving her, she'd finally concluded that he must have found himself stranded there after his sister had returned to London without him. So he probably wasn't doing her a favor a'tall, as he'd implied. Which was just as well. She did *not* want to feel indebted to *him*.

But she wouldn't mind having her name linked to his, which would happen if anyone she knew saw him driving her coach once they reached London. And the people she knew looked for her coach—well, the men did anyway. That could only be to her benefit, as esteemed as his family was. She did still have to find a husband for herself, after all, and preferably before the Season ended.

Without the threat of an unwanted "arranged" marriage hanging over her head, she could devote the proper attention to finding the right man for her this time. Her criterion wasn't that unrealistic. She merely wanted, needed, to meet one man who didn't worship her beauty instantly, one man who would make an effort to know her, the real her, one man who didn't profess undying love ad nauseam when he couldn't possibly love her— yet. Not too difficult at all, she thought bitterly.

"There you are," Raphael said from the bottom of the stairs, only to add, "I could have sworn you said early."

Ophelia gritted her teeth. So much for dazzling him to make him regret his harshness with her. He barely looked at her as he slipped his greatcoat over his wide shoulders!

She'd actually been up for hours after going to bed so early last night. She'd delayed coming downstairs merely so everyone else could get a little more sleep before another long day on the road. Next time she'd save her consideration for someone who might appreciate it.

"I was exhausted yesterday," she merely said, "or I would have come down to meet your aunt. Am I going to have that pleasure before we depart?"

"Oh, indeed, in fact she's coming with us. Didn't think you'd mind sharing your coach."

"Afraid to be seen with me without chaperonage?" Ophelia smirked as she reached the bottom of the stairs.

"I knew you'd understand. No one likes having a favor back-fire on them."

"If they're actually doing someone a favor. I doubt you are," she said drily. "Why don't you fess up that your sister left you stranded at Summers Glade, so in essence, I'm doing *you* the favor—"

"Of letting me ride in your nice warm coach?" he cut in with a raised brow.

She actually felt a blush coming on. What the devil? She never blushed. Pink on her ivory cheeks looked like a splotchy rash. It was *not* becoming.

But having disconcerted her, he at least didn't expect an answer and continued, "Why don't we agree to suffer each other's company for the duration and let it go at that?"

"Fine," she retorted. "Since the duration will be a short one, I suppose I'll survive it."

"Ouch," she thought she heard him say, but she wasn't quite sure.

An elderly lady came out of the parlor just then to join them, a young maid close on her heels, both dressed to travel. Ophelia assumed this was Raphael's aunt. Heavily bundled in not just a coat but a heavy cape over that, and thick woolen scarves about her head, it was hard to see the cherub face beneath all that covering.

"You must be Lady Esmerelda," Ophelia said with a smile, extending her hand in greeting. "I'm Ophelia Reid. It's a pleasure to meet—"

"Speak up, gel," Esmerelda said in a testy tone. "I'm quite deaf, you know."

"I said it was—!"

"You don't have to shout," Esmerelda interrupted. "I'm not quite *that* deaf yet."

Ophelia grinned. "Shall I help you to the coach?"

"There's nothing wrong with my feet, gel."

Ophelia didn't take offense at the lady's cantankerous replies. She found them rather amusing. "Very well. My maid went out earlier to start the brazier. It should be nice and warm for you."

"Excellent. Do appreciate it," Esmerelda said, then added to the butler standing off to the side, "Hold the fort, William. I have a feeling I won't be gone long."

"Of course, m'lady," the butler replied as Esmerelda marched outside.

Ophelia noticed Raphael's wince over his aunt's remarks. If she didn't detest the fellow, she would have assured him that she understood how the infirmities of old age could and did make some people quite disagreeable. But apparently she was mistaken about the source of his discomfort because he held her back from following Esmerelda, his grip on her arm quite firm. This wasn't the man who usually had a jaunty air about him even when he was being his most sardonic. This was the serious Locke, the devil she'd met twice before when anger had removed all semblance of civility from him.

"What in the bloody hell was that about?" he demanded, adding in the same breath, "Don't think you can use my aunt for any of your machinations. I won't tolerate it."

She blinked, then she understood. He thought the worst of her, after all. Seeing her being nice to his aunt must have shocked him, she thought derisively.

"What an amusing idea. I hate to correct you, Lord Locke, really I do, but I happen to like older people. They're the only ones who don't try to compete with me or otherwise take advantage of an acquaintance with me. So your aunt and I will get along just fine, I do assure you. You needn't be concerned that I'll turn my viperous tongue on her. You on the other hand—"

"I got the point, no need to belabor it," he cut in, not nearly so sharply now. "Just get in the coach. The sooner we get this over with can't be soon enough for me."

"How odd that we agree perfectly," she retorted on her way out the door.

Chapter Seven

OPHELIA HAD THE ANNOYING HABIT of having to get the last word in. Of course he enjoyed the same habit, which was why he found hers so annoying.

Raphael was beginning to have reservations. Well, he'd already had quite a few, but damn, watching the woman interact with his aunt had been quite a surprise. Ophelia, being nice, was such a bloody contradiction of everything he knew about her. And his aunt had noted it too, even remarked on it for his benefit when she told William she was sure she wouldn't be gone long.

Ophelia's explanation had sounded quite reasonable, too reasonable. It had given him doubts that he shouldn't be having, when he knew what a schemer she was. He just didn't know her well enough to be able to tell if she was being honest or lying. But come to think of it, she had to be an expert liar or she wouldn't have been able to get away with half the transgressions laid at her door.

He'd sent a letter off to Sabrina late last night, getting his aunt's permission to use her one footman to deliver it and then bring him the reply. Sabrina knew Ophelia much better than he did, having stayed with the Reids when she'd gone to London for her own come-out. Someone had mentioned that Sabrina's aunt and Ophelia's mother had been childhood friends. But in either case, she was sure to have a much longer list of Ophelia's misdeeds than he did, and he wanted to know it all before he began his campaign to turn her about. Hopefully, Sabrina wouldn't take too long to reply.

They spent another long day on the road traveling through Durham and deep into Northumberland to his grandfather's retreat. It was a bad time of the year to come so far north. Actually, it was just a bad time of the year for him to take up coach driving.

He'd had Esmerelda pack a basket of food for the ladies, so he wouldn't have to stop for luncheon. She'd given him some food as well, though he had a hard time eating it with his gloves on. But he was wishing he'd stopped at that last hostelry he'd passed around midmorning, if just to get warm for a while. The farther north they went, the more patches of snow he came across, and the more biting the wind became.

There were no other inns. He'd known there wouldn't be. The Nest really was in a secluded area of the uplands, far removed from any other habitations. But he finally reached it by late afternoon, and smoke was coming from at least one chimney to assure him his caretaker was in residence and there would soon be a nice fire where he could thaw the cold from his bones. But before he could reach that warmth, he was going to have to deal with Ophelia's outrage, which, for once, would be warranted.

Steeling himself for an unpleasant confrontation, he opened

the coach door. "You might want to hurry into the house, ladies," he warned. "It's more than just chilly out here."

"It's been overly warm in the coach," Ophelia complained. "The heat put me to sleep when I wasn't the least bit tired."

She was the first to step down with his assistance. She didn't hurry off as he'd hoped. She stared at the large manor house in front of her and demanded crossly, "*Now* where are we? Another aunt's house?"

"No, this one belongs to me."

"But why have we stopped here? Surely we're close enough to London now that you can get us there before nightfall."

"We're a long way from London, m'dear. Welcome to Alder's Nest."

While she digested that with a confused frown, her frown deepened as she looked beyond the coach at the barren moors, which stretched as far as the eye could see. When he'd come here in the summer, the view had been magnificent with the heather in full bloom. But right now the scene was rather desolate.

"I hope you have some servants retained here," Esmerelda said as he helped her down from the coach, then she warned him, "I don't cook."

"Rest easy, Aunt Esme. There's a caretaker who's taken good care of the place for many years, previously employed by your father. His wife acts as my housekeeper and cook when I am in residence. I believe he has a few daughters, too. I'm sure we'll have a nice staff by tonight or tomorrow at the latest."

Esmerelda nodded and hurried to the door that Bartholomew Grimshod, the middle-aged caretaker, was holding open. Her pretty young maid followed, giving Raphael an appreciative smile as she passed him. He barely noticed, his mind too much on Ophelia at the moment.

The London beauty stood her ground, looking quite incredulous now.

"Why does it sound like we're staying here for an extended visit?" she demanded.

"Because we are."

"The devil we are. I demand you take me to London as you said you would."

"You can demand all you like. I'm staying here. And I never said I was taking you to London, merely that we were going in the same direction, which we were. That direction was here."

He helped Sadie down from the coach. Wiping sleep from her eyes, the maid gave them both confused looks, having heard some of what was said. Ophelia grabbed her arm. "Don't go in there. We're leaving."

Raphael ignored Ophelia's announcement and actually walked away from her. She probably wasn't used to men doing that, and he heard her outraged gasp. But he wasn't about to stand outside in the cold to answer her questions.

"Lord Locke," she called after him, then in a louder voice, "Raphael!" Then even louder: "Dammit, Rafe, stop this minute!"

He didn't, but he did pause at the door long enough to greet Bartholomew and tell him, "Just leave all the baggage out front here before you put the horses—actually, take the horses away from here, to your house for now. I'll help you carry the trunks in after I warm up a little."

"Certainly, my lord," the man replied. "And how long will you be staying?"

"To be honest, I have no idea, but I'll need some household staff for the duration. See what you can do in that regard. Oh, and the lady making all that noise behind me—it's a complicated situation, but just ignore her—"

"I heard that," Ophelia snapped as she reached him. "And I will *not* be ignored!"

The caretaker hurried off to do as he'd been told. Ophelia immediately turned and ordered her maid, "Stop him from un-hitching my coach."

The maid was starting to look outraged herself by now and, with a curt nod, marched off after Bartholomew with a deter-mined look in her eyes. Raphael knew it wouldn't do any good, but he wasn't going to stand there in the cold and wait for her to find that out.

With a sigh, he extended an arm, indicating for Ophelia to follow him inside. "If you'll calm down, I'll explain fully, Ophe-lia, I promise you, just as soon as we can find a moment alone. You're not going to embarrass my aunt with the scene you're sure to make. So a little patience, if you please, because I'm going to thaw out first. You might have been comfortably warm on the way here, but I certainly wasn't."

He headed toward the parlor, where he was sure his aunt had gone. Ophelia's hiss stopped him. "Don't you dare walk away from me again!"

He glanced back at her. "Did I mention patience?" he said drily. "I'm sure I did."

"What makes you think I have any? I don't, you know. None a'tall."

"Then I suppose that is something else we'll need to work on, and we can begin immediately. Pay attention, Ophelia. You will come into the parlor here, sit down, and remain quiet until the rest of the house is opened up and everyone is situated."

"And if I don't?"

"Well then, I just may keep to myself the reason why you're here. Come to think of it, an explanation isn't necessary—"

"This is ridiculous!" she cut in. "Keep your bloody explanations to yourself. I'm going home!"

She turned about to leave and nearly collided with her maid, who had returned, mumbling, "The caretaker wouldn't listen to me. He'll only follow his master's bidding."

Raphael heard the low growl that Ophelia emitted with that news. He smirked, "Which of you would have driven the coach if my man had been obliged to ignore my orders?"

Ophelia swung back around and glared at him. He shrugged and added, "If you'd like an explanation, and there is a perfectly good one, I'd suggest you do as I say, because I really don't have to explain myself in order to accomplish what we're setting out to do. Of course, that would leave you in the dark, floundering your way through, but I'm sure you can manage."

"You can't be serious!" she gasped.

"Patience is a virtue. Since you don't possess any—patience or other virtues for that matter—we'll let this one be the first you learn. Practice, m'dear, beginning now."

Chapter Eight

Ophelia was still fuming. The viscount was out of his mind! Why had no one mentioned that to her sooner?

Ophelia glared at Raphael's back as he stood in front of the fireplace, warming his hands. She might as well not even be in the room, he was ignoring her so completely. She'd sat there in the parlor, practicing patience, for what seemed like an hour now, without saying a single word to anyone.

Esmeralda had been taken to her room upstairs as soon as it was heated. She'd only had a few words to say about Ophelia's seething silence before she left.

"Don't pout, gel, it doesn't become you. Play your cards right and you'll come out the winner here."

What did that mean? She didn't ask because Raphael was in the room. She would find out later when she could speak with the older woman alone, because she obviously knew what was going on. Did Raphael's aunt condone what he was doing? It would seem so, but Ophelia hoped not. She could use someone other than Sadie on her side. But until he gave her that promised explanation, she was going to remain silent, even if it drove her mad with frustration.

The two maids had been shown to the servants' quarters. Sadie had returned to tell her that her room was ready, but Ophelia had merely waved her away. She wasn't going anywhere until Raphael explained himself, and that damned devil was making her wait, deliberately she didn't doubt, much longer than was necessary.

She stewed. She seethed. She'd never been quite this angry before. She thought about ways to make him pay for this outrage. And she tried to figure out for herself, without asking again, what she was doing here—she didn't even know where they were!

Earlier, as she'd gazed out the coach window, she'd vaguely wondered why they were traveling through such empty countryside. There were only a few houses here and there, and then not even a few, but she'd merely assumed, before she'd nodded off, that Raphael must know some back roads that avoided the heavy traffic flowing into London. But from what she'd seen outside, which was nothing but an empty horizon, this house of his was the only one for miles around, so she couldn't begin to guess where it was located.

She'd find out where they were and what the man thought he was doing, bringing her here instead of taking her home. Was he so full of his own lofty consequence that he thought he could— what? What *was* his motive?

The only thing that occurred to her was the same motive she was so used to dealing with, that he wanted her for her beauty just like all the other men, and because of the prestige of his family, he was in a position to sweep her away and think he could get away with it. To compromise her? To convince her he loved her when he couldn't possibly?

"Have we learned patience today?"

Ophelia's icy blue glare returned to Raphael's broad back. Such a superior tone he'd just used. He knew he held the upper hand here. And he hadn't even turned around to face her, to ask her that!

Stiffly, with every bit of the fury she was feeling, she snarled, "No . . . we . . . have . . . not!"

"That's too bad." He started to walk out of the room.

She watched him incredulously for a moment. He really was going to leave!

She leapt to her feet, intending to place herself between him and the door. But the table in front of the sofa she'd been sitting on had been pushed closer to her when a tray of food had been brought to her. She hadn't eaten the food, but now her knees knocked against the table, causing a teacup and saucer to crash to the floor, making her gasp.

Raphael stopped immediately. "Are you all right?" he asked, his tone actually sounding concerned.

"Yes—no, I'm not."

She was referring to her rage, not the minor bump on her knees, but he replied with a sigh, "Sit down. We can work on patience another day, I suppose."

She wasn't going to correct his misinterpretation of her answer, not when it appeared that he was changing his mind about denying her an explanation of what they were doing here. He sat down on the same sofa she'd been occupying, albeit at the opposite end of it. But he did turn to face her as she resumed her seat.

"You're going to tell me now why I'm here, instead of back in London?"

"Indeed. You and I are going to—"

"I knew it!" she cut in sharply. "You plan to compromise me in order to force me to marry you. Well, I won't—!"

She stopped her tirade when he began to laugh. He sounded genuinely amused. If she weren't so angry, she would have been embarrassed that she'd obviously been off the mark. He was quick to confirm it.

"Good God, where did that appalling idea come from?" he asked.

With less heat she demanded, "What other reason can you have for bringing me here?"

"I was explaining that before you interrupted. But since you mentioned it, let me assure you that my aunt's presence will guarantee that no scandal of any sort will result from your stay here. You won't be the least bit compromised, I promise you that."

"Until my father hears about this outrage," she predicted.

"What outrage would that be, m'dear? That you've been invited by the Locke family for a visit? That I've taken a personal interest in your launch this Season? He's already aware of it by now. I sent off a note to him before we left Summers Glade."

"A visit? Without asking me?"

"Would you have declined?"

He seemed to expect only one answer. She was glad to give him a different one. "Yes, I would have."

"Would your father?"

"No, he would have pushed me out the door," she replied, unable to keep the bitterness from her tone.

She immediately wished she'd kept that to herself when Raphael said smugly, "As I thought."

With a scowl, she reminded him, "But I'm the one whose permission you needed."

That didn't dent his smugness at all; he even smiled as he corrected her, "No, actually, as you recently found out with your first engagement to my friend Duncan, only your parents' permission is required. Terribly unfair, I'm sure you're thinking, but quite true nonetheless."

He was back to his jaunty, sardonic self. The blasted man was enjoying telling her how little control she had over her life.

"This isn't exactly your 'family' home," she pointed out. "And where the deuce are we, anyway?"

"Northumberland."

"But that's nearly to Scotland!"

"Not quite a stone's throw away. It's a big county. But, yes, it borders Scotland."

"So you lied to my father in your note to him?" she said triumphantly. "This isn't where your family lives. When I tell him the truth—"

"You haven't even heard yet what the 'truth' is, Ophelia," he cut in, finally revealing a little annoyance with her. "But by the time you see your father again, we can hope you'll have a much better outlook on things."

"You mean *you* can hope," she said with some smugness of her own.

"No," he replied thoughtfully. "I think I phrased it right the first time—since you won't be leaving here until you *do* have a better disposition."

She gasped at what that implied. "You can't keep me prisoner here."

"Why ever not?"

That reply was so far removed from anything she might have expected that she shot to her feet to shout at him, "Because you have no right!"

"Do you always react so extremely?"

"You are provoking me beyond my tolerance!"

He tsked, unimpressed with her rage. "I'm doing no such thing. And we're going to have this conversation without any more theatrics, if you please, so sit down, behave, and quite possibly you will learn that there is a very good reason for you to be here."

"What?"

"Your own happiness," he said simply. "Or are you going to try to tell me that you're already as happy as you can possibly be?"

She wasn't the least bit happy, but that was none of his bloody business. "I'll see to my own happiness, thank you very much."

"As you have so far? Ruining other people's lives? That makes you happy? Or is it making other people miserable? Oh, wait, it must be starting rumors that don't have a jot of truth to them. That must make you ecstatic."

She felt a blush sneaking up her cheeks. Defensively she said, "You know nothing about any of that other than what you've heard others say. But what has that to do with making me happy? And why would you even want to? But even more to the point, how can *you* make me happy when I despise you?"

"Do you really?"

She stared at him incredulously. "Were you not sure? You had doubts? After the nasty things you said to me at Summers Glade?"

He shrugged. "Warning you not to start a rumor about Sabrina and me wasn't being nasty."

"You assumed I was going to start a rumor when I wouldn't have done any such thing. I was merely trying to be helpful so she wouldn't get hurt. I really did think you were bedding her because of all the attention you were paying her. And if I had come to that conclusion, others would have too. But instead of just telling me I was mistaken, you threatened to ruin me if I mentioned it again!"

"With good reason, considering your well-known predilection for starting rumors."

"We haven't really gone full circle back to matters you have no firsthand knowledge of, have we?" she retorted, only a slight dryness to her tone. "But we *have* established that you, personally, can't contribute to my happiness. So tomorrow, you will take me home."

He didn't even pause to consider it. "No, I don't think so. And I never said I was going to make you happy. However, I am going to help you find your own happiness, to be at peace with yourself, as it were."

"I am at peace!" she snarled.

"Yes, you sound it, indeed you do," he said as he stood up.

"Where are you going?" she demanded.

"To find my dinner and get a good night's sleep. I have a feeling tomorrow will be an exhausting day."

"But you haven't finished your explanation!"

He raised a brow. "Didn't I? Well, here it is in a nutshell, m'dear. We're going to turn you into a kind, considerate woman who people will want to be around. Their delight in your company will have nothing whatsoever to do with your amazing beauty, and everything to do with how wonderfully sweet and nice you are. When you can convince me that we've succeeded, *then* I'll take you home."

Chapter Nine

Hᴉꜱ ᴍᴇᴇᴛɪɴɢ ᴡɪᴛʜ Oᴘʜᴇʟɪᴀ ʜᴀᴅ gone much better than he had anticipated, Raphael thought as he lay in the ornately carved oak bed in the master suite. Shocking Ophelia Reid into silence hadn't solved anything, but it had certainly been enjoyable. At the least, it had let him escape her company for the remainder of the night.

She'd gone to bed. He'd made sure of that before he retired himself. After all, she *might* have run off into the cold night, stupid as that would have been, just to make a silly point. But he wasn't getting the good night's sleep he'd hoped for.

He shouldn't have let her outrage make him so defensive that he hadn't made a clean breast of it. He hadn't intended to keep his bet with Duncan a secret. But did she really need to know that this campaign to improve her character had started with a bet? No, she didn't. What he'd told her ought to suffice for them to work together. Once she stopped being angry. Once she admitted that her behavior was reprehensible to everyone—except herself, of course. Duncan had been right. She obviously felt that she had nothing to be ashamed of, that there was nothing wrong with her behavior. But then maybe she'd never stood back and taken a good look at her own actions and how they were perceived by others. Good God, was he making excuses for her? Those damned doubts were intruding again.

He hadn't counted on her incredible beauty being so difficult to ignore. He'd rather be admiring her than disliking her. He'd rather be kissing her into silence instead of—where the devil had that thought come from? But he knew. And it had taken every ounce of will he possessed tonight to keep her from noticing just how attracted he was to her. But it was only a visual effect, he was sure. Now that he knew what was contributing to his doubts, he could take steps to—yes, that would work well, he thought drily. Don't look at her a'tall. They'd get a lot accomplished that way.

He turned over and slammed a fist into his pillow, disgusted with the thoughts that were keeping him awake.

*   *   *

"Why are you doing this?"

Raphael didn't pause on his way to the dining table or glance at Ophelia, who was sitting there alone. Broadsided the moment he stepped into the room. He wondered how long she'd been waiting for him to show up. Her plate only had a crust of toast left on it.

"Mind if I eat first, before we begin?"

"Yes. I do mind."

"Then this is an excellent time to practice yesterday's lesson, isn't it?"

Hearing his voice, Nan came in with a platter of breakfast choices for him. She and her mother, Beth, had arrived yesterday in time to serve a cold dinner. They were good country people, happy to help out.

"The pickings are lean, m'lord," she warned as she set the platter in front of him. "M'father's gone to market to stock the pantry, but he probably won't be back until late tonight or tomorrow. He had enough stores here to last a few days, just nothing fancy."

"No need to apologize." Raphael smiled at the girl. "I know our visit wasn't anticipated."

She nodded and hurried back to the kitchen. Ophelia was tapping her fingers on the table. He stared at them.

"I wouldn't call that patience," he remarked to his houseguest.

"I already warned you I have none. It's one of my flaws I don't mind admitting to. No patience whatsoever."

At least her tone was moderate—for the moment. "You admit it's a flaw. Wouldn't you like to get rid of it?"

"Of course I would, but I don't need *your* help to do so," she retorted.

He buttered a chunk of freshly baked bread, nicely toasted. "How old are you? Eighteen? Nineteen? And you still haven't mastered patience? You *do* need help. I don't mind playing the teacher."

"You mean playing the devil, don't you?"

He glanced at her with a chuckle. "I've been called worse, and, yes, I'm sure *you'll* think of worse before we're done. But in the meantime, you'll accept my help graciously."

She snorted.

His chuckle turned to a laugh. "Very well, not so graciously."

She was glaring at him now. He shrugged and went back to ignoring her, or trying to. The food at least gave him something else to look at. Damn, she looked radiant this morning in her pink tulle morning dress with corded lilac trim, not a hair out of place in the tight coiffure she preferred, bangs across her brow, several perfect ringlets at her temples. He wondered if she ever didn't look magnificent. Anger certainly didn't detract from her beauty.

After a few more minutes of finger tapping, she asked, "Where is your aunt?"

"No doubt hiding from your sour disposition."

"Must you insult me with every word you utter?" she snapped.

"Have I been doing that? I wonder why."

He saw the slight color climb her cheeks. It was quite becoming. He wondered why she didn't wear makeup to achieve that effect—no, it was just as well she didn't. The woman was too beautiful as it was.

He relented enough to answer, "It's her habit not to appear before midday. She's awake, I'm sure. She just enjoys spending mornings alone in her room with her knitting. And she's an avid reader. Prefers solitude for it. One of her trunks was probably filled with books, I don't doubt."

"I didn't need that much information, thank you."

"Not used to simple conversation that doesn't revolve around you?"

Her blush got much brighter. Aha! Finally something that removed the ethereal glow from her and made her appear more normal. And that's obviously why she didn't wear makeup. A little too much appeared like splotches on her pale cheeks.

To get his mind off her looks, he said, "Were you hoping to talk her into your camp? You needn't bother. She's firmly in mine."

She didn't deny it. "She can't condone what you're doing."

"She doesn't need to. She knows I'll have your parents' blessings, which is good enough for her. That *should* be good enough for you as well."

"Blessings you've falsely obtained by taking advantage of my father's ridiculously high regard for titles more lofty than his own."

He heard the bitterness that crept into her tone, and it wasn't the first time he'd heard it when her father was mentioned. Apparently, she didn't like her father very much. But then the Earl of Durwich couldn't have much love for her either, having tried to shove her into a marriage she obviously didn't want.

She didn't expect a reply and actually fell silent for a few minutes. The finger tapping even stopped. She was staring at him, though, which made him quite uncomfortable. She'd flirted outrageously with him at Summers Glade, after all, before she'd got reengaged to Duncan. It had prompted him to warn her at the time that the men in his family did the pursuing and they didn't tolerate being pursued by marriage-minded females. But she'd obviously felt some attraction to him or she wouldn't have put herself forward. That had occurred prior to the setdown he'd given her though, when she'd made him so furious with her insinuation that he was bedding Sabrina.

He'd spoken quite sharply to her and she'd disliked him ever since. Not that he liked her either, but their mutual dislike *was* going to make this campaign much more difficult, for both of them. But he wasn't about to try to make her look upon him more favorably again just to make this task easier. Hell no. He was having enough trouble ignoring her beauty without her batting her pretty blue eyes at him.

"If you've finished your breakfast," she finally remarked, "I'd like an answer to my original question."

He was only half-finished eating, but she'd asked so many questions that he hadn't exactly answered that he replied anyway, "Which was?"

"Why are you doing this to me?"

"Ah, that again. For a number of reasons."

"Just give me one."

"You are universally disliked, except by a seemingly endless stream of men who haven't discovered yet that you're a shrew."

"I'm not a shrew. But that has nothing to do with you, so give me another reason."

"Very well, I find it quite odd that anyone as beautiful as you are could be so obviously unhappy. I've taken it upon myself to correct that, my good deed for the year, you could say. And I must disagree with your response to my first reason. I lean toward the underdog, always have, and help them when I can. In your case, I can."

"It's well-known that you champion the underdog," she allowed. "Even I heard it mentioned. But I am *not* an underdog! And for you to insinuate that I am—"

"Of course you are, m'dear," he interrupted calmly. "Name me one person who likes you, aside from your parents and that stream of idiots we've already mentioned."

"My maid," she retorted looking rather triumphant to have come up with that answer.

He rolled his eyes. "Maids don't count."

"Go to hell," she said, and surprised him by leaving the table.

"Where are you going?"

"I'm going to walk home," she informed him without looking back.

He started to laugh. That halted her before she reached the door.

"I'm serious." she swung around to tell him, in case he doubted it. "I'll find someone who can help me get back to London."

"I'm sure you will, but probably not before dark. And then

what will you do? Aside from freeze or get hopelessly lost *and* freeze."

She stood there bristling. He took pity on her and said, "Come back and sit down and I'll explain why that isn't such a good idea. Here, have another piece of toast," he added as she passed him on her way back to the other side of the table.

She ignored the offering. She lifted the chair she had vacated, slammed it down on the floor just to show how angry she was, if he hadn't guessed, then after all that, sat down in it demurely.

"I'm listening," she growled.

His urge to laugh again was almost irrepressible. He managed to contain it, but not without taking a bite of the toast still in his hand. That, of course, made her wait for the answer, and they'd already established she wasn't good at waiting. But her theatrics really were amusing, because they were real, not contrived. He had a feeling this was how she was used to getting her way. He was going to have to add "spoiled" to her long list of flaws.

"Well?" she bit out, her glare much more icy.

He put his eyes back on his plate before he said, "Did I fail to mention just how remote Alder's Nest is? My grandfather bought this huge tract of land up here in the wilderness of Northumberland for the very reason that it was quite far removed from any other habitation. And then on top of that, he had this house built in the center of it."

"Why?" she asked with some genuine curiosity.

"An excellent question that our family has asked more'n once as well. His idea was to have a retreat for himself that the family would think twice about visiting. He didn't mind admitting it. He had a house full of very noisy children at the time."

"He didn't need anything so grand as this just for a place to get away to."

"Of course not, but, well, he was a duke, after all," he said with a grin. "A modest abode just wouldn't have befitted him."

"He kept a mistress here, didn't he?" she asked in a smirking tone.

It was a good thing he'd swallowed his mouthful of toast, or he might have choked. "Good God, the way your mind works is beyond comprehension. No, he adored his wife and children. He never stayed away from them for long. He just felt a need for complete solitude—and quiet—for a week or two every year."

She shrugged nonchalantly, as if she hadn't insulted him and his family with her baseless speculation. "It was just a guess."

"No, it was a firsthand demonstration of your reputed spite."

She gasped. "It was nothing of the sort!"

"When you don't know my family and certainly never met my grandfather, that was indeed a petty, malicious bit of slander you call a 'guess.' By the way, if a man keeps a mistress, he doesn't put her where she's so inaccessible it would take him more'n a day to reach her."

"You speak from experience, I suppose."

She was doing it again. Did she not even realize it? Was being snide and spiteful so ingrained in her that it was the only way she knew how to be?

She guessed what he was thinking, accurately. "Oh come now, you don't expect me to be cordial to you, do you? I haven't even begun to insult you. Give me time, I'm working up to it."

He had to bite back a laugh. Good Lord, he hadn't counted on her being witty. "Of course I don't expect you to be cordial—yet. That's what *I'm* working on, remember? But, yes, I was speaking from experience. I am a renowned rake, after all, or hadn't you heard?"

"I'd heard. I just didn't believe it."

"Why not?"

"Because you're going to be the next Duke of Norford," she said primly. "Which means you would be circumspect enough to not come into the title with any scandals hanging about your coattails."

"Ah, I see. You think an unmarried man keeping a mistress is scandalous?"

She frowned. "Well, no, I suppose I was thinking of a married man."

"It's all right, m'dear. You can admit you simply weren't thinking a'tall. You do that a lot, don't you? Speak without thinking first?"

There was that becoming blush again. He was going to have to try harder to rile her in order to get the splotchy one instead.

She hissed, "*If* you're done dragging me through the mud, let's get back to the issue at hand."

"The reason why it wouldn't be a good idea for you to walk away from here?"

"Well, that too. You don't *really* expect me to believe that this house is so far removed that I can't find help somewhere in the neighborhood?"

He chuckled. "There is no neighborhood. But you're welcome to ask the servants. They'll tell you that Bartholomew's house, which was built for a caretaker, is the only one around for a good fifty miles, and the nearest market is much farther than that, or didn't you hear Nan mention that her father would be gone all day because he was going to market?"

"This is intolerable!"

"Well, it *is* why I brought you here rather than to one of my other estates. At least here you are free to roam the house and grounds."

"As opposed to being under lock and key?"

"Exactly!"

She blinked. "I wasn't being serious."

"I know, but I am. Most serious. And the sooner you realize just how committed I am to helping you, the sooner we can both leave."

"And just how do you propose to *help* me?" Her tone dripped sarcasm. "Are you opening a charm school here? You have to abduct students for it?"

"Don't be ridiculous."

"Your entire scheme is preposterous, but if there isn't a schoolroom for me to report to, just what will the agenda be?"

"I haven't exactly tried anything this daunting before, so why don't we just take it one step at a time and see how it goes."

Daunting stung. "Since you obviously see me as a lost cause, why don't you admit you've made a mistake and take me home instead?"

"If I thought you were a lost cause, we wouldn't be here. And, no, taking you home isn't an option—yet."

She gritted her teeth. "You still haven't answered, to my satisfaction, why you have decided to meddle in my life. Did you even consider that I might love being the way I am? That I wouldn't want to be any other way?"

"Rubbish. You're miserable, and because of it, you strive to make everyone else around you just as miserable. It's so bloody obvious, Ophelia, that a child could see it. Oh, good God, don't you dare cry!"

She ran out of the room, effectively hiding the tears that had just showed up in her eyes. He didn't try to stop her. Damned tears! Real female tears were his downfall, and he didn't want her to know that and use it against him. But he hadn't expected to hit the mark quite so accurately about why she was the way she was. The question now was, what had made her that way?

Chapter Ten

"HERE NOW, STOP THAT," SADIE said in her stern, motherly tone as she entered Ophelia's bedroom. "You'll be making your eyes all red."

Ophelia sat up from where she'd been crying on the bed. She wasn't sure where those tears had come from, but she felt somewhat better for having shed them.

"Red will go well with this dress," she remarked to make light of it.

"Red doesn't suit you under any circumstances. It's not your color, dear. And what brought that on, or do I need to ask? You were so angry yesterday you wouldn't even speak to me, and now you're crying again?"

"He's not a nice man. I can't believe I considered him for a husband, even if only briefly."

"It's a grand title he'll be inheriting," Sadie offered as an excuse.

"As if I care a jot about that. The title was just for my father.

He won't approve any husband for me who doesn't have a title more exalted than his own."

"You know, even I heard gossip about him when he returned to town, about all the girls' hearts he broke when he left, and the hearts of their mamas! It wasn't just his title and wealth, you know, but because he's quite the charmer."

Ophelia snorted. "Not around me he isn't."

"Then you must have been attracted to the viscount's pretty face. He is passing fair, after all."

Ophelia would have liked to deny that, but she couldn't. It just made her even more angry that a man that handsome could be such a high-handed bastard.

"Did you have any luck?"

She'd sent Sadie to find out where her coach had been taken. Not that she thought either of them could drive it, but the horses had been an option, at least they had been before she'd found out just how deep into the wilderness Raphael had taken them.

"The coach is in the stable," Sadie replied. "No horses, though. And his servants were warned not to talk to us about leaving."

"That doesn't surprise me." Ophelia sighed. "We really are stuck here, you know."

"I'd gathered as much. But for how long?"

"Until he admits he's stepped way out of bounds in bringing me here."

"So he didn't bring you here in order to compromise you?"

Ophelia could feel the anger coming back. "I thought the same thing, but I couldn't have been more wrong. He doesn't even like me! So it makes absolutely no sense that he'd want to *help* me."

"Help you?" Sadie frowned. "How is stealing off with you supposed to help you? I'd like to know."

"He intends to show me what a mean, horrible person I am," Ophelia said sarcastically. "And it doesn't sound like he'll be satisfied until I've turned about and am dripping sweetness all over his marble floors."

Sadie gave a hoot of laughter. "Is *that* what he told you, dear? What a crock of—"

"He was serious."

"Well, then, show him how sweet you can be."

"I will not!"

"You're too upset to, I know, but if it will get us home . . . Well, never mind. I don't believe it anyway. Are you sure he's not secretly in love with you and brought you here to court you to his favor? That sounds much more likely. You two got off to a bad start, after all."

"And we've gone downhill ever since. He admits he doesn't like me, Sadie."

Sadie wasn't convinced. "That could just be a strategy, you know. It's a pretty old trick."

"What is?"

"To make you think you can't have him," Sadie said sagely. "For some people, it works to make them want the person all the more."

Ophelia snorted. "That wouldn't work on me."

"But he doesn't know that—yet."

Ophelia frowned. She might have to give that some thought—no, it was a silly notion. But then Raphael's explanation was even more silly. To change her? When he didn't know the first thing about her or what motivated her?

She shook her head at her maid. "Trust me to know if a man

is harboring secret affections. Locke insults me with every word out of his mouth. He delights in telling me that no one likes me. He's called me mean and spiteful. He's as nasty as Mavis was. He even called me a 'shrew'!"

"You know you can be shrewish at times."

"With reason! I'm so sick of all the insincerity, and it grew much worse with the opening of the Season. There's been so much of it that I can't trust anyone anymore—well, aside from you and my mother. Besides, you know that at least half the things I say and do are deliberate. I just can't control this bitterness sometimes."

"I know." Sadie sat beside Ophelia and put an arm around her shoulder.

"It hurts."

"I know," Sadie said soothingly, adding, before the tears started again, "Did I mention it's snowing? That's what I came to tell you."

"Is it?"

Ophelia would ordinarily have been delighted by the news. Ophelia loved to watch the snow fall. But she was too distraught at the moment to enjoy one of her few pleasures. She did glance toward the windows though, all four covered in sheer white drapes that let daylight into the room. She wished now that she'd let Sadie open the drapes this morning, instead of telling her not to bother since there was no view whatsoever to look upon.

Ophelia had been given a corner room, with many windows that looked out on nothing more than the empty countryside. It was a serviceable room, but not exactly designed for a woman. If Raphael had been truthful about his grandfather's only coming to Alder's Nest for solitude, then all of the bedrooms were probably like this. There was no vanity, but there was a lovely desk in cherrywood with ornate scrollwork along the edges and legs, and a plush velvet, cushioned chair to go with it. A large stuffed reading chair sat between the windows on one wall. A long bookcase was on another, with a tall wardrobe with a mirror on the inside door. The lamps on the two side tables by the double bed were plain, but gave off a nice bit of light in the evenings when they were lit.

A carpet covered the entire floor, its pattern woven in shades of brown and purple. That coupled with the marble-manteled fireplace allowed her to move about the room with her feet bare. There were paintings on every wall, which depicted scenes as varied as children playing in a field, a busy city street, a woman who looked rather sad, a vase with a single flower in it, among others. They certainly brightened up the room.

It was quite an extravagance to fully furnish a house of this size, and it was very large merely for one man to enjoy it for a few weeks out of a year. She'd heard the Lockes were quite rich. It must be so. Not that it mattered to her. The heir apparent could choke on all his family's money for all she cared.

She'd resisted taking a look outside for as long as she could. She walked over to the closest window and moved aside one of the drapes and stared out at the falling snow. The flakes were quite large. When she looked below, she saw that the ground was almost covered.

"How lovely," she said.

Sadie came up beside her to enjoy the same view. "I thought you'd think so."

"At least it's thick enough to hide that there's nothing beyond it to look at."

"The cook mentioned that it's beautiful up here at certain times of the year, when the heather is in full bloom. Can you imagine, looking at nothing but heather for as far as you can see?"

"I suppose that would look nice," Ophelia allowed, though flowers didn't interest her nearly as much as snow did.

"If this keeps up, there may be a deep carpet of pristine white out there tomorrow," Sadie predicted.

Now *that* interested Ophelia. "Do you think?" she asked excitedly.

"We're far enough north for it to even stick around for a while. It's coming so hard I wouldn't be surprised if it continued into the night. Should I unpack some of your warmer clothes?"

Sadie knew her well. Ophelia loved walking in freshly fallen snow if it was deep enough that her footsteps wouldn't uncover the ground beneath it.

"You might as well unpack everything now," Ophelia said with a sigh.

She hadn't let Sadie do so last night, insisting they wouldn't be staying. "I don't think we're leaving—for a few days at least," she added, then turned to Sadie, opening her eyes wide so the maid could examine them. "My eyes didn't really get red, did they?"

"Planning to jump back into the fray, are you?" Sadie guessed.

Ophelia didn't deny that she was going to seek Raphael out again, now that she was back in control of her emotions. "Just tell me?"

The maid tsked and pointed out, "You could just look for yourself. There's a mirror right over there that is *not* your enemy."

"Sadie," Ophelia said warningly.

"Not red a'tall, which is too bad. Wouldn't hurt for him to know you were crying. A little guilt works wonders on a man."

"He knows," Ophelia replied in a disgruntled tone. "But a man has to have a conscience to feel guilty. Devils don't have them, I'm sure."

Chapter Eleven

AT FIRST OPHELIA DIDN'T EVEN notice Raphael in the parlor, though she'd been looking for him and he was sitting right there on the sofa. But the drapes were open on a long bank of windows on the front of the house. She smiled to see that it was still snowing quite hard.

"Feeling better?" Raphael asked.

She located him on the sofa. Her smile left her. He was just setting down a book he'd been reading. He'd removed his jacket, probably because the fire was roaring in the fireplace. Esmerelda was there as well on another sofa. The room was large, with three sofas plus an assortment of comfortable chairs. The older woman glanced over the rim of her own book to give Ophelia a nod.

"Morning, gel. Or is it still morning? Actually, it must be later than that, since I'm getting rather hungry. I don't eat breakfast, you know. But skipping it just means I can't wait too long for luncheon."

Ophelia's smile returned for Raphael's aunt. "They're making a racket in the kitchen, so it probably won't be long, Lady Esme."

"Eh?" Esmerelda said, not quite hearing her. "I'll just go hurry them along then and wait in the dining room. Join me?"

"In a moment," Ophelia said a bit louder, trying not to shout. "I'm just going to have a few words with your nephew first."

"Why did that sound ominous?" Raphael asked as soon as his aunt left the room.

"You jest, Lord Locke, when nothing about this situation is remotely humorous."

"No jest a'tall, since you've done nothing but shout, rant, and complain since we got here."

"All with good reason, or did you really think I'd say thank you for holding me prisoner?"

He let out a long-suffering sigh, which she was sure was quite contrived. "Come and sit down. And do call me Rafe. All my friends do." She stared at him pointedly, causing him to chuckle and add, "Even my enemies do. No, really they do. And I'll call you Pheli if you don't mind. Less formality between us will—"

"I do mind."

"Too bad. But as I was saying before you rudely interrupted, less—"

"I really do mind," she cut in again. While she could care less that it appeared she was annoying him, this was something she wasn't going to give ground on, so she decided to explain. "It was a childhood name my friends gave me. When I thought they were my friends, it didn't bother me in the least, but I found out they weren't. So it's a name I associate with lies and deceit, and every time I hear it, it reminds me of that betrayal."

She didn't expect to shock him into silence, but he had nothing to say to that, and the look he was giving her was a mixture of confusion and—pity? He better not pity her. She wouldn't tolerate it.

He recovered enough to ask, "Was your childhood really so—unusual?"

"Don't go there," she warned. "I mean it."

He shrugged. "Well, this won't do a'tall. The name Ophelia is much too standoffish, and as I *was* saying, twice as you'll recall, we'll get a lot more accomplished, and much quicker, with less formality. How about Phelia then? No, I have it! Phil. A bit mannish, but—"

"Fine!" she snapped. "Phelia will do."

"Thought so." He grinned.

She narrowed her eyes on him. He looked back at her innocently. His tactics were deplorable, but at least they were obvious. He wasn't really trying to trick her into compliance, just putting his jaunty affectation to good use.

He stood up, since she hadn't taken the seat he'd offered, and asked, "Was there something specific you wanted to discuss, as you implied to my aunt?"

"Yes, but—can we step into the foyer? I don't know how you tolerate this heat."

"Because I enjoy my aunt's company. She needs a little more warmth than we do."

"I know. It's why I turned the brazier up in the coach. But, well, never mind. I suppose I'll get used to it."

"So you *can* make concessions?" he said with exaggerated surprise. "I'm impressed."

"Don't be. I told you, I like older people. But listen here, *Rafe*. If you are sincere, which I still doubt, mind you, but if you *are* sincere in wanting to deal with me for a specific goal, you'd do well to stop making me furious with your insults every time we converse."

He put a finger to his lip in brief speculation. "You don't look furious," he concluded.

"Give me a moment."

He laughed. "You're going to have to stop being so witty, Phelia. It's not one of the things you're known for."

"Of course it isn't. But then I'm not presently among friends where I need to guard every word I say."

"I agree we aren't friends, but I think you have that backwards. When you're among friends you don't need to be guarded."

"No, I stated it correctly."

"Ahh, I see," he guessed. " 'Friends' as in not really friends?"

"How astute of you. Now *I'm* impressed."

He laughed again, even harder. Well, devil it, she wasn't trying to amuse him. She turned about to stare out the window, which reminded her of what she had come to warn him about. She was looking forward to a brief outing in the snow and wanted to make sure he wouldn't ruin it by stopping her because he thought she was trying to escape.

"If this snow keeps up, I'll be going out for a walk in it tomorrow. That's what I wanted to tell you."

She turned again to watch his reaction. There was the remote possibility that he'd try to keep her from leaving the house, which was why she was telling him she planned to go out. But he merely looked curious.

"Why ever would you want to do that? I assumed most women were like my sister, who refuses to go anywhere if it's snowing. She swears she'll melt."

"I didn't mean if it's still snowing," she corrected him. "I'd wait until it stops. I just didn't want you to think I was going anywhere other than for a walk."

"So you like fresh snow, do you? Didn't think anyone enjoyed it as much as I do. As it happens, I was thinking about taking a walk in it m'self."

"No, don't disturb it until—"

"You do?" he cut in.

She grinned. She couldn't help it. "Yes," she said, not realizing that she was blushing.

Chapter Twelve

LUNCHEON WITH OPHELIA AND HIS aunt was surprisingly pleasant. Raphael was actually able to relax and for a short while not think about the monumental chore he'd set for himself. He didn't need to keep the conversation flowing. He was, for the most part, excluded from it!

But then Ophelia was in her element, talking about London. And as soon as she found out that Esmeralda had only been to the city twice in her life, once for her come-out, and once to visit her brother's solicitor when her husband died, Ophelia took it upon herself to give the older woman a verbal tour of the London she knew best. Bond Street! Good God, when two women started talking about shopping, a man might as well not be present. But she described the city's parks as well, the Seasonal social events, the theaters, even the palace, since Ophelia had toured it when she was a child.

He realized, over dessert, that the conversation hadn't once revolved around Ophelia. Hadn't that been one of Mavis's allegations, that the beauty wasn't happy unless she was the center of attention, that she made sure everything revolved around her? And yet Ophelia hadn't talked about herself at all, had merely made an effort to entertain his aunt by chatting about things she was familiar with.

She'd even laughed and got his aunt to hoot a few times as well. One of the stories she related was about her mother.

"She'd taken me shopping for hats, to match the new wardrobe I'd just ordered for this Season. We'd brought along samples of the materials, and this one haberdashery had quite a good selection to choose from, already made. The owner was sure he had exactly what I needed in blue velvet in his back room, so he invited us to follow him. But it was an old shop. The doors weren't very wide. My mother actually got stuck in the doorway!"

"You're pulling my leg, gel," Esmeralda replied doubtfully. "Admit it!"

"No, really. She has a sweet tooth that she's indulged over the years to the point that she's now quite wide of girth. She'd never gotten stuck in a door before though, since she usually steps through them sideways, just to be safe, mind you. But that day she was distracted and was simply following me, and unfortunately, finding the door too tight a squeeze, she *thought* she could merely push her way through it."

"And made sure she was good and stuck?"

"Exactly!" Ophelia chuckled. "And the poor shopkeeper panicked. There was no other way out of that back room, you see."

Esmeralda was laughing uproariously at this point. "And how was the situation rectified?"

"Well, with no one else coming along to help, the owner and I made a combined effort to push my mother back out the way she'd come in."

"And that worked?"

"No, it didn't."

"Then what did?"

"My mother finally belched."

"Oh, good God," Esmeralda said, wiping tears of laughter from her eyes. "She was that full of hot air?"

Ophelia laughed again. "We'd stopped for lunch before going to the haberdashery, you see. She simply hadn't had enough time to digest it!"

What an amazing experience, hearing Ophelia laugh! It put a twinkle in her blue eyes and softened all of her hard edges. A lock of her white-blonde hair had come loose while she was laughing. Somehow he'd imagined her running off to find the nearest mirror to fix it, but she merely flicked it out of the way with the back of her fingers and seemed not to give it another thought.

He was shocked, though she didn't notice, since she'd pretty much forgotten that he was even there. But it made him realize that he'd never seen her enjoy herself before, as she did today in his dining room. Then again, he'd never heard the ice queen laugh in genuine pleasure before either. No, after today, he couldn't very well call her that anymore.

Those damned doubts were showing up again. He had a feeling he was seeing a side of Ophelia that no one else ever saw. He'd thought the same thing in the parlor when she'd made him laugh. And when she'd admitted that she enjoyed one of life's little pleasures—leaving fresh footprints in newly fallen snow—she'd nearly bowled him over with her bashful smile. Why did she keep the vivacious, amusing woman under wraps, for no one else to appreciate?

It was just as well that Esmerelda's footman arrived with Sabrina's letter late that afternoon. Sabrina had to be busy planning her wedding to Duncan by now, and yet she'd taken the time to answer him right away. And that letter definitely erased those pesky doubts he'd been having.

He waited until after dinner. He probably shouldn't have. His sobering mood put a damper on the meal, which made it quite different from the lively luncheon they'd shared earlier. Esmerelda went upstairs as soon as she could, the silence making her uncomfortable. Ophelia tried to do the same, but he wasn't about to let her escape.

"Join me in the parlor for a nightcap?" he suggested when she rose from the table to follow his aunt out of the dining room.

"I'd rather not," Ophelia replied. "It's been a long day."

"It's been nothing of the sort. And join me anyway. You've had time to settle in. Now it's time to begin—"

"What?" she cut in, her tone turning sharply defensive. "Dissecting me?"

"I prefer to think of it as examining motives." He extended an arm toward the door. "Shall we?"

She preceded him into the parlor, her back stiff. She took a seat on the first sofa she came to, just as stiffly. Raphael moved to the rolltop desk off to the side where he'd stocked liquors during his last visit. He poured two shots of brandy and joined Ophelia on the sofa before he offered her one. She waved it aside.

"Just as well," he said with a shrug, and downed one of the shots. "I have a feeling I'll need it more'n you."

"Humph."

"You know," he said thoughtfully, "if you take this defensive attitude, we aren't going to get anywhere. I assumed you'd like to get back to London sooner than later."

"I would. But this whole charade is your idea, not mine, so just get it over with."

"Very well. I have a list of your transgressions, Phelia. I'm not going to lay them all on the table at once or we'd be here all night, but we are going to pick them apart, one by one. Tonight let's begin with one of the main charges against you, as I and most others see it, your propensity for spreading harmful rumors."

"Ah, yes, I'm such a rumormonger," she said drily. "You've mentioned it more'n once now. But in fact, I've only ever spread one rumor."

"Three," he corrected.

She gasped. "Three? What other rumors do you think I've started?"

"Patience, m'dear. Remember? Tonight we're just going to deal with the rumor you admit to starting, which, I assume, was your slandering of Duncan."

"Who was hurt by the rumor that he was a barbarian?" she demanded. "He certainly wasn't."

"No thanks to you."

"Nonsense. People only had to meet him to see that it was mere speculation, that there's nothing *really* barbaric about him."

"Did that give you the right to blacken his name?"

"How did I do that? By calling him a barbarian? He was from the Highlands! Everyone, well, except for my father, knows Highlanders are barely civilized."

He stared at her without replying. After a few moments she sighed. "Very well, so it's just a myth. Obviously, Highlanders can be quite civilized. I'll admit that if I weren't so desperate I could barely think what to do, I never would have done that."

"How were you desperate?"

She mumbled something so low he didn't catch it and had to ask, "What?"

"I *said* I was afraid he really was going to be a barbarian. I'm not the only one who believed that myth about Highlanders, you know."

"So your excuse was fear? Fear is almost understandable."

"No."

He was incredulous. She'd just given him a somewhat acceptable reason for what she'd done and now she was denying it? "No?"

"It wasn't just fear. I was also furious, too. I didn't spread that rumor to hurt Duncan. I started the rumor for my father's benefit. I didn't want to marry a man I'd never even met. There was the fear of *who* he was, but besides that, I wasn't even asked if I wanted to be engaged to him! I was furious with my father because he wouldn't listen to reason. So I wanted him to hear the rumors and get me out of that damned engagement."

"Which didn't happen, so I assume he never heard the rumor?"

"Oh, I'm sure he did, he just didn't care," she said in a low voice.

"Did it never occur to you to simply tell Duncan how you felt instead of taking matters into your own hands and insulting him so he'd break it off?"

She laughed bitterly. "Duncan asked me that too, but I feared once he saw me, I'd never get rid of him."

"Because of your beauty? I hate to say it, m'dear, but some men actually value goodness and honesty over a pretty face."

She rolled her eyes. "I can see why you and Duncan are such good friends. You even think alike."

"How so?"

"He said nearly the same thing, though he called them sterling qualities that men prefer. But I'll tell you what I told him. I've had hundreds of marriage proposals, which proves what most men prefer. Many of those proposals were from men who barely knew me. What did you call them? 'A stream of idiots'? I quite agree."

He couldn't help grinning. "In defense of men in general, I'm going to suggest that most of them were smitten with you, and with good reason. And because of your popularity, they would see a need for haste, in order to outrun the competition. I believe that's why the men proposed before they had a chance to get to know you."

"Oh, of course, and by your contention, once those men got to know me, they'd despise me the way you and Duncan do. Though Duncan did admit he would have tried to win me over if I hadn't insulted him when we met. He was delighted to be engaged to me after he clapped eyes on me. You're the only man I've ever met who wasn't smitten by this face at first sight."

She seemed surprised by her own words. She even gave him a thoughtful look that made him quite uncomfortable.

"No need to go off on a guessing tangent," he warned her. "I simply have no intention of getting married in this century."

"So never?"

"An exaggeration," he said with a sigh. "Just not for another ten years at least. My father is very understanding in that regard, probably because he didn't marry early himself. So he's not pushing me onto the marriage mart yet."

"Was that really why you left England? Because every mama in London had you earmarked for her daughter?"

"You make it sound worse than it was, but yes, I was hounded more'n I cared to deal with. It seemed as if I couldn't turn around without some young chit being shoved in my face. I simply got fed up with it. And I hadn't done the grand tour yet, so decided that would be a good time to escape, as it were. But let's get back to the matter at hand."

"Certainly," she replied tartly. "I just love being raked over the coals. Let's do get back to that."

He frowned. "You're not taking this seriously, Phelia."

"Aren't I? Perhaps because I see no reason to belabor it when I've already admitted that I never would have started that rumor if not for the mixture of fear and rage I was beset with at the time. But here's another confession for you. Flaw number two is my temper. I can't help it and I'm rarely able to control it once it snaps."

"No surprise there, m'dear," he said drily. "I've already figured that out, indeed I have."

"Really? Then you've gone out of your way to provoke my temper deliberately?"

"Not a'tall. You're just too touchy about your own flaws."

"Because I hate them, every one of them!"

Thrown out there as it was in a burst of heat, they stared at each other for a long moment, until he finally asked quietly, "Then why are you fighting tooth and nail my effort to help you get rid of them?"

"Have I refused to talk to you? Have I told you to go to hell—lately?"

He burst out laughing. "No, not lately. Then you're saying you're going to cooperate? For your own benefit at least?"

"For my own benefit, no. To get me out of here sooner, yes."

He sighed. "Not exactly the attitude I'd hoped for, but better than no cooperation at all. Let me ask you this. If you had it to do over again, would you have handled breaking your engagement to Duncan any differently?"

"Why don't you ask me instead if I felt I had any other choice? I didn't, you know. What part of *desperate* didn't you understand?"

"So you don't regret any of it?"

"Of course I do. There was no spite or malice involved as you seem to think. I wasn't *trying* to hurt him, I was just trying to get rid of him! I even concluded later that he'd do well enough. At least his title would have delighted my father."

"But not you?"

"There's only one thing I'd like in a husband, and, no, it's not a title. That's my father's criterion for a son-in-law, not mine."

"What's that one thing?"

"I don't believe that information pertains to your goal, does it?"

"No, but you have me curious now."

"Too bad," she said with a little smirk.

Chapter Thirteen

"ANOTHER PETTICOAT?" SADIE SUGGESTED. "I stuck my nose out the door; it's colder out there this morning than I figured it would be."

"Have you ever been this far north before? I haven't, but that's obviously why it's much colder than we're used to. And I'm already wearing three!" Ophelia complained.

"You did find those woolen stockings I laid out for you?"

"Yes, now stop fussing."

"I wish we'd thought to bring your riding boots. They would have insulated your calves better than those short traveling boots."

Ophelia finally chuckled. "There wasn't room for them, and will you stop worrying? I'll be fine in this thick velvet dress as well as my coat. I'm only going for a little walk. If I get too cold, I'll come right back inside, I promise."

A few minutes later she was hurrying downstairs, her fur-rimmed cap in place, her powder-blue coat buttoned to the neck, her fur muff hanging from a cord on her wrist so she wouldn't lose it. It was still early. She was hoping to enjoy the walk she'd been looking forward to without running into her nemesis first.

Later this afternoon would be soon enough to continue with that long list of transgressions Raphael had mentioned. Last night had been painful enough. She didn't like being reminded of her regrets. She didn't have many, but those she did have made her sad, and she hated being sad. Was that what he was hoping for? That she'd be sad and miserable and—voilà!—she'd be a changed woman? She snorted to herself.

But their first foray into her supposed wickedness hadn't been as bad as she'd thought it would be. She'd decided to be truthful. She wasn't always. She didn't see that as a flaw, but as a convenience, since the truth rarely worked for her. But lies always did. It was a habit she'd picked up from her "friends" since they were never truthful with her, always pandering to her and telling her what they *thought* she wanted to hear. Besides, if she'd ever been truthful with them, they would have been so insulted they would have gone away for good, and false friends were better than no friends at all she'd long ago concluded.

She was amazed, though, that she'd decided to be truthful with Raphael. She wasn't even sure why, other than that he seemed a bit more astute than most people she met, making her suspect that he'd see through any lies she might offer. Not that she needed to offer any. She had flaws. Everyone did. That hers governed some of her behavior wasn't exactly something she could help. But she'd admit to them, and that bloody well better be enough to get her out of here.

Sadie had been right, she discovered when she stepped outside and closed the front door behind her. It wasn't the air that was frigid, though, but a slight wind, which she probably wouldn't have felt if the sun were shining. But the sun hadn't made an appearance yet to melt anything. It was firmly tucked behind a solid sheet of dark clouds that predicted more snow.

She scowled at the shoveled walkway leading up to the door and around to the right where the stable was. The caretaker was doing his job, no doubt. Tucking her hands into her muff, she carefully moved through the snow that hadn't been disturbed, off to the left side of the house. Now here was a view she had to admit was lovely.

No other buildings were on this side of the house that the dining room and parlor looked out on, just a lot of barren trees looking much prettier now with their branches coated with white, and a few piney bushes and trees, still quite green, drooping with the snow clinging to them. And her footsteps.

She grinned as she made several large circles of footsteps around the trees, then stopped to stare off at the rolling hills, all beautifully white. It was almost blinding, the snow was so pristine and undisturbed, the air so brisk.

She took a deep breath, then gasped it out when she felt something hit her back. She thought it must be a bird, though there weren't many left at this time of year. But the poor thing could be half-frozen and unable to fly accurately. She turned around, expecting to find it lying on the ground by her feet— and caught sight of Raphael forming another snowball in his hands.

She stared at him openmouthed. That wicked grin he was wearing spoke for itself. The very idea, deliberately throwing a snowball at her! How utterly childish.

"Are you mad?" she called out, then immediately shrieked as the second wad of snow flew past her head.

She ducked behind the bush next to her, indignant—and yet determined to get even. She shook off her muff and gathered a big scoop of snow, packing it firmly before she straightened up and let it fly in his direction. She scored a hit! White splattered on the side of his chest all across the greatcoat he had on. She hooted with laughter, only to get a mouthful of snow. She sputtered and ducked down again. His aim was too bloody on the mark, but she'd already proven hers wasn't that bad, and at least she had cover from the bush. He was boldly standing out there, probably thinking she'd merely gotten lucky with that hit. She'd show him!

She laughed again as she wound up to throw her second snowball. He'd just been waiting for her to show her head! His third snowball knocked her cap off. Perhaps hiding behind a bush wasn't such a good idea after all, since she couldn't see what he was doing. She decided a hit-and-run approach might serve her better.

She peeked over the bush, ducked his next missile, immediately stood up to launch her own, then ran. And ran. She slipped, she slid, she ran some more, laughing all the while.

She felt two more snowballs hit her back before she heard him call out, "Coward!"

She turned around to give him a brilliant smile. "Come closer—if you dare!" she taunted back.

"So it's to be like that, is it?"

He started toward her. She quickly scooped up more snow and lobbed it at him, then ran again, but not before she'd seen white splatter on his forehead and down his cheeks. She laughed delightedly and spared a moment to scoop up another ball, but shrieked again when she glanced up and saw that he'd narrowed the space between them too much. His damn long legs!

With a laugh she ran off, but he dove at her and didn't miss. They both hit the snow and slid across the ground quite a few feet. She had to gasp for breath, she was laughing so hard.

The kiss was so unexpected, it took her a few moments to realize that it was his lips that were warming hers. She was shocked, just long enough for her to actually experience that kiss to the fullest—before she got indignant over it. It felt nice. Even nicer was the thrill that shot through her because of it. Like butterflies fluttering around in her belly, and she'd never felt anything quite like it.

Quite naturally, her arms slipped about his shoulders. If she had felt the cold before, she certainly didn't now with Raphael's large body on top of hers. Steam from their mingled breath warmed the rest of her face, making her realize his lips were quite hot as they moved seductively over hers. Her breasts tightened, tingling. Her toes curled in her boots. Heat seemed to be spreading all over her as her blood began to race swiftly through her limbs.

That might have continued indefinitely if he hadn't got carried away and slipped his icy fingers along her neck. The shock of the sudden cold brought her indignation straight to the fore. She pushed away from him and stumbled to her feet, dusting off some of the snow that clung to her velvet coat. She was covered in it everywhere, of course, but that was to be expected and was not what had her bristling.

"I *knew* that's what this was all about," she said in an aha! tone. "You could have just asked me to marry you. My parents would be thrilled, no doubt."

"But you wouldn't be?"

"Don't be ridiculous."

"And you might want to stop making guesses that are even more ridiculous, when I merely wanted to see if you tasted as sour as you always sound."

She stared at him still lying there on the ground in such a casual pose that he could have been comfortably stretched out on a sofa. She started to frown, then raised a brow at him instead.

"Do I taste sour?"

"Oh, absolutely," he said with a grin.

Good God, he was teasing her! No one ever teased her. The holier-than-thou attitude she'd worked so hard to achieve made sure of that. But then no one had ever thrown snowballs at her either.

She'd just enjoyed herself too much to have it end on this bad note, so she took a moment to examine her response and realized that she shouldn't have gotten nearly as huffy as she just had over a mere kiss that obviously meant nothing. He was an admitted rake, after all, probably quite used to doing things like that.

"I scored more hits than you did," she said with a little grin of her own, her way of admitting she'd overreacted, an unspoken apology, as it were.

"You did not!" He laughed and got to his feet. "But you *were* pretty good at that. You must have had a lot of practice as a child."

She went very still. "No, there was never anyone willing to play with me in the snow."

The amusement left him as well. "I hope you're lying, Phelia."

"Yes, of course," she agreed just to get him off the subject.

"You weren't, were you?"

"I warned you not to go there, so don't!"

She walked off. The interlude had ended on a bad note after all.

Chapter Fourteen

HER LAUGHTER HAD CARRIED ON the wind to him. Raphael had a feeling he'd never forget the sound of it, or that particular experience with Ophelia today.

Throwing that first snowball at her had been a complete impulse on his part. He'd been finishing his breakfast when he saw her taking a walk and decided to go out and join her. What followed certainly hadn't been premeditated.

He'd barely recognized her today. Such an amazing difference between the woman who'd thrown snowballs back at him, and the woman that everyone hated. It hadn't been contrived. He was absolutely sure her behavior had been nothing but spontaneous. She wasn't trying to fool him into thinking that he'd miraculously "changed" her. She'd merely shown him yet another side to her that no one else ever saw—a playful side that had been delightful.

While he didn't regret his first impulse, he would probably regret the second one. Kissing her had been foolish. It had given her the wrong impression, while it had been no more than a nat ural inclination on his part. Her lips had been close, her laughter ringing in the air, and she was so damn beautiful. There was simply no way he could have resisted. But wanting to see if she tasted sour? What a whopper! He could at least have come up with a better excuse than that and would have if he hadn't been so bemused by that kiss.

He found her alone in the parlor, standing in front of the window that looked out on the side yard. Quite a mess they'd made out there during their snow fight. Their tracks were everywhere, and the deep indent where they'd slid across the snow when he tackled her—was she thinking about the fun they'd had, or about that kiss they'd shared? Actually, it was a bit conceited of him to imagine she was thinking of him now.

What *did* she usually think about when she was alone? Bloody hell, he was getting much too curious about her and things that had nothing to do with the reason he'd brought her there.

"Are you ready for those coals again?" he said lightly by her side.

She wasn't startled by his presence; she must have heard him approach. And she didn't need to ask what he was talking about. "Being raked over coals" had been her own remark.

But he did hear the sigh and her tone was rather forlorn as she said, "By all means."

Guilt! It rose up and nearly choked him as he watched her walk toward the sofa with drooped shoulders. What the devil? How could he possibly feel guilty for trying to help her? She was going to benefit from his efforts, not him—well, he'd win his bet with Duncan, but that was so minor in the scheme of things now, when he'd more recently come to realize that he simply wanted to help her. Something had made her the way she was and perhaps he ought to add finding out what it was to the agenda.

He joined her on the same sofa, noting that she moved away from him as he sat down. "I don't bite, you know," he said with a degree of annoyance.

"Actually, I believe you do."

"Was that in reference to kissing you, or raking you over hot coals?"

"Both." She poured herself a cup of tea from the tray on the table. A basket of sweets was there as well, but she didn't even glance at it.

"I'll take a cup of that."

"Pour your own," she retorted.

Much better. A forlorn Ophelia was as bad as seeing her in tears. Quite out of his league.

He did pour his own tea, and just to make sure she didn't throw him off with any more sighs, he remarked, "I'll leave those pastries for you. You're too skinny."

She hadn't really looked at him yet, but she certainly did now. "I am not!"

"And you're too pale," he added for good measure. "You've got no color in your skin."

"As it should be."

"I would have thought you'd want to be at your best."

"There's nothing wrong with the way I look. I'm so damned beautiful it's disgusting."

Whoa. Take a step back. Did he hear that right? And in such a bitter tone?

"Yes, quite," he agreed jauntily. "Very disgusting. Extraordinarily so."

She narrowed her blue eyes on him. "You needn't belabor it."

"Was I? Beg pardon. Let's discuss another one of the rumors you started then."

If he'd thought to put her off guard by tossing that out there so abruptly, it didn't work. She sat back and looked nothing but curious now. "Yes, please do, since I don't recall starting any others."

"I believe your friend, or rather, ex-friend would disagree. What was it Mavis said you spread about her? That she was a liar and a backstabber?"

"No, she called me a backstabber. I merely called her a liar in front of Jane and Edith, our mutual friends. She provoked me one time too many. My temper snapped. But it went no further than that. I knew Jane and Edith wouldn't repeat it. They happen to like Mavis."

"But not you?"

She glanced away from him. "I know you overheard that second conversation between Mavis and me. No, Jane and Edith have never really been my friends. They pretend to be, but they aren't."

"That bothers you?"

"Hardly. I don't want people to like me. I tend to make sure they don't."

That statement was so bizarre, it rendered him speechless for a moment. Of course he didn't believe it. But why would she even say it? A defensive excuse?

He pointed out the obvious to her: "No one goes out of their way to be disliked—deliberately. It's against human nature."

She merely shrugged as she glanced at him again. "If you say so."

She wasn't going to argue her case? Quite annoyed with this new indifferent attitude of hers, he said, "Very well, for what conceivable reason would you deliberately alienate your friends?"

"So I don't have to wonder if they're sincere when I'm sure they aren't."

"You don't trust anyone? Is that what you're saying?"

"Exactly."

"I suppose that includes me?"

He was actually hoping for a denial, though he wasn't sure why. He didn't get it.

"Of course it does. Like everyone else, you've lied to me."

"The devil I have," he said indignantly. "I've been completely honest—"

Her snort cut him off. "You told me you were driving me to London, not in so many words, but you certainly implied it. That wasn't lying?"

He flushed with color, guilty as charged. "That was an exception, merely to avoid your theatrics until we got here."

"Oh, I see. That it prevented me from finding help until you got me to this place, which is so remote there is none, was merely a bonus? But one exception or a dozen, what's the difference? I rest my case."

His flush got a little darker. "I apologize for misleading you for mere convenience, but I won't apologize for trying to help you."

"You don't need to apologize for lying, either. And certainly not for the sake of convenience. I do so quite often myself."

"Is this flaw number three?"

"No, I'm not a compulsive liar. If I lie about something, it's quite deliberate. My flaws—my impatience and my temper—I have no control over, lying I do."

"You don't see that as a bad trait?"

"Don't be a hypocrite and say you do."

"Actually I do, but I suppose therein lies the difference between us. I prefer to be honest, you seem to prefer dishonesty."

"I don't *prefer* it," she retorted, then admitted, "I even used to feel guilty about it."

"What changed that?"

"Everyone around me lying *to* me. That's actually why Mavis was the only real friend I ever had. She was the only one, out of all of them, that I could trust to be honest with me—at least she was up until I hurt her."

"Would you like to discuss that?" he asked carefully.

"No."

She wasn't going to say any more. And now that she'd admitted that she had no qualms whatsoever about lying, he had to wonder if she'd been at all truthful with him about anything so far. It was a daunting thought. If she'd decided to lie to get back to London . . .

"I didn't deliberately hurt Mavis," she started to tell him, then burst out, "Oh, God, you see!"

He frowned. "What?"

"*That's* my third flaw."

She had him utterly confused now. "What is?"

"That I can't keep my mouth shut! It's ridiculous, how I react to silence!"

He started to laugh. "You see that as a flaw?"

"Of course it is," she said, annoyed. "How would you feel if you had a nice story to relate and you wanted to draw it out, but when met with a little silence, you got right to the point? It totally ruins what could otherwise have been quite an entertaining anecdote."

He was definitely laughing now. "As flaws go, that's a bloody minor one, m'dear."

"I don't happen to think so," she replied indignantly.

"You had a story to relate?"

"No, I just used that as an example. It happens when I don't want to discuss something too."

"Ah, I see. Good to know." He grinned. "But let's get back to Mavis."

"Let's don't."

"Need I be silent again?"

She glared at him. He managed to resist laughing this time. Like his sister, Amanda, Ophelia was proving to be too easy to tease. But the new subject he was going to introduce was sobering.

"Mavis said you've ruined lives. Was that statement broader than it should have been?"

"Not at all. I'm sure many of the men I've turned down think their lives are ruined because of it. Duncan was the only one who thought the opposite, that marrying me would have been a fate worse than hell. I thought the same thing, after his grandfather pointed out what drudgery living at Summers Glade was going to be."

Duncan had been willing to marry her to prevent Ophelia from being ruined if Mavis spread the rumor of what she'd seen when she walked in on them in Ophelia's bedroom. It was quite innocent, but who would believe that once the rumor got started? Raphael doubted he would have been so noble, at least not for her.

"You really didn't contrive that compromising situation that Mavis walked in on, did you?" he said.

"No, but don't get the wrong impression. At that point I was willing to marry Duncan just to get it over with. I'd decided he would do well enough—at least for my father. And I thought, erroneously as it turned out, that Duncan would be willing as well, once he recovered from my calling him a barbarian. If I had known at the time that he was reluctant to marry me, I probably would have arranged a compromising situation like that."

He was bemused now. Why the deuce did she own up to that? He'd actually thought she'd been innocent in that situation.

"And you don't see anything wrong with that?" he asked curtly.

"When I thought he'd be pleased enough with the match in the end? No, I don't."

He shook his head, but allowed, "I suppose you can't be blamed for that reasoning, when women have been trapping men into marriage since the dawn of history. I personally see it as the worst sort of machinations, but then that's from a man's point of view, you understand."

"Of course. I wouldn't expect you to feel any other way. But as long as we're on the subject, you might as well know, also, that I wouldn't have done any such thing if I had known that there was no chance of Duncan ever being happy with me."

Could he believe her? He supposed he could, after what she'd already admitted.

"Now let me ask you something," she continued, giving him a pointed look. "If I *had* contrived those machinations of the worst sort, as you called them, how is that different from what you're doing here, keeping me prisoner until my behavior changes—to *your* satisfaction? You've taken matters into your own hands, quite high-handedly, without asking if I wanted your help, which I didn't. So answer me that, Rafe, if you can. What is the difference?"

She was looking rather smug, probably thinking she'd just cornered him into a spot he couldn't get out of. "I see the similarity, but you're overlooking the broader picture. Trapping a man into a marriage he doesn't want would make you both miserable for the rest of your lives. There's no escape from that without a serious scandal. Do you really want to compare that to a few brief weeks where no one gets hurt, no one ends up miserable, and you go about your merry way a much better person when we're done here?"

"Go to hell!"

He managed not to grin. "You can keep trying to send me there, m'dear, but this halo is rather firmly attached to my head. And don't be a poor loser."

"Why not?" she shot back furiously. "What's one more thing to add to your bloody long list of my despicable behaviors? And you are *not* an angel! You are the veriest devil and you know it!"

He tsked at her. "Your temper is showing, Phelia. This would be an excellent time to work on controlling it, don't you think?"

She gave him a tight little smile. He had no idea how she managed that when her eyes were staring daggers at him.

But her tone *was* dripping sarcasm when she replied, "How's this? And what were we discussing? Ah, yes, how many lives I've ruined. Let's do get back to that."

She shot off the couch and began pacing, which completely distracted him from their conversation. Watching the swish of her skirt and how it moved over her backside . . .

"Who is that?" she asked, stopping to stare at the portrait above the mantel.

He reluctantly drew his eyes off her derriere to follow her gaze. "My grandmother Agatha."

She glanced back at him with a raised brow and a smirk in her tone as she asked, "The woman your grandfather came here to get away from?"

"No, the one he always rushed home to. In fact, when their children were grown, he often brought her here with him, to be alone with her."

"I'm sorry," she said, amazing him. "I was actually just teasing with that remark. But I guess I don't have a knack for it."

She really did look contrite, so he decided to try to put her at ease. "There's actually a little story behind that painting. I noticed the artist trying to drown himself in a river I was riding past."

"You mean swimming?"

"Well, that's all I thought he was doing. It was a warm day, after all. But, no, he was trying to drown himself, he was just failing at it. He kept bobbing back to the surface! But he didn't see the dead tree floating his way. I shouted to warn him. He didn't hear me. And the tree took him under."

"You saved him, didn't you?"

"To his fury," he said with a chuckle. "He even took a few swings at me after he got done coughing up all the water he'd swallowed. And then he started crying his woes and explaining why I'd done him such a disservice in saving him. Turned out he was so dedicated to his art that he refused to do any other sort of work, and he was starving since no one would buy his paintings. Silly chap lived in a tiny village where no one could *afford* his art, and he hadn't even thought of moving."

"So you commissioned him to paint your grandmother to help him with his finances?"

"No, actually, he found a miniature I carried of my grandmother and painted that portrait for me as a gift. I merely dragged him and his art off to the nearest city, where he's now so much in demand he has to turn commissions down. But he's that good, you see." Raphael gestured to the painting. "I realized that as soon as I saw his painting. The miniature didn't do Agatha justice, but with his artist's eye he saw through to the real her. The portrait is nearly her exact image when she was younger, according to my father. I would have had it hung in

Norford Hall, but it made Grandmother melancholy when she saw it."

"Why, if it is such a good likeness?"

He shrugged. "Lost youth and that sort of rot, I suppose. She's getting up there in years."

Ophelia came back to rejoin him on the sofa, seeming a bit more relaxed now. Clearing his throat to signal he was returning to their previous subject, he guessed, "You're going to contend you've ruined no lives, aren't you?"

"On the contrary. I did ruin Mavis's life, obviously. I should have let her marry that bounder she fancied. She might have been quite happy with an unfaithful husband, certainly more happy than she is now."

"I take it you stole him away from her?"

"There was no stealing involved. I wasn't even sixteen when he asked me to marry him, long before he'd even met her. He became such a nuisance, always trying to steal kisses from me, I finally asked my mother to stop including him on her guest lists, which she did. So he started courting my best friend, which got him invited to the same parties we all attended, and he *admitted* to me it was just so he could get close to me again."

"You didn't tell her?"

"Of course I did, repeatedly. She laughed it off every time. She refused to hear a single word against him, she was so infatuated. Finally I allowed him to kiss me, when I knew she would walk in on it. She wouldn't listen, so I gave her the proof she needed."

"I would think that would have severed your relationship with her."

"It did, briefly. She cried. She said some nasty things. She blamed it all on me. But then she came back and said she understood, that she forgave me."

"Obviously not."

"No, obviously not," Ophelia said in a small voice. "It was never the same again between us."

Regret was written all over her face, making him feel like a cad. He wanted her to own up to the things she'd done wrong, but this obviously wasn't one of them. She'd tried to help a friend and lost that friend because of it.

He'd prefer to deal with her anger at the moment, and the quickest way to get that back was for him to point out, "There now, it wasn't so difficult to get your temper under control, was it?"

She stood up. "By making me sad with painful memories? If that's what it takes, no thank you."

She marched out of the room. He wasn't about to try to stop her. She'd just given him too much to think about, in particular that she'd come up with somewhat acceptable excuses for each of the transgressions he'd laid on the table so far. Of course, the worst was yet to come, her appalling treatment of one of the sweetest, kindest women he'd ever met—Sabrina Lambert.

Chapter Fifteen

OPHELIA WENT NO FARTHER THAN the top of the stairs and sat down there. She didn't want to encounter Sadie, who might be in her room and would want to know why she looked so miserable. She didn't want to talk to anyone other than Raphael. She actually expected him to follow her and apologize. She was giving him a chance to do so by not going far. More fool her. He didn't follow her.

"A penny for your thoughts, gel?"

She'd heard the footsteps coming down the corridor behind her, but she'd hoped it was one of the servants. No such luck.

She stood up to address Raphael's aunt. "You wouldn't want to know."

"So it's going to cost me a pound note?"

That managed to make her grin, however briefly. "Your nephew is impossible to deal with, utterly high-handed, obnoxiously stubborn. He won't listen to reason."

"I would have thought he'd have you charmed by now. He's good at charming the ladies."

Ophelia snorted. "Perhaps in another life. I find him about as charming as a rogue boar."

Esmeralda chuckled. Ophelia found nothing amusing about it. She'd been serious.

"Let me ask you something, Lady Esme. I was going to broach this yesterday, but Rafe convinced me I'd be wasting my time because you're firmly in his camp. But are you? Can you really condone his keeping me here when I want to go home?"

"He assured me your parents would be quite agreeable to your brief stay here. Did he exaggerate?"

"No, he didn't. I don't doubt they were thrilled when they received his note. But doesn't it matter what I think and want?"

Esmeralda squinted her eyes at her. "Are you old enough for your opinion to count in this regard? Or do your parents still hold full authority over you? If you're old enough to make your own decisions, gel, I'll take you back to London m'self if that's what you want."

Ophelia let out a bitter sigh. "No, I'm not that old. And that is *so* unfair. I'm old enough to marry, but not old enough to have a say in whom I will marry. I'm old enough to bear children, but I haven't sense enough to pick out the father for them?"

"Don't be surprised if I don't agree with you. Course it's all well and good for me to say that now, when all decisions about m'self are my own to make. But I *do* understand, and I confess I felt the same way you do when I was younger. When I found the man I wanted to marry, it was quite upsetting that I couldn't have him without my father's permission. There was the chance, him being a Scotsman, that my father would have said forget it, find yourself a nice English lad. He didn't, but he could have, and there wouldn't have been a thing I could have done about it."

"You could have run off to be with the man you loved."

Esmeralda chuckled. "I'm not a wild card, gel, as you seem to be. I don't break rules or thumb my nose at the dictates of society."

"I don't either," Ophelia protested.

"But you'd like to," Esmeralda guessed. "Therein is the difference."

Ophelia couldn't very well deny that. "This is still so—so outrageous."

"My nephew's motives are well-intentioned. He likes to help people. He usually doesn't even think twice about it. And this certainly isn't the first time he's gone out of his way to do so. He didn't take the typical tour of the Continent when he was away from England, you know. He single-handedly saved a bunch of orphans from abuse when one of them picked his pocket and explained he'd done so in order to get his sister out of the dreadful orphanage he'd run away from. It took half a year, but Rafe found every one of those orphans a good home. He also helped to evacuate a whole town in France that got flooded. Saved a few lives, according to Amanda, to whom he wrote about it. Those are only a couple of examples of how he tends to help when help is needed."

That was supposed to make what he was doing to her all right? "I didn't ask for his help!"

"No, but he claims you made a big mess of things at that gathering you both attended recently at Summer's Glade. If I were you, I'd want to make sure I didn't muck things up like that again."

"I have a few flaws," Ophelia grumbled. "I don't deny them."

"We all do, gel."

"Mine might be a little excessive."

Esmerelda chuckled. "A little, eh? Then maybe just a few lessons in restraint might be in order? Just to curb the excess, mind you."

"How do you control an uncontrollable temper?" Ophelia knew it was a hopeless question.

But the older woman actually answered from experience. "By biting my tongue."

Ophelia grinned. "You don't have a temper."

"I did, oh, quite a nasty one."

"Really?"

"Indeed. It used to amuse my husband no end, him being a Scotsman with no temper a'tall!"

Ophelia laughed. The sound drew Raphael out of the parlor. Seeing her at the top of the stairs with his aunt and apparently in a much better mood, he asked, "Feeling better?"

She scowled at him. "Not in the least."

He rolled his eyes and went back into the parlor. Esmerelda tsked beside her.

"He really does get your hackles up, doesn't he?"

"Without even trying," Ophelia said in a lower tone, just in case Raphael was still within hearing distance. But then she amended, "No, I take that back. He does seem to make a concerted effort to do just that."

"Is it strategy, perhaps? To help you deal with your temper in a more acceptable fashion."

"Then he needs another lesson in strategies, because it's not working."

"Are you even trying to curb this infamous temper you've mentioned?"

Ophelia sighed. "I have curbed it, actually. I stopped screaming at him."

Esmerelda grinned, but then her look turned thoughtful.

"Let me ask you this: Why don't you want to be here? You have one of the most eligible bachelors in all of England going out of his way to try to help you. I'd think you'd want to take advantage of that."

"I don't."

"But why not? He tried to tell me you don't like him, but I don't see how anyone can *not* like that boy. He's personable, he's witty, he's pleasing to look at, and he comes from one of the most prestigious families in the realm, if I do say so m'self."

"I hate to point it out, but you are in fact quite prejudiced. Perfectly understandable, with him being your nephew. But none of what you've mentioned makes a jot of difference when he had no right to interfere in my life like this!"

Esmerelda frowned. "So you're not going to cooperate and benefit from what he's trying to do?"

Ophelia let out a long sigh. "It may not seem like it, but I *am* cooperating. It's the only thing I could think to do, to get this over with so I can go home."

Chapter Sixteen

"A MANDA! WHAT THE DEUCE ARE you doing here?"

The last person Raphael expected to see, was his younger sister. She'd never come to the Nest before, and now she was standing just inside the door to the parlor, briskly wiping off the dusting of snow on her coat. The snow had started up again about an hour ago, just after Ophelia had left him. Amanda didn't like snow, but he doubted that was why she was looking quite put out.

She spared him a glare. "What am I doing here? Missing a very nice ball to come here to find out what *you're* doing here. You were supposed to follow me to London. Why didn't you?"

"I never said—"

She wasn't finished, interrupting him, "Everyone was asking after you. All my friends were quite disappointed that you didn't return to town with me."

"I warned you I wasn't escorting you to any more parties. The one at Summers Glade was the last. We have numerous cousins and two aunts who live right in London, quite enough escorts for you, m'dear. So it hardly matters when I get to London, now does it?"

"Yes, but you're the one everyone wants to see."

He raised a brow at her. "*Everyone* as in that gaggle of giggling chits you call friends?"

"Well, they do adore you. All the ladies do."

"Not all," he replied, thinking of his houseguest. "And remove your coat. It's quite warm in here. Or are you not staying?"

She missed the hopeful note in his voice and huffed as she marched directly to the fireplace and stuck her hands out toward the heat. "I'll keep it on a bit longer, thank you. I am quite frozen, I don't mind telling you. The coals in the brazier didn't last for this long of a trip. They died out about two hours ago. My maid and I had to bundle under the same lap robe to try and keep warm, but it barely worked. And why the deuce do you only have one lap robe in your coach?"

"Because the brazier usually keeps it warm enough that none are needed. You came here in my coach?"

"Well, of course I did. I don't have one of my own. Never needed one, now did I? It's not as if father doesn't have a half dozen of them in the carriage house at Norford Hall that I could use, *if* I had left from there. But I came here straight from your town house in London."

Before he'd met Ophelia, he could honestly have said that his sister was the most beautiful girl he knew. It wasn't familial loyalty that had made him think so. It was quite true. With her blond hair, shades darker than his, her blue eyes quite lighter, more a powder blue, and the aristocratic bones that ran in his family, no one had doubted that she would outshine all the other debutantes this Season. But then no one in his family had ever met or heard of Ophelia Reid before the party at Summers

Glade. And no one, including Amanda, could hold a candle to Ophelia's beauty.

"And we got lost," she added in a mumble.

"Did you? That must have been interesting."

"Not in the least."

"You got lost because of the snow covering the road up here?"

"No, that was the only thing that got us here. We finally found wagon ruts left in the snow and followed them. But I assumed your driver had been here before. Only after he got us lost did he admit he hasn't worked for you for very long and he's never been this far north in his life. The odious fellow *could* have said something about that sooner."

"Most of my servants are new, Mandy. I didn't retain too many of the old ones when I left for Europe. Now how did you find out I was here?"

"I assumed you went home to Norford Hall. I sent your footman there to find out what was keeping you, and he came back to say you didn't go home a'tall after Summers Glade, that you sent them word that you were coming here instead. I couldn't believe it. Why would you come here, of all places, and at this time of the year?"

He shrugged. "Why not?"

"But you're missing the Season!"

He chuckled at her. "I could care less about the Season. You're the one looking for a good matrimonial match, not I. Did you find one yet?"

She made a look of disgust. "No. Half the men I'm interested in barely notice me."

He laughed. "What a whopper!"

"Thank you for the vote of confidence, but it's quite true. All they want to do is talk about that haughty Ophelia Reid and ask if I know why she hasn't returned to London yet. It didn't take long a'tall for the news to reach town that she didn't marry Duncan MacTavish after all. Do you know why?"

"They decided they wouldn't suit" was all he was going to say about that.

"That is *so* disappointing."

"Why?"

"Don't be obtuse, Rafe. Obviously because now she's back in the competition again and there aren't that many perfect men to go around, you know."

He grinned at her reasoning. "Does your husband have to be perfect?"

"No, of course not—well, a little. But I'll be second in line now, with *her* shopping for a husband again."

"Vanity and jealousy in the same breath. Shame on you, Mandy."

She blushed. "Don't tease. We're discussing the rest of my life here."

"No, we aren't, we're discussing your impatience. If you'd just relax and enjoy your first Season in London, the right man for you will come along before you know it."

"And fall in love with her instead," she said in a petulant mumble.

"You really *are* jealous, aren't you?"

She let out a long sigh. "I can't help it. Good God, she's so beautiful she glows with it. It's bloody well blinding!"

He choked back the laugh that that comment elicited from him and merely said, "I quite agree."

She blinked, then narrowed her eyes on him. "Don't you dare say you were smitten too."

"Not a'tall."

"Good, because she's not a nice woman, you know, certainly not nice enough for you. She's vain and snide and too proud for her own good."

"Is that the current gossip making the rounds?" he asked curiously.

"No, the only gossip about her right now is that she's back on the marriage mart and has delighted *so* many men because of it. That was my own observation from when I met her at Summers Glade. You know she had the nerve to tell me I was wasting my time there? She wasn't even reengaged to MacTavish yet when she said it. She was just positive that he would take her back."

"As it happens, you were wasting your time there. Duncan was already in love with his neighbor Sabrina. It just took him a while to realize it."

"Well, good for him. So *that's* why he and Ophelia broke it off again?"

"Part of it. But getting married was never their own idea, it was arranged by their families, so they were both glad to find a way out of it. Now, remove your coat, have a spot of tea, then go home."

"Don't be a bore, Rafe. Did you forget you invited me to spend the Season with you?"

"Not here."

"No, course not."

"And not even with me," he corrected. "The invitation was for you to use my town house, since Father doesn't keep a house in London. I didn't mean that I'd be spending the Season there with you."

"Well, I like that!" she huffed. "I assumed you would be there. I've missed you. You were away on the Continent for nearly two years. I thought you'd want to spend some time with me, now that you're back."

"And I will, when I return to London."

"But *when* are you coming back? You still haven't said what you're doing here, of all places."

"It didn't occur to you that I might be here with a guest?"

She blanched. "Good God, I never thought! I am *so* embarrassed. I'll leave at once—as soon as I warm up."

"Good."

"Good? You aren't going to try to convince me to stay—at least the night?"

"Not a'tall. It's early enough for you to reach an inn before dark."

She sighed as she finally removed her coat and joined him on the sofa. She took a small pile of letters out of her pocket and handed them to him.

"I brought your mail, in case any of it was important."

"You mean you were hoping there was an invitation to a party here that would interest me." He glanced briefly through the letters. Only the one from Ophelia's father interested him. He opened it and quickly read exactly what he'd expected.

"That too," Amanda agreed, then got right back to the previous subject. "And it's not that early, you know. The inn I used last night is a good six hours from here."

He glanced back at her to point out, "You got lost, remember?"

She sighed again. "Very well, four hours from here. But it will be close to dark by the time I get there. I'd as soon get an early start in the morning. And who is she? Anyone I know?"

She tossed out those last questions abruptly, hoping to catch him off guard, no doubt. It didn't work. And he could only hope that Ophelia wouldn't pick that moment to make an appearance.

"Yes, you know her, and, no, you can forget about finding

out who she is. That, m'dear, is none of your business. But it's not what you've just assumed. I'm not having a lovers' tryst here."

"Oh, certainly," she said doubtfully. "You come to a place with a woman that's so remote it could be in another country, but it's all perfectly innocent?"

"Exactly that. Aunt Esme is even here to make sure of it."

"She is?" Amanda exclaimed in delight. "Wonderful, I haven't seen her in ages! You really have to let me stay now and visit for a few days."

"You saw her just two months ago at father's birthday party. And, no, you're not—"

He broke off, staring out the window. He'd had his nose in a book before Amanda walked in, so he hadn't seen her coach arrive, but he had no trouble seeing it leaving now.

"Tell me you aren't up to tricks, Mandy, to force me back to London? Did you send my coach home?"

She huffed indignantly at his accusing tone. "When I'll be riding back in it? Certainly not."

"Bloody hell," he said as he shot off the sofa.

Chapter Seventeen

O PHELIA WAS SO NERVOUS WONDERING if she'd made good her escape that it was quite a while later before she noticed how cold it was in the coach. Finding nothing but cold ashes in the brazier wasn't alarming, but after a quick search under the seats and even inside one that lifted up, she was definitely disturbed. Not a single chunk of coal to be found anywhere in the coach.

There was a lap robe. Small consolation but she quickly curled into it. Would that be enough? Not to make her comfortable, but it would have to do. The driver had even less warmth, she reminded herself, so she could withstand a little cold. And she didn't need to tell him to hurry. She'd made it perfectly clear that haste was imperative.

She still couldn't believe that she was actually on her way home! But the immense satisfaction and triumph she was feeling had nothing to do with going home, and everything to do with the simple fact that she'd outwitted Raphael!

She had come downstairs and heard the voices in the parlor. She'd almost entered the room, sure that it was Raphael's sister's voice she was hearing, not his aunt's. A stroke of luck made her pause long enough to realize that if his sister was there, she had to have come in a coach, and that the coach might be right outside, still hitched to its horses, and providing her with a means of escape.

Getting past the open parlor door to find out wasn't a chance she could take though. Nor could she leave as she was, wearing no more than her day dress. So she'd run back upstairs for her coat and reticule, then raced down the servants' back staircase, hoping to find Sadie in the kitchen. No luck there and she had no idea where her maid might be at this time of day. Such a dilemma! Should she look for Sadie and risk losing the opportunity to leave, or leave without her, feeling reasonably certain that Raphael would make sure that Sadie got back to London.

There really was no choice to make. This was her only chance to get away from this place, and it wasn't even a certainty yet that she could. She had to act at once, before the horses from the new coach were led away to the stable as the others had been.

She slipped through the kitchen and out the side door while the cook was busy rummaging about in the pantry. And just in time! The new coach was just now being driven across the side path toward the stable.

She hadn't realized it was snowing again, but it was, lightly. The previous snow had been melting before the temperature dropped again, so there was now ice too to contend with, but not enough to change her mind.

"Wait up!" she'd called to the young man on the driver's perch.

He heard her and stopped. He even hopped down to the ground as she hurried toward him, trying not to slip on any ice under the newly fallen snow. He would probably have doffed a cap if he'd been wearing one, instead of a bunch of woolen scarves under the hood of the extra cloak he had on. His expression was typical of most men who saw her face for the first time—dazzled and incredulous at what he was seeing.

And to keep him that way, she gave him her most brilliant smile. "I need someone to drive me back to London. Would you be able to help me?"

It took the young man nearly a full minute to recover from his bedazzlement. She only had to repeat herself once.

He finally frowned regretfully and said, "I don't think I can do that, ma'am, not without Lord Locke's permission. This here is his coach."

"What's your name?"

"Albert, ma'am."

"Will twenty pounds change your mind, Albert?"

He winced. "That's a lot o' coins to a bloke like me, but it's sure to get me fired or tossed in gaol if I take off with this coach."

Her impatience was rising. She didn't have time to cajole him. At any moment, Raphael might show up, and then she wouldn't be going anywhere.

"You wouldn't be arrested," she assured the fellow. "I can promise you that."

He was still frowning regretfully. "I brought his sister here. She'll probably be returning home in a few days. She's a nice lady. She'd let you join her for the ride, I'm sure."

"That won't do. I need to leave *immediately*. Fifty pounds!"

"I don't like this job much," he admitted. "Took it in the summer when it weren't so bad. Now I find I'd rather be working indoors this time o' year. But fifty pounds ain't enough to get me tossed out on the street."

The devil it wasn't. That was more money than he was likely to see in two or three years. "One hundred pounds," she said impatiently.

"Where did you want to go?" he asked, and immediately opened the coach door for her.

"London. With all speed. And I mean that. Haste is mandatory."

"Don't worry, ma'am. I'll be racing to the nearest inn and a warm fire, since I won't be getting warmed up here. We *can* stop at an inn, right?"

"Yes, certainly," she said, guessing that's why it had cost her so much. He simply wanted out of the cold. "I don't expect you to drive at night."

It was a good thing she'd already told him to make haste, she thought, her teeth chattering. The inside of the coach probably wasn't getting any colder than it had been, yet it certainly seemed to be, now that she'd been sitting in it for several hours. The lap robe wasn't really much help when her velvet coat was so thin. How long before they reached a town and a warm inn? Probably no more than another hour or so considering the reckless speed at which Albert was driving the team of horses.

At least Raphael wouldn't be able to stop her now before she reached civilization again. He'd made sure no one, himself included, could leave his Nest immediately when he'd had all the horses hidden away. She smirked at the thought, and how annoyed he was going to be when he discovered she'd escaped. He might find her before morning if they stayed at an inn, if he was persistent. But it wouldn't do him any good. She'd be back among people who didn't know him and wouldn't tolerate his trying to force a screaming woman into a coach, and she would most definitely be screaming.

It was just annoying that she'd had to leave Sadie behind, as well as her own coach and her clothes. But Raphael would have no reason to stay at Alder's Nest now, and he'd have to use her coach to get him and everyone else back to their respective homes. If he didn't actually return the coach to her, well, she'd worry about that once she was home and was assured that she'd never have to deal with that devil again.

It was the last thought she had before she was bumped off her seat onto the floor. Briefly tangled in the lap robe, she barely noticed the coach oddly sliding to the side. But the floor was a good place to be as the coach bounced about on its way into a ditch.

She'd barely gotten to her knees when the door was thrown open and Albert, looking horrified, asked, "Are you all right?"

"Yes, barely bruised," she assured him. "Just tell me that you didn't really slide us off the road into the ditch, did you?"

His face turned quite red. "I didn't see the bump, I swear I didn't. If I wasn't pushing the horses to top speed, I might've, then again, there's new snow covering the old, so I might not have seen it either way."

"And?"

"Coming off the bump, the wheel lost its traction and slid. The ditch didn't look that close, but I guess it was. And then it broke."

"What did?"

"The wheel," he said, embarrassed. "Snapped right off as it landed in the ditch."

"Are the horses all right?"

"They're fine, ma'am."

"Then they can pull the coach back on the road?"

"Yes, but it isn't going anywhere with that broken wheel. Of all the bloody rotten luck!"

He could say that again, she thought with a sigh. In hindsight, it had been stupid of her to tell him to push the team in weather like this. But hindsight only helped to avoid future disasters, it did nothing a'tall for current ones.

"What would you normally do in a situation like this?" she asked.

"Get a new wheel."

"Well, go and get one."

"We're not exactly close to town yet. It might be dark before I get back."

Her first thought was she didn't want to be left alone there on the side of the road, in the cold, especially after dark. But the alternative was to try to ride one of the horses herself, without a saddle, and more than likely fall off it repeatedly, get hurt, and be in even more dire straits. Or wait for the weather to improve and freeze in the meantime? Or wait for Raphael to show up and gloat that he'd found her? That was if he showed up. He might not bother to come after her. He might just as easily decide that he'd given it his best shot and wasn't going to any further lengths to try to "help" someone who obviously didn't want his help.

So she said, "Then don't waste any more time." And hoped she wasn't making yet another mistake.

Chapter Eighteen

RAPHAEL COULD BARELY SEE TWENTY feet in front of him, the snow was coming down so heavily now. It could have been called a blizzard if the wind were a little stronger, but thankfully, there was hardly any wind at all, just enough to make him *feel* just how cold it was—and make him think about giving up. After all, considering how long it had taken him to fetch a horse from Bartholomew's home, get it saddled, and gather some coal, since he knew the brazier in the coach was empty, he didn't really expect to catch up with Ophelia before she reached the nearest town. He merely wanted to find her before she got back to London, but he could have done that tomorrow, after the snow stopped—if it stopped.

He almost didn't see the coach in the ditch. Covered in white, it blended in with the snow around it. It was the horses that drew his eyes in that direction. The snow wasn't sticking to their warm, dark-coated bodies any more than it was to his own mount. Fear rushed through him as he took in the wreck. It was stronger than any he could ever recall feeling, but thankfully it was brief. As soon as he realized one of the four horses was missing and saw that the coach was upright, if tilted a bit, but not wrecked at all, he was sure no one had been hurt. Ophelia and his driver had obviously decided to share the one horse to continue on.

That was his only conclusion, so he almost didn't go down in the ditch to check. But he knew he'd be kicking himself, wondering about it, if he didn't, so he dismounted long enough to open the coach door for a quick look inside. Nothing left in it but a bundle of . . . *Why the deuce do you only have one lap robe in your coach?* his sister's words came back to him with a shock. One lap robe wouldn't make a pile that big.

"Good God," he burst out. "He left you here to freeze? Where the hell did he go?"

Ophelia poked her head out from under the lap robe, not all of it, just enough for him to see her eyes and to notice that she wasn't wearing her cap. Even her usual elegant coiffure was missing. She'd let her hair down? She was scrunched down on the seat so tightly into a little ball under the lap robe that she'd even had it covering her head.

"He went to fetch us a new wheel to replace the broken one."

Raphael sat down next to her and glanced at the cold brazier. "Did he know he was leaving you here with no heat?"

"Probably not," she said, then snapped, "And shut that bloody door!"

He reached back to pull the door shut. It didn't help much. His every breath was releasing a cloud of steam in front of him.

She was unwinding, now that she had company. She put her feet back on the floor and sat up straight. The lap robe really was just a miniature blanket, only long and wide enough to reach from lap to feet. She spread it over her lap again. Her hands were bare. Her hair really was loose and longer than he could have imagined. A single lock of it curled by her hands in her lap. Her fingers were trembling with cold! A wave of anger that she'd put herself in danger like this washed over him.

"Where are your muff and cap?" he demanded.

"They weren't with my coat. I didn't have time to look for them."

She said it so primly, it just annoyed him all the more. "I thought you had more sense than to pull a stunt like this," he snapped as he removed his gloves, then grabbed her hands and rubbed them between his own.

She didn't try to stop him. She simply said, "Desperation leads me to do stupid things. I thought you and I had already established that."

"You weren't desperate. You're just afraid to face the woman that everyone else encounters when they meet you. And what happened to your hair?"

She took one hand back from him and pushed an errant lock behind her back. "I needed the extra warmth for my neck and ears."

She was so cold she'd tried to warm herself with her own hair! That made him so furious he snarled, "I'm going to kill that idiot Albert for agreeing to this."

"No, I promised him a hundred pounds."

"That's no excuse." He grabbed both her hands again and blew his own hot breath on them.

"It is if you've never seen a hundred pounds."

A good point, but still he narrowed his eyes on her. "You're determined to take full blame, aren't you?"

"Of course I am—no, I'm not. *You're* to blame."

He almost grinned. "I was wondering when we'd get around to that."

"Well, you are. If you hadn't been so ridiculously stubborn in keeping me prisoner, when you didn't even have my parent's permission yet, when you only *assumed* you'd have it—"

"I have it now. My sister was thoughtful enough to bring my correspondence with her."

Ophelia slumped back. "How nice for you, exonerated on all counts."

"Yes, quite nice, since we aren't anywhere near finished raking you over the coals."

He was teasing. She must have guessed as much, or she would have lost her temper over that remark. But the mention of coals reminded him that he had a sack of coal tied to his horse for the brazier.

"Speaking of which, I did bring some coal," he added. "Let me fetch it."

He left immediately and was back within moments. Nor did it take long to light the coal. But it was going to be quite a while before it actually heated the coach, he realized, and Ophelia was sitting there with her teeth still chattering, her lips nearly blue! He was going to have to try something else in the meantime. . . .

"Actually," he said, as if their conversation hadn't been interrupted, "we have made progress. You aren't nearly as abrasive as you were to begin with, and I've personally seen no evidence of spite. Now don't be alarmed, but I'm going to try something else to warm your hands, since that coal isn't burning quickly enough."

He opened his coat and pulled his shirttails out of his trousers, then placed both her hands under his shirt on his chest.

She tried to pull her hands back, but he held fast to them despite the chill it gave him.

"That isn't going to work either," she said. "You aren't exactly warm right now."

"Let's try this then." He placed her fingers under his arms.

"Only marginally better, but that won't last. This is merely making you cold too."

"I was already cold, m'dear. It *is* snowing out there, you know. But you're probably right. The only way we're both going to warm up is with a little exertion. You know, get the blood flowing, work up a little sweat. It works every time."

She gave him a doubtful look. "There isn't exactly room in here to exercise, and no thank you, I'm not stepping outside to run about just to work up a sweat." She added primly, "Besides, I don't sweat. Ladies never do."

He wasn't going to laugh at that silly statement. If it killed him, he wasn't. But it took a few moments to get the urge under control.

"I was thinking of a more pleasant form of exertion." Her eyes flared wide, so he quickly added, "No, I draw the line at making love in a coach in the dead of winter—well, at least without a brazier burning more strongly than this one."

He grinned to show her he was just teasing. He didn't want to alarm her or outrage her maidenly sensibilities. But this was an opportunity he simply couldn't pass up.

From the very beginning he'd restrained his natural inclinations with her because his motives had been pure. He'd brought her to Alder's Nest to help her, not seduce her. But a little kissing wouldn't hurt, and at the moment it would actually help to take her mind off the cold.

He'd been good. He'd been damned good. He honestly

didn't know how he'd managed to resist keeping his hands off her, as desirable as she was. His dislike of her had helped. But as soon as she'd started explaining some of her actions, his feelings had turned neutral. He didn't exactly like her, she still had a lot to account for and to change about her behavior toward others, but he didn't have to like her to want her, and good God, he did want her.

Chapter Nineteen

S HE'D BEEN CURLED UP, BREATHING so hard against her knees to get a little warmth back to her face, that Ophelia hadn't even known Raphael was there until he'd first spoken. He hadn't gloated as she'd expected when he'd found her. He'd shown nothing but concern and anger, not at her, but for her.

She'd been beginning to fear that the coach driver wouldn't return today. If he didn't reach the town before nightfall, he might not. But all her fears had departed with Raphael's presence. She didn't doubt for a minute that he'd get her back to warmth and safety. She no longer cared that she'd failed to escape him.

"I'm merely going to kiss you, Phelia. I guarantee after a few moments you won't notice the cold, and after a few minutes, you'll start feeling quite warm."

She started to feel warm just thinking about it. Not really warm, but the thought of kissing him was already taking her mind off the cold.

She'd been sitting there trying to keep her teeth from chattering while she talked to him. Every few seconds she had to fight down a chill. She wished he'd just kissed her as he did before, instead of mentioning it. Discussing it implied he was asking her permission first, and she'd rather not have to say that she wanted him to kiss her. In fact she did and had been quite disappointed that he hadn't attempted to do so again, after that first kiss in the snow.

"You're speaking from experience, no doubt?" she said.

"Of course. Passion generates its own warmth. Shall we give it a try?"

He *was* asking permission. How unrakish of him. When the deuce was the man going to live up to his reputation? But she supposed he only tried to bed women he liked, and they'd long ago established that she didn't fit in that category.

"By all means," she said with a sigh. "I'll try anything to get warm again."

"Anything?" He grinned.

"*Most* anything."

But he was still grinning as he came closer, and then their lips were touching. His weren't cold. Hers probably were, though not for long. But he wasn't touching her in any other way, as if he was deliberately restraining himself. Or maybe he just didn't really want to kiss her! She still felt an unexpected thrill to have her lips pressed to his, even though the kiss was rather tepid, as kisses went.

"Don't be alarmed," he warned, barely moving his mouth away from hers. "But when I suggested this, I didn't have chaste kissing in mind. Exertion is the key, and that comes from passion."

She drew back. "What do you mean?"

"This."

This was an entirely different sort of kiss indeed. He drew her flush against his chest, then wrapped his arms around her to keep her there. His mouth fastened hard on hers, forcing hers open with his tongue. That was a shock. She'd had more kisses stolen from her than she could count, but they usually ended abruptly with a slap from her. None had ever progressed to this amazing intimacy that stole her breath and started her heart pounding.

He leaned back against the side of the coach, lifting her into his lap so their mouths didn't part. It felt as if she were lying on him now, which was quite an exciting feeling. One arm still held her fast, but his other hand slipped into her loose hair, his fingers threading through it against her scalp. Shivers shot down her spine that had nothing to do with the temperature.

"Have you stopped feeling the cold?" he asked as he rained a few kisses over her cheeks and chin.

"Yes."

"Do you want to feel my hands on you?"

"Not if they're cold."

"I do believe there's nothing left on me that's cold. I'll show you."

His mouth slanted across hers again while his hand cupped her cheek. It wasn't just warm, it was rather hot as he moved it down along her neck then began unfastening the top of her coat. He didn't open her coat far, just enough for his hand to slip inside and cup her breast. She made a sound deep in her throat. She wasn't even sure if it was a protest or merely a sound of pleasure she couldn't contain, because it felt wonderful, having his hand there, tingly, sensually stirring, making her want to curl even closer against him.

"Not thin everywhere," he noted.

His tone was only half-teasing at the reference to his earlier comment about her being too skinny. The other half sounded quite pleased. The remark still caused her to blush, which just heated her all the more. But although he was managing to say things, he wasn't giving her many chances to reply, because his kiss wasn't actually ending, was merely pausing before his tongue thrust deeply again.

And then he drew her tongue into his mouth to gently suck on it. She moaned and she wrapped her arm around his neck without even thinking about it. Her knees curled upward on his chest. She did make a sound of protest when he stopped kneading her breast, but it was brief, because his hand wasn't leaving her, was just moving in a new direction, down along her waist, then he was cupping her derriere with it to draw her even more tightly against him.

"Think of me as a pillow," he whispered against her lips. "It's all right to curl up and stretch against me."

How did he know she wanted to? It was the most amazing urge she had, to crawl all over him! And she was learning quickly, this new sort of kissing. She even took over the lead in it, couldn't seem to help herself, though he quickly took it back. They dueled with their tongues! They seemed to fight over dominance, or more accurately, they shared it. And heat was pouring off them both now.

He somehow got that roving hand of his under her skirt. She did feel a slight draft as he did so, but barely noticed it as his fingers felt their way along her thigh. And then she literally jumped in his lap when his finger touched her directly between her legs. He held her tighter. He wasn't going to let her deny herself the immense pleasure he was capable of giving her, but she had no thought of stopping him, was too caught up in the novelty of the new sensations he was evoking.

She had grasped a handful of his hair, didn't know she was pulling it. She was kissing him voraciously as the pleasure swiftly escalated, her entire body trembling with desire, not cold. But what suddenly burst upon her was beyond her comprehension. She would probably have screamed. As it was, he trapped a loud moan in their kiss as her orgasm pulsed against his finger.

Utterly drained, luxuriously replete, toasty warm in his arms, she could have stayed there all night. He was dropping soft kisses on her brow. His hand was merely gently caressing the outside of her thigh now. He made no attempt to move her, just held her in his lap. She could probably have slept. He would have let her, she didn't doubt, and kept her warm, his body was giving off so much heat.

But he must have heard the movement outside. She did as well and lifted her head from his chest just before he set her back on the seat. So they weren't touching when the door burst open. And poor Albert, ready to assure her that he'd succeeded at his task, didn't get a chance to. Raphael's fist caught him squarely in the face and sent him sliding through the snow to the bottom of the ditch.

Chapter Twenty

"I s'pose I'm fired?" Albert asked warily as he picked himself up off the ground.

"Damned right you are," Raphael replied as he untied the wheel hanging from the horse Albert had just ridden back on. "After you fix the coach wheel and drive us back to Alder's Nest."

The stipulation turned Albert indignant. "And why would I be doing that if it ain't my job anymore?"

"Possibly because the alternative is for you to walk away from here on foot?"

Albert snorted. "I'll bleedin' well walk, and I'll be taking the money with me, that the lady promised."

Raphael pinned Albert with a look, some of the rage he'd felt earlier reflected in his tone when he said, "You think I'm going to let you anywhere near her without killing you, when you left her out here to freeze? Don't mention money again when you didn't complete her task, which you should have refused in the first place!"

Albert didn't know Raphael well enough to be wary or was too disappointed to care. "Fine then, I'm going," Albert grumbled, but took no more than a few steps before he swung around and demanded, "You ain't going to try to stop me?"

Raphael almost laughed at that point. Instead he raised a brow and said, "Why ever would I do that?"

"Because I'll probably die out here on foot!"

"And your point is?"

Albert flushed with angry color and marched back to take the wheel from Raphael, conceding, "Here, I'll do that, m'lord. I'll have us back on the road in a few minutes."

"I thought you'd see it my way. And you might want to put some snow on that swelling cheek," Raphael added before he turned back to the coach.

He didn't miss the mumble "Bleedin' *nabobs,*" he just chose to ignore it.

He didn't doubt Ophelia had heard every word, and in fact the first thing she said when he helped her step out of the coach was "Don't fire him."

"Give me one good reason why I shouldn't." He drew her against him to keep her warm while Albert replaced the broken wheel.

"Because I used my best smile on him."

She didn't really need to elaborate. He could only hope she never used that particular smile on him, because he could just imagine how dumbstruck and willing to do her bidding Albert had been.

In a teasing tone, Raphael said, "That vanity of yours must be a wearisome burden. Quite out of control, isn't it?"

She snuggled closer to him to get warm again. "Don't think I consider it a flaw, because I don't. I actually don't like the effect I have on men, but that effect is entirely predictable. Except where you're concerned, of course."

"Really? Why am I an exception?"

She glanced up at him. "Don't pretend you don't know. You don't see this face when you look at me, you see the monster you think I am."

He chuckled. That wasn't the least bit true, but he'd rather not correct her other than to say, "I never called you a monster, m'dear."

"Not in so many words. But you've implied it a number of times."

She didn't sound the least bit huffy or otherwise indignant over that reminder; in fact, she'd been agreeably mellow ever since she'd expended some of her passion. Not only that, having her hair loose and flowing about her seemed to make her softer, more accessible. It wasn't his imagination. Or maybe that too was because of the passion she'd released. Actually . . .

"I believe I've figured out why you have so little control of your temper. You have a great deal of passion in you, which can be a wonderful thing, but you've had no outlet for it, except for your temper."

She slipped her hand inside his coat to keep it warm on his chest. "D'you really think so?"

"Indeed. But then there's one way to find out." And then he groaned. "Just not here."

A while later when they were back in the coach on their way to Alder's Nest, she said, "Now that I'm nice and warm, I've noticed that I'm famished."

"So am I." He wasn't referring to food. She'd woken a sleeping dragon tonight. There was simply no way he was going to be able to keep his hands off her now. In fact he'd been softly caressing her ever since she'd settled back against him again.

"We'll be at the Nest soon," he added. "And I probably should warn you that there will be no way to prevent my sister from finding out who my houseguest is now."

"You didn't tell her?"

"I avoided doing so."

"Why? Were you intending to keep it a secret?"

"No, it's just she isn't likely to understand."

"That you could want to help someone like me?"

"No, that I haven't made you my mistress yet. She'll think I've lost my finesse."

Ophelia leaned back and gave him a curious look, then she actually chuckled. "That's a bad habit you've gotten into, teasing me."

"What makes you think I'm teasing?" He gave her a roguish look. "Did I mention I know a way to make you forget that you're famished?"

She burst out laughing.

Chapter Twenty-one

"THERE YOU ARE," ESMERALDA SAID perkily as Raphael and Ophelia stepped into the parlor together. "What an odd time of year to go off for a country drive. But at least you're not too late getting back. We held up dinner for you. Shall we?"

Raphael smiled at his aunt as she stood up to lead the way into the dining room. It was a nice attempt to make Ophelia's failed escape seem like an ordinary outing when it was anything but. It just wasn't going to work with his sister, and in fact, Amanda, who had been sitting next to Esmeralda on the sofa, didn't move an inch and was staring incredulously at Ophelia.

Ophelia was probably too accustomed to odd reactions from people to remark on Amanda's open mouth. She merely said, "Hello, Amanda. How nice of you to leave the gaiety of London for a visit in the country."

Amanda hadn't yet sufficiently recovered to reply or even realize that she was sitting there with her mouth hanging open. Raphael sighed to himself.

"You two go ahead," he said to his aunt. "I know Phelia is

famished, so don't wait any longer. Mandy and I will come along in a moment."

Ophelia's departure didn't snap his sister out of it, she was just staring wide-eyed at the empty doorway now. Raphael rolled his eyes and said, "It's a good thing there aren't any flies in my house at this time of the year."

"What?" Amanda said, then leapt to her feet in her usual exuberant way and exclaimed, "Good God, Rafe, I love you to pieces, but you really didn't need to go to such lengths to help me out."

Since that wasn't exactly what he was expecting to hear, he said, "I'd go to any lengths to help you, m'dear, you know that—if you needed help. But since you don't need help, what the deuce are you talking about?"

Her frown showed up immediately. "But that's why you did it, isn't it?"

"Did what?"

"Invited that woman here. You did it to remove her from the competition for me. So I'd have a chance to find a husband without having to compete with her."

He shook his head. The way the female mind worked sometimes was quite beyond his comprehension.

"Mandy, think about what you just said for a moment, would you? You're implying that any man interested in you would immediately turn his interest to Ophelia instead, if she showed up. Is that the kind of man you want?"

"No, of course not, but—"

"There are no buts in that analysis."

"There are some things that would tempt a man beyond good sense. She's one of them."

He would have liked to argue with that statement, but since

he was already experiencing some of that temptation, he couldn't. "Perhaps. But if a man is going to be that fickle, I'd think you'd want to know about it before you drag him to the altar."

"Drag?" she started to sputter.

"You know what I mean. Before you get a proposal. Before you fall in love."

She gave him a thoughtful look. "That would be a good test, wouldn't it?"

He lifted his eyes toward the ceiling. "I said it before, why don't you stop worrying about finding a husband and just let it happen naturally."

"Because the Season is half-over. I'm running out of time!"

"It wouldn't be the end of the world if you don't find a husband in your first Season."

"Are you mad!" she gasped. "Of course it would be. Two of my best friends are already engaged!"

"I swear, Mandy, if you follow the pack and settle for a husband you won't really be happy with, just because your friends are getting married—"

"I wouldn't. I'm not that stupid. But I'll be mortified if the Season ends without my at least getting engaged."

"No, you won't, you'll just start ordering a new wardrobe for the summer Season and begin again. Now let's go have some dinner. I'm—"

"Wait just a minute," Amanda said without budging. "If you didn't invite Ophelia here for my benefit—oh, good God, Rafe, don't tell me *you've* followed the pack and are enamored with her too!"

"That's a bad habit you've developed, jumping to wrong conclusions. No, I'm not enamored with her. I barely like her."

"Barely? The last I heard, you didn't like her a'tall."

He shrugged. "So I'm finding out she isn't quite the prima donna I thought she was."

"But *what* is she doing here? Did she just show up without an invitation and you don't know how to get rid of her? I'll take her back to London with me if that's the case."

"There you go, doing it again. Stop guessing, and stop trying to wheedle information from me that is none of your business."

As if she hadn't heard him, she guessed again, "She's hiding here, isn't she? She thinks her second breakup with MacTavish made quite the scandal, which it should have done, but didn't. I can assure her that it didn't."

"Amanda."

She caught the warning tone this time and protested vehemently, "You can't leave me in the dark! She's too beautiful, too well-known, and too sensational to just be here for no good reason!"

"There's a perfectly good reason," he relented enough to say. "I'm helping her to develop a few good qualities to add to the pitifully few she has now."

"Oh, sure you are," his sister snorted.

He wasn't going to try to convince her it was true. He said instead, "And you are not to repeat that or mention to anyone that she's here. I do *not* want my name linked to hers or have the entire town of London going through the same sort of ridiculous speculating that you've just done. Am I quite clear about that?"

"Then give me a crumb!"

He sighed to himself. When did his little sister become so bloody stubborn?

"I'll give you dinner instead, a bed for the night, and see you on your way back to your husband-hunting in the morning. Amanda, her parents know she's here and Aunt Esme is acting as her chaperone. There is absolutely nothing out of the ordinary occurring here. So keep your pretty nose out of what doesn't concern you."

"Fine, so don't tell me!" Amanda huffed on her way out the door.

Chapter Twenty-two

Iᴛ ᴡᴀsɴ'ᴛ ʜᴀʀᴅ ᴛᴏ ᴅᴇᴅᴜᴄᴇ that Amanda Locke was annoyed about something from the way she marched stiffly into the dining room without removing her glower. Ophelia had toyed with the idea of enlisting the girl to help her get back to London, despite Rafe's warning not to.

"She's a scatterbrain," he'd told her as they arrived back at the Nest. "She'll end up causing a scandal about your being here without meaning to. So it would be better for all involved if she not know that you'd rather not be here."

That wasn't what made Ophelia decide to say nothing. The animosity that kept coming her way from Amanda during dinner was just a small part of it too. Obviously the girl didn't like her at all. Mere jealousy? Perhaps. So many young women she met reacted that way to her. But because of it, like Mavis, Amanda would no doubt gloat over Ophelia's predicament instead of helping her out of it. But that wasn't why she wasn't going to ask the girl for help.

Incredibly, she didn't really *want* to leave now. What had

happened in the coach after Rafe had found her today was such an amazing experience, she simply had to examine further what she'd felt and experienced. And what if he was right?

When her worst flaws showed up, her temper, her ridiculous jealousies, she couldn't recall ever being able to keep those horrid emotions from spilling out to someone's detriment, even her own. Not even her regrets could prevent the same vicious cycle from occurring again. Because she'd never had any other outlet for her passions? That was Rafe's guess, and it seemed so plausible, she could find no way to disagree with it.

Having found a new outlet, as it were, she felt remarkably tranquil and at peace. Every one of her vitriolic emotions was quite dormant. She felt that nothing could disturb her this evening. Even her worst emotion was noticeably missing, the bitterness that had been her constant companion since she was a child.

It had begun with her father. She was barely out of swaddling clothes before he started plotting how he could benefit from such a remarkable child. She just didn't know it until the day she found out everything she'd believed to be true wasn't true at all. The memory was still so painful she usually shied away from it. But she was so content just now, even, dare she say, happy, that she could face even that memory.

*   *   *

It was her eighth birthday. She could barely contain her excitement. Her birthdays meant lots of presents from her friends. And her mother always gave her a wonderful party to celebrate the occasion. This party was no different, or it wouldn't have been if she'd just remained in the dining room where all the guests were seated enjoying the luncheon that had been prepared for them. But she'd received a new trinket from her mother for

her birthday, a pretty locket. She'd been going upstairs to fetch it to show one of the girls at her party when her parents' raised voices drew her toward her father's study instead.

"This can't continue," her mother was saying. "You can't keep buying her friends."

"You'd prefer to explain to her why you can't fill a guest list for a simple birthday party?" her father said in an annoyed tone.

"That was *your* guest list," Mary reminded him. "Filled with lofty titles. Half of those children are too jealous of Ophelia to want to be around her, the other half have never been here before. Of course they wouldn't come. And this new list you gave me is no different. She doesn't know any of these children, not a single one. I should have canceled this party when those original names you gave me all turned down my invitations. She's going to know something is wrong."

"Nonsense. This is excellent exposure for her. I should have thought of it sooner. Inviting only lesser titles as you've been doing is pointless. None of them will do for *my* daughter."

"But those are her real friends!"

"Are they? Or do their parents only come here to curry favor with me."

"Not everyone thinks the way you do."

"Of course they do," Ophelia's father scoffed. "It's all about who you know in this town and who you impress. And we have a gem that can impress anyone. Her looks are priceless, and she gets prettier every year. I still can't believe it m'self. You were a beauty when I married you, but I never dreamed you'd produce such a remarkable child!"

"And I never dreamed your only thought would be how you could benefit from her. Why can't you just love her as I do and—"

"Love her?" her father snorted. "Children are a nuisance and

she's no different in that regard. If it weren't necessary for her to be here to show off—well, you can be sure she would have been shipped off to some school instead of being taught at home with private tutors."

"And trotted out at every party I give as if she were your pet doing tricks for the entertainment," her mother replied bitterly.

"Stop making so bloody much of it. Entertaining is what *you* live for. Watching your guests stare at our daughter in disbelief is what *I* live for." Her father laughed. "And did you really look at the new guest list I gave you for this party? That one boy is in line for the title of marquis. She could catch his eye, you know."

"She's too young to catch anyone's eye! For God's sake, why can't you let her grow up first before you start shopping for her husband."

Having heard every word, the child was too shocked to cry yet. She didn't go upstairs for her trinket. In a daze, she returned to the dining room where her friends were all seated at the long table. Friends?

She'd known the children gathered there were all strangers to her, but that was nothing out of the ordinary. She'd merely thought her real friends would still be coming, that they were just late. So she hadn't thought anything was amiss. She was so accustomed to meeting new children who came to dinners with their parents. Her mother entertained weekly. Even when there were no children for her to meet, she was still summoned to the parlor or the dining room or wherever the guests were gathered, to be introduced. . . .

She stopped by a boy much older than she was, slumped in his chair, talking to no one. "Why are you here?" she asked him frankly, as children will do.

"It's a party. I usually enjoy parties," he replied petulantly.

"You're not enjoying this one," she said, pointing out what was obvious.

He shrugged and said candidly, "They said if I came and pretended to like you, I'd have a new horse. The one I have now is getting old. My father wouldn't buy me a new one, but he said yours would if I came here today and pretended to have fun."

A tightness filled her throat as she replied, "I guess you didn't really want the horse."

"Of course I do!"

"Then you should have pretended."

He glared at her. "There's no point in my staying then, is there?"

"No, there isn't," she agreed, and turned to the boy sitting next to him, who appeared to be closer to her age, and asked him also, "Why are you here?"

With the first boy already on his way out the door, this one was just as candid. "Your father paid mine twenty pounds so I was told I had to come. I'd rather be in the park sailing my new boat."

"I'd rather you were in the park too," she replied, her voice more quiet, the words more difficult to get out past the lump in her throat.

Her eyes were starting to sting with tears now. Even her chest was hurting when she glanced at the plain-looking girl across the table from him. This one was older than all the others, too old to be attending an eight-year-old's birthday party.

"And you?" she asked the older girl. "Why have you come here?"

"I was curious," the girl replied snobbishly. "I wanted to know why it took bribery to get me here. I understand now. You're too pretty to have any real friends."

Ophelia didn't need to ask any of the others her question. And she couldn't hold back the tears any longer. Before they spilled down her cheeks to her further mortification, she shouted, "Get out, all of you!"

*   *   *

Ophelia had never looked at a friend the same way after that day. She doubted them all and easily caught them in their placating lies. And usually those very lies provoked her to do exactly what others tried to prevent by lying. She'd come across a few of those birthday guests again over the years. All of them had apologized to her and swore they wouldn't have needed to be bribed to come to her party if they'd just met her first. She didn't believe them and scorned the lot of them.

She never looked at her father the same way either. She had adored him. Finding out that he bore her no love in return, that he saw her only as a tool in his social-climbing schemes, had ripped her heart out and left only bitterness in its place.

But it was all gone today—because of Rafe. It surprised her that she was even thinking of him as Rafe now, but then formality between them would seem silly after today. And his theory was easy enough to test. That's really why she didn't want to leave the Nest quite yet. This new outlet for her passions not only tempered her emotions, it had been too pleasant not to want to explore it again.

She ignored Amanda, who pouted through the meal, but she couldn't ignore Rafe. Her eyes were drawn to him repeatedly whether he was speaking or not, though he did try to put some normalcy to the meal by keeping up a conversation with his aunt. He tried several times to draw his sister into it, but she would just glower at him, so he gave up the effort. Ophelia found it easy enough to join in, though, when the new snow-storm was mentioned.

"I think I'll have to trample through the snow again in the morning, now that it's thoroughly covered up my earlier tracks," she said, then added with a grin, "Care to have another snow fight, Rafe?"

He laughed. "You lost the last one."

"I did not." She chuckled as well. "That was a draw and you know it!"

That was apparently too much familiarity between them for Amanda to stomach, because she stood up angrily and warned Ophelia, "Don't try to seduce my brother into marriage. Our father would never approve of a woman like you."

Ophelia actually blushed. She hadn't intended to do any such thing, but the unprovoked attack did jar her tranquillity a notch. Rafe, on the other hand, was appalled at his sister's remarks.

"Good God, Mandy, have you taken leave of your senses? I am utterly ashamed of you."

"So am I, gel," Esmerelda added.

"What?" Amanda protested in a whine. "You might not be tempted by her beauty or have designs on her, but that doesn't mean she hasn't set her cap for you. You don't see the way she looks at you?"

"There can be no excuse for such rudeness and you know it," Rafe said. "Apologize this instant."

"I will not!" Amanda refused. "Don't be blind. It needed to be said!"

"The devil it did."

Red-cheeked now, Amanda threw down her napkin. "I'm not going to sit here and watch you being led to the slaughter.

When you've finished wasting your time doing whatever it is you won't confide in me about, you'll know where to find me. And I'll apologize to *you* when you've regained *your* senses, but I won't apologize to *her*! And don't you dare apologize for me!" she added on her way out the door.

Amanda must have known her brother quite well, because he did just that. "I'm sorry, Phelia—"

"Don't be," she interrupted with a weak smile. "I am so very used to jealousy, it doesn't bother me in the least anymore."

"You think that's all that was?"

"Certainly. Unwarranted in this case, but then jealousy doesn't need truth or facts to rear its head. Believe me, I know that better than anyone."

"Commendable attitude, gel," Esmerelda put in. "But my niece knows better than to make outbursts like that."

Ophelia chuckled. "I can hardly hold her at fault for that when I'm the one usually making outbursts. But perhaps you can escort me to my room, Rafe? I would rather not be ambushed by your sister again tonight."

Chapter Twenty-three

IT WAS RATHER BOLD OF her to ask Rafe to walk her to her room. It was a bedroom, after all. The proper form would have been to ask Esmeralda instead. But Ophelia hadn't hesitated. She didn't ask to be here, she was being kept from leaving, so the normal rules of etiquette could be suspended for the duration as far as she was concerned. And that was all the reasoning and logic she needed to proceed down the path of ruination, as it were.

The thought amused her, since she didn't for a moment think that any such thing would happen if she dallied a bit with the next Duke of Norford. They were too secluded here. And he'd seen to it that she had a proper chaperone. So no one would ever know.

She might have to mention it to her future husband, if she was lacking her virginity, but she could do so without providing names. If she was lucky enough to find a man who really loved her and wasn't just smitten by her face, then she didn't think it would matter all that much, and if it did, well then, he wouldn't really be in love with her, would he?

How easy it was to make excuses when something she really wanted was involved. But then she was a London girl and far more sophisticated than most debutantes. Every scandal in her fair city for the last ten years had passed by her ears. She knew how they were started, how they were avoided, and how to defuse them.

She slowed her step at the top of the stairs now that she had Rafe completely alone. The excitement that had shown up the moment she'd made her decision to test his theory was new to her and still present. She was going to make love with him. The thought was absolutely thrilling. But she couldn't just pounce on him there in the hall. A little more subtlety was called for.

She began, "I suppose I should assure you, after your sister's allegation, that I don't have designs on you."

"Believe me, Phelia, you've made that perfectly clear from the very beginning. Actually . . . ," he started to amend, but she easily guessed that he was remembering that she'd approached him at Summers Glade.

"That was before I knew that you don't play by the rules, and to be honest, any man would have served at that point, even you. I was impatient and simply wanted to get it over with, and you were one of the few men I knew, without a doubt, that my father would approve of."

"I do believe I should feel insulted."

They had stopped to talk, so she couldn't miss his grin. "Yes, you certainly look offended," she replied. "But, no, I didn't know you yet, so my reasoning had nothing a'tall to do *with* you, and everything to do with your title. But that was for my father. Your wealth, on the other hand—" She paused to chuckle. "I confess that is my own personal criterion. I have every intention of being a social matriarch and to give the grandest balls London has ever seen, and that will require a lot of money. So I won't be marrying a pauper if I can help it. But there are many more wealthy men to go around than there are titles as esteemed as yours will be."

He feigned a forlorn sigh. "As assurances go, m'dear, I'm afraid you've failed miserably."

She blushed slightly. "I don't think I phrased that properly. What I meant was, there are more men that would suit me than there are to suit my father, but I'm not all that keen on taking his preferences into consideration anymore. And that means you're the very last man I'd put on my list, because you're definitely on his. Does that make better sense to you?"

"Rather convoluted, but I'm getting the drift that you'd spite yourself just to spite your father."

She rolled her eyes. "Sure, bring my renowned spite into it."

"You don't see it that way?"

"I can understand why you do, but you don't know how it is between my father and me."

"I could hazard a good guess that you don't like each other."

"That isn't the case at all. I don't hate him, I just lost all love for him long ago. We tolerate each other, I suppose is a good way to put it. But I'm tired of being used to further his own ambitions. If you doubt me, just look at what he's done to me this year alone. Engaged me to a barbarian and thrown me to the wolves!"

"Are you calling me a wolf?"

"You noticed that, did you?"

He laughed. "I think I get the point now."

"Good, because if I find the perfect man for myself, I wouldn't think twice about marrying him without my father's permission. I am well aware that there are places we could go to accomplish that."

"Now *that* reassures me."

"I thought it would."

She turned away and took another step down the hall. It took a moment for her to get up the nerve to add, "Having said all that, don't be alarmed when I tell you I'd like to test that theory you raised today."

She glanced back to see he'd gone very still. He knew exactly what she meant. "I think—perhaps—you should give that more thought." And then he groaned. "I don't believe I just said that."

"I have thought about it, and I must tell you I've never felt such—such—"

"Sublime ecstasy?" he supplied with another groan.

"No, not *that*," she said with a blush. "Though that was very nice. I meant the tranquillity that followed and is still with me. You don't know how rare it is, for me to feel this way."

"You know I wasn't completely serious today, when I mentioned other outlets for your passions?"

"Weren't you? But it makes perfect sense! Especially considering this lingering effect it's had on me. Look at your sister, for example. She didn't disturb me a'tall tonight, when I usually react to that sort of jealous hostility with pointed barbs of my own. So I *am* going to test this, Rafe, with you or with someone else. If you were right, then I have hope now of getting rid of at least half of my flaws for good. That isn't something I'm going to pass up."

"At the risk of losing this golden opportunity, I feel it only fair to point out that making love right now, while you are already at peace, will test nothing."

She frowned, then gasped. "I didn't think of that! But you're quite right. And perhaps what happened today will have a permanent effect—?" He was shaking his head at her. "No? Well, I suppose I'll just have to see how long it does last. Good night."

"Phelia."

She pretended she didn't hear him as she hurried to her room. How utterly embarrassing. He probably thought she'd merely been making advances toward him, that she'd known all along that her suggestion would be pointless just now. But damn, why did he have to point that out?

Chapter Twenty-four

RAPHAEL STOOD AT THE PARLOR window watching Ophelia take her walk outside. He wasn't going to join her this time. His mood had turned sour last night and still was, which was hardly conducive to gay antics that she might expect out in the yard. But he still couldn't help watching her.

The sun had come out. The fresh snow on the ground that she enjoyed wouldn't last long now. Bartholomew had remarked that while they got their fair share of it in the winter, they didn't usually get this much snow all at once. Raphael was glad they had. If there hadn't been snow on the ground yesterday, Ophelia's coach wouldn't have landed in a ditch and she might have made good her escape.

Amanda had left early that morning, still too angry to even bid him good-bye. He'd given Albert a letter to take to his factor, who would give him a year's pay before he "quit," as long as he got Amanda back to London safely. It wasn't the hundred pounds he'd risked his job for, but much more than the fellow deserved.

While his eyes followed Ophelia's every step, he unwittingly put his raw knuckles to his mouth to suck on them. He'd slammed his fist against his bedroom wall last night to commemorate what a bloody fool he was. Passing up an opportunity to make love to *her*? And it had even been her idea!

He still found that remarkable, though after some thought, not all that surprising. Ophelia could in no way be compared to an average debutante, and not just because of her exceptional beauty. She'd had too much exposure to the London sophisticates, long before she should have had any. She'd even been receiving marriage proposals before she was out of the schoolroom.

While that was her father's fault, no doubt, it still gave Ophelia a more worldly outlook than a normal girl her age would have. Nor did he doubt she'd been serious last night. What he was sure of, and wished he wasn't, was that she didn't really care with whom she tested his theory. He merely happened to be handy. And that was the biggest source of his current disgruntlement.

He had no intention of forming an attachment to her or even having a brief affair, but he *was* used to fighting women off, and his experience with Ophelia thus far was in the exact opposite direction. She wanted nothing to do with him, would prefer to get as far away from him as possible. The few overtures he'd been unable to resist making hadn't changed that at all. She could at least have given him some indication that she wanted him personally, instead of saying any man would do for her damned testing.

"I'm sorry about last night," she said behind him. "I simply wasn't thinking."

His thoughts had distracted him long enough to miss her return to the house. He turned around and saw her shrugging out of her coat, which she laid over a chair as she made her way to the fireplace.

"Don't give it another thought," he said. "All the snow off your boots? Letting it soak in will delay your feet getting warm."

"Yes, I'm good at stomping my feet."

"I can imagine."

She glanced at him, but must have decided not to respond to his dry tone. She held her hands out to the fire. She was wearing a dress today he hadn't seen before. Like most of the dresses he'd seen her in, it was more suited to summer weather with its low neckline and short capped sleeves. But then most young women of his acquaintance dressed the same because houses were usually overheated in the winter and they remained mostly indoors. The lavender color seemed to enhance the rosiness of her cheeks, which was no doubt due to her walk outdoors. The dress was becoming, though perhaps a bit too snug across her breasts. He groaned inwardly. He had a feeling his every thought about her now was going to be sexual.

He moved over to close the door she'd left open when she entered. "We need privacy?" she asked.

"No, just keeping the heat from escaping into the hall." However, privacy *was* on his mind, and the fact that his aunt wouldn't be coming downstairs for several hours yet assured him that they'd have some privacy for a while. "You appear chilled."

"Yes, I was, thank you." But with her hands warmed now, she moved over to the nearest sofa and took a seat. "I missed bidding your sister farewell."

He crossed the room to join her. "No, you didn't. She left in a snit without saying good-bye to anyone. And how is your sublime tranquillity today? Still holding up?"

She gave him another curious glance, but still answered, "Indeed. I'm beginning to think you were wrong, that it is permanent."

He shrugged. "My opinions are merely that, hardly infallible."

"So what is on the agenda for today?"

"Why don't we try a day where neither of us lies about anything."

That brought an immediate frown to her brow. "That implies you've been lying to me. About what?"

"Quite the contrary, m'dear. After you admitted you don't mind lying, I found myself assuming that's what you've been doing here."

"You assumed wrong. I decided that telling the absolute truth was the only way I was going to get out of here."

"But you see, even that could be a lie," he pointed out. "How would I know the difference? Once you start down the path of dishonesty, no one will trust what you say. You don't see that?"

She sat back with a little smirk. "What I see is you're trying to provoke my temper. A good try, but it isn't going to work."

Was he doing that? Actually, that was a damned good idea, though he insisted, "I just made a valid point."

"Yes, it was, and I quite agree. But then you see I've lived with that sort of distrust most of my life. And once you believe that no one is honest with you, not even your parents, then you no longer care if you're believed or not. It simply doesn't matter. Tit for tat, as it were."

"You really think it doesn't matter?"

She blushed. "Very well, *sometimes* I suppose it does. Like now. I really did decide that honesty was the only way to deal with you, but to *be* honest, that was because I couldn't think of a single way to lie my way out of here."

He couldn't help laughing. Sometimes she was simply too candid. But then she surprised him by taking exception to his amusement.

"That isn't funny. This entire situation hasn't been. And I'll have you know that it isn't easy being completely honest when I'm accustomed to—"

"Hurting people with your lies?"

She gasped and glared at him "You really are two-faced, aren't you? You deceive and lull with your amusing jocularity only so you can sneak up from behind and go straight for the jugular! I can't believe I was lulled into forgetting that about you."

"No longer quite so tranquil?"

"No, damn you!"

"Good," he said, and dragged her across his lap.

Chapter Twenty-five

Her anger reappeared with shocking speed. It was as if she'd been shielded by a curtain made thick by her own delusions that was abruptly opened, and there in the audience were all her bitter emotions applauding that she could no longer hide from them. And that absolutely infuriated Ophelia, who directed her rage right where it belonged, at the instigator who'd drawn open that curtain.

But just as quickly, Rafe's mouth was on hers, and while her fist hit his shoulder once before he gathered her too close for her to reach it again, she was soon gripping his head instead with both of her hands and kissing him back in an explosion of passion. Damn him! She didn't doubt he'd deliberately provoked her, she just didn't care at the moment.

He leaned back on the sofa and without much ado positioned her so she was lying on top of him. Not for a moment did he break the kiss that was inciting her. The position gave him full access to her body, and since it was obvious that he didn't need to keep her trapped there, that she was fully involved in that kiss, his hands were free to wander over her back and lower. And he went lower indeed. Before long he was gripping both her nether cheeks and moving her carefully against the hardness between his legs.

In doing so, he somehow found an incredibly sensitive spot—on her. And every time it pressed against his hardness, she felt a little shock that caused her to bounce against him. She couldn't prevent it, had no control over that reaction at all, but it was raising her passion to new heights, so much so that she was soon grinding her body against him.

The heat emanating between them was growing much hotter. She wished it were cooler in the room, that he hadn't closed the . . . door. A quelling thought, and once it arrived, it took precedence.

She was loath to end what was happening, but propriety had reared its ugly head and she gasped out finally, "Someone might come—"

"I locked the door."

The anxiety that had briefly mounted in her left her immediately. That was all she needed to hear to remove the worry of discovery and just experience to the fullest what he was doing to her.

He'd slowly been raising her skirt. When he suddenly changed their positions, there was no cloth to hold him back from settling between her legs. What a thrilling sensation, having him there! It stirred inside her and seemed to uncoil, spreading a new heat that increased the sensual tension mounting in her.

All of her senses were heightened to acute awareness. She was tasting him, minty from the tea he'd drunk earlier, smelling him, spicy musk! The hair she was still gripping wasn't coarse at all; it felt like fine silk. She would never have imagined that. And every time she heard *him* groan, she felt a corresponding need to do the same, it thrilled her so much that she was having the same effect on him that he was on her. But what it did to her when she opened her eyes to see such intense heat in his—how could just seeing how much he wanted her excite her so much?

Every breath was becoming labored. It wasn't due to his weight on her, oh, no, that gave her a unique thrill in itself and was mostly centered between her legs. But she caught herself holding her breath, she couldn't seem to help it, each time he touched a new sensitive spot on her, and he seemed to find so many! His hips weren't still for a moment, nor were his hands.

His fingers curled about her ear, traced a teasing path along her neck, which made her shiver deliciously, and it was easy for him to slip the top edge of her dress below her breasts. His palm pressing against one plump globe was exceedingly hot, but that was nothing compared to the heat of his mouth when he suddenly broke their kiss to suck on her breast. She forgot to breathe. Her arms wrapped about his head, her body arched against him. It felt as if she were going to go up in flames at any moment!

He fumbled with the clothes still between them. She heard a tear—her drawers? Such impatience! She almost laughed, but he was kissing her again. And then there was a new pressure between her legs that made her purr in her throat, but no sooner did it feel wonderfully pleasant than it started to hurt. She pressed back away from the pain, but it followed her, increased to where she started to cry out. But with a swift thrust from him, it was suddenly gone, leaving just a tight fullness behind that she didn't yet know what to make of.

The mood was broken however, and he'd leaned back slightly to see her reaction. She was understandably glaring at him, feeling somehow betrayed.

"That was—," he began, but amended with a sigh, "It won't happen again, you have my word."

"What won't? The pain?"

"Yes. That was your body fighting to retain its innocence. You didn't really want to keep it at this point, did you?"

She understood now and said with a good deal of annoyance, "No, but my mother should have mentioned to me that there would be pain involved, instead of just telling me that if I was lucky, I'd enjoy the matrimonial bed or, more to the point, love-making. She said that not all women do. I suppose I didn't get lucky."

She could see he was fighting to hold back a laugh. The urge rose up to hit him. This was *not* funny. To have such pleasure end on such a bad note . . .

"Are we done then?" she asked stiffly.

"Good God, I hope not. But I have a feeling your mother rushed through that conversation. She should have told you luck has nothing to do with it."

"What does?"

"The skill of your partner," he said with a grin. "Shall I prove it?"

He moved in her as he said it. Her eyes flared wide. The sensation he evoked with his fullness was nothing but pleasant, and in fact, it was nearly too pleasant. That quickly, her passion returned to take full control of her again. And what he was doing went beyond her meager experience. Had she thought she'd discovered the ultimate pleasure yesterday in the coach with him? The exquisite slow thrusting he was treating her to was sliding across nerves she didn't know she possessed. So deep the pleasure went in her, so stirring, that she seemed to feel it everywhere, until a tension built that would have to explode, and it did, blissfully pulsing, draining her to repletion.

She was barely aware that he'd reached his pleasure with her. Such sensual languor filled her now she didn't want to move. And she felt a moment of profound tenderness for the man still wrapped in her arms. This odd emotion almost brought tears to her eyes, no sadness, just the opposite, utterly unique, certainly nothing she'd ever felt before for anyone.

"That was wicked of you," she remarked once her breathing had calmed down. She was still running her fingers gently through his hair.

"Yes, it was," he said against her neck. "But did it work? Are you at peace again?"

"I have no idea, I'm too filled with pleasure at the moment to feel anything else."

He leaned up to look at her. He was grinning. "Enjoyed that, did you?"

"Yes! You simply can't imagine."

"Ah, but I can, or do you think men do this just to pass the time?"

She laughed. She was in such a bubbly mood now, she was surprised she hadn't started giggling. But then she had a disappointing thought.

"It's rather obvious that my temper is still going to show up, isn't it?"

"Yes, but I'll wager a guess that you'll find that you have much better control of it now. That was the point, m'dear. Not that you'd never get angry again, which is unlikely for anyone, not just you, but that all of your volatile emotions wouldn't be channeled into only one outlet, which was making them too abrasive and detrimental."

"So I didn't need to really test it—this way?" she guessed.

He was grinning again. "At the risk of ending a beautiful moment—he kissed her lips softly so she couldn't doubt what he was talking about—"probably not. However, you only need to recall the tranquillity you experienced yesterday to realize that lovemaking does have certain additional benefits, at least for you. As testing goes, it was already proven that for a while it will drain your passions for you. It did so nicely, didn't it?"

"Indeed. I was quite incredulous."

"And now?"

"Sublimely peaceful again."

He nodded. "So in that regard I would say further testing was necessary and proved successful. And I will, of course, offer my help anytime you feel a need to release some of those passions again."

"How generous of you."

"I thought so."

His teasing brought on the urge to hug him. Actually, the urge had shown up at his first grin. She was so pleased with him at the moment and felt a closeness she'd never experienced before with any other man. Friendship or . . . ? No, she wasn't going to go there. She didn't want to examine more deeply what she was feeling for him now, when nothing more would ever come of it. She ought to assure him of that. There was no need for him to worry needlessly that she'd take advantage of what had just occurred.

She moved her gaze away from his, even felt a blush mounting over the subject she was going to broach. "About what we did, I'm not compromised, so don't give that another thought. As it happens, I wouldn't marry you anyway. I refuse to make my father that happy. So what happened here will remain strictly between us. No one needs to know."

He was giving her an odd look. "That's rather—noble of you."

"No, it's not. It's quite vindictive, just not against you."

"I see." He started to frown.

She guessed the direction his thoughts just went. "Don't even think of discussing my relationship with my father or the lack thereof, or any resulting vindictiveness on my part because of it. What's between him and me is just that, none of your concern."

"A sweet, kind woman wouldn't have such thoughts," he pointed out, despite her warning.

"A sweet, kind woman wouldn't have a father like mine, either."

He winced. "Touché."

Chapter Twenty-six

Iᴛ ᴡᴀs ᴇᴀsʏ ᴛᴏ sᴛʀᴀɪɢʜᴛᴇɴ her clothes, as if nothing unto-
ward had happened in that parlor. Rafe even helped, lifting the
bodice of her dress back over her breasts and depositing a brief
kiss on the upper edge that didn't get quite covered and wouldn't,
because of the low neckline. She pulled up her stockings, which
were bunched about her ankles, and almost laughed that she was
still wearing her boots. That he'd removed none of her clothes to
make love to her was rather tawdry by all accounts, if she cared to
think about it. She didn't, but he obviously did.

Before he unlocked the door, he drew her into his arms and
kissed her one last time. "We really should do this in a bed sometime." His smile was somewhat embarrassed. "Where I can
devote the proper time to your pleasure. Rushing like a wet-
behind-the-ears schoolboy—"

She put a finger to his lips. "Your ears are quite dry, I do assure you."

"That's kind of you to say so, but I do seem to lose my finesse
when I'm around you."

"Fishing for more compliments, are you?"

"Was I?" He grinned.

"And I'd be careful about calling *me* kind," she teased. "Or you might have to take me back to London immediately, task finished."

He coughed, opened the door, and gently shoved her through it. "Go change your dress before luncheon. My aunt will be down soon."

"I just need to dispose of the evidence." She was grinning now.

"Would you like me to?"

She'd bunched her torn drawers in her hand, since she had no pocket on this dress to stuff them in, but she'd prefer not to be caught running up the stairs with them in hand. She glanced at the fireplace behind him.

"Would you toss them in the fire for me? Sadie can't be allowed to find them."

"Certainly."

She handed them over with a slight blush, then rushed upstairs. It wasn't as easy to dispose of her stained petticoat. Water alone wasn't going to remove the splotches of virginal blood, and Sadie knew well it wasn't her time of the month. She ended up hiding the petticoat under her mattress for now. When she had more time, she would cut it up and feed it to the fire as well. Evidence gone. No one the wiser.

She did change dresses, though, after getting a better look at the wrinkles they'd managed to put on the lavender one. But it was amazing how quickly she rushed through doing so. She was back downstairs in less than fifteen minutes, to spend more time with Rafe today. So she was quite disappointed to find that he was no longer in the parlor, where she'd left him.

She moved over to the window to wait for him to return. She

kept stealing glances at the sofa behind her, where they'd made love. She didn't think she'd be able to sit there again without blushing.

It was starting to sink in. She was a woman now. She'd had the sophistication of one for several years, but now she really was one. Oddly, it felt no different—no, that wasn't true. It felt wonderful. No, actually, what she was feeling had nothing to do with crossing the line into womanhood and everything to do with who had helped her across it. That first time could have been a horrible experience, she realized now, but Rafe hadn't let it be. He'd made sure she could look back on it with a smile. And she had a feeling it was going to be quite a wide smile for a long time.

Rafe came back downstairs with his aunt beside him. He'd changed his clothes as well and combed his hair—she'd made it look rather wild threading her fingers through it. She hoped no one had noticed before he was able to fix it. The man *never* looked untidy, certainly not the way he was when she'd left him earlier.

With Esmerelda present, there was no further opportunity to talk about what they'd done together, though Ophelia did catch the secretive grin he gave her *and* returned it. And her wonderful mood lasted through luncheon. Nor was it daunted when he suggested afterward that they adjourn to his study, rather than the parlor.

"I don't believe I will be able to concentrate just now in the other room," he admitted in a low voice as he escorted her across the hall.

She understood perfectly. And she didn't think he had another intimate tryst in mind, more's the pity. Every time he'd suggested they adjourn to another room by themselves, it was to discuss her past peccadilloes. Today she didn't even mind. Today she could probably withstand any subject he felt like introducing.

"Let's discuss Sabrina," he said as she took a seat across from his desk.

Well, any subject except that one. "Let's not."

She smiled at him as she said it. She didn't want him to think she was being difficult. But she had such mixed feelings about Sabrina Lambert, she didn't really want to delve into them.

Rafe didn't say another word, was staring at the letter opener he'd picked up and was now twirling through his fingers. She knew what he was doing, using silence against her. It wasn't going to work this time. . . .

"I was fool enough to give her a chance, you know," Ophelia said after a few more moments of his ignoring her. "When she arrived in London with her aunts to stay with us for the Season, she seemed so sweet. I doubted it at first, but then I realized her sweetness probably wasn't false because she was a country girl, so I actually broke my own rule. I thought we could be real friends."

He let out a long-suffering sigh. "So this is a case where you really did backstab a friend? I must admit I was hoping to hear a valid excuse."

He looked so disappointed in her it actually brought a tightness to her chest. What the devil? And she didn't even know what he was talking about!

"Explain that remark, if you please. How exactly did I backstab her?"

"You reintroduced her family scandal, which had been long forgotten, and you did so maliciously."

"Don't be absurd," she said curtly. "I was doing her a favor."

He raised a skeptical brow. "By ruining her chances for a good match in London? I think I'd prefer to decline favors like that."

Ophelia sat back with a sigh of her own. "Very well, I see I'm going to have to explain. You probably won't believe this, but I was trying to save the girl a lot of grief later."

"Grief?"

"Yes. I didn't want to see her get hurt by falling in love with someone, then not being able to marry him because of the scandal. It was bound to come out on its own. After enough people had met her, someone would have remembered the Lambert name. And it was such a silly scandal. To assume that just because a few ancestors killed themselves everyone else in her family was bound to do the same, herself included, was preposterous. Yet you know how people are. Some will believe such nonsense. So my idea was to get it out in the open and point out just how silly it was. I would have laughed down anyone fool enough to give credit to it. It would have died a quick death and no more would have been heard about it."

"Good God, you're trying to say that you were championing her?"

Ophelia gritted her teeth. "You don't have to sound quite that incredulous. That was the idea—originally."

"Ah." He nodded. "Are we going to get to the malicious part now?"

"No, I see what we are going to get to is my final flaw. Coupled with my temper, it's probably my worst flaw."

"And that would be?"

"Jealousy."

"Do you realize how absurd that statement is?" he said incredulously. "You are quite possibly the most beautiful woman in England. Every woman you meet is probably jealous of *you*. Even my sister is! Out of all of them, you are the one woman who would have no conceivable reason to be jealous of anyone."

"Everything you've said is true. I'm well aware of it. But that has absolutely nothing to do with it. Knowing I have no reason to be jealous doesn't stop me from becoming jealous. I *know* it's ridiculous. And it can happen over the most silly things. But it still happens! Once that emotion shows up, it's there, and I don't deal with it very well."

"So you're telling me you got jealous over Sabrina?"

"Yes. It was Mavis who provoked my jealousy when we saw three of my admirers flocking around Sabrina at a ball. So while I had intended to introduce the Lambert scandal with good intentions, I did so jealously instead. I would have gotten over the jealousy and I would have continued with the original plan, but Sabrina and her aunts were determined to return home. And since my family received the summons from Summers Glade for me to meet Duncan, we all traveled there together. By then I was afraid of meeting the "barbarian," so I forgot about laughing down Sabrina's scandal. Not that it matters now if, as you say, she's soon to marry Duncan."

"I still find it hard to believe that you could be jealous of Sabrina." But then he appeared thoughtful and added, "That wasn't the only time you became jealous of her, was it?"

She blushed. "No, it happened again when I kept seeing Duncan with her, but I thought he was merely trying to make *me* jealous."

"And?"

"Oh, very well, also when I kept seeing you with her. So, yes, I was jealous that day I told you it looked like you and she were—"

"You needn't go into that again."

"Very well, but since you've brought this up, I'm going to tell you why I didn't want to discuss Sabrina. Because I have very mixed feelings about her. When I'm not in the midst of a jealous snit over the girl, I actually *like* her."

"That's understandable. Everyone likes Sabrina."

She raised a brow at him when he didn't add to that. "You're not going to finish that statement and remind me that everyone *doesn't* like me?"

He grinned at her. "Actually, m'dear, that wouldn't be a true statement anymore, so, no, I can no longer say it."

She started to blush, sure that he was talking about himself, that he no longer disliked her. But he added, "My aunt has grown quite fond of you."

She wasn't sure why she felt hurt, but she quickly shook it off and said, "You've missed the point I was making. Everyone else I've become jealous of, I don't like. Sabrina is the only one I do like. So each time I got jealous of her, I felt as if I were betraying her, which made it quite worse. But as soon as the jealousy would pass, I'd chide myself for being so silly, and I'd be back to liking her. Quite unusual feelings for me."

"Not unusual a'tall."

"That might be the case for other people, but for me, this was very unusual," she insisted.

"Perhaps you were still hoping you and she could be friends."

"I don't think there is any *perhaps* about that. I did still think we could be *real* friends, and I still found myself *wanting* to help her."

"When did she need help?"

"When it looked like she was making too much of Duncan's interest in her."

"His interest was quite real."

"I know that *now*," Ophelia said impatiently, "but at the time, how the deuce was I supposed to figure out that they were falling in love with each other? I told her that Duncan kissed me at the inn the day I met him there to apologize to him."

"A lie."

"Indeed, but just a minor one, intended to keep her from being hurt, not hurt her."

"As it happens, I was going to bring up a few of your lies. That was one of them."

She rolled her eyes. "Why does that not surprise me? And the others?"

"There's just one other that I know about."

"Not a long list? I thought you were better prepared than that."

"Are we getting angry this soon?"

She blinked, then actually smiled. "Not a'tall. Merely a little annoyed, but now that you've pointed it out—" She shrugged. "It's gone."

He sat back, looking surprised. "I'm amazed. That's quite a turnabout, Phelia. How do you feel about it?"

She grinned. "I love it. It is so nice not to have my temper take over. Now what was this other lie you mentioned?"

"There were so many you don't know?"

She gave that a moment's thought, then said, "I don't think so. I can only think of one other time when I deliberately lied to Sabrina. You've called me spiteful and I've denied it, but this was probably one time I was, because of my jealousy. She was making too much of the timing of when Duncan and I got reengaged. It annoyed me, smacked of her interest in him, so I told her that he insisted upon it right after she left the house. In fact, Duncan's grandfather wanted us to feed people that story, so that wasn't even my lie! But for some reason the information devastated Sabrina. I have no idea why, do you?"

"No, that's between Sabrina and Duncan and is none of our business. So you admit you've been spiteful?"

She wasn't surprised he latched onto that. "Yes. Are you happy now?"

"Not really. The question is, and this is a really important question, m'dear, now that you're no longer in denial, have you learned anything from our discussions? Or will you return to London and revert to—"

"Stop right there," she cut in . . . "Apparently *you* haven't learned anything from these discussions. With my temper, which was responsible for exacerbating my jealousies, in better control, nearly complete control for the time being—and I'll allow I have you to thank for that—how can you think that I won't be different now?"

"A good point. Then I see no reason for us to remain here any longer. We will set out for London first thing tomorrow morning."

Chapter Twenty-seven

O PHELIA SHOULD HAVE BEEN ECSTATIC, jumping for joy to finally be going home. Instead she found herself fighting back tears more than once on the trip back to London, and otherwise feeling quite down. She couldn't even fathom why, other than that she'd been introduced to the most exciting experience of her life and she'd *thought* she'd be able to enjoy it again, but there wouldn't be any other opportunities to do so once she was back at home. She couldn't be feeling so odd simply because her time with Raphael Locke was coming to an end.

Rafe didn't need to drive the coach this time. Esmerelda's footman was still with them and had been given that chore, so Rafe was able to ride inside with the four women. But Esmerelda's home would be reached before the day was out. And while she kept up a steady stream of chatter that Ophelia tried halfheartedly to take part in, Esmerelda wouldn't be with them for the rest of the journey. Not that that would leave her alone with Rafe for the remainder of the trip. Sadie did make a good chaperone, after all.

They agreed unanimously to spend the night at Esmerelda's again rather than to look for an inn. They had a nice dinner together, their last, and the older woman got emotional there at the end of it.

"I won't see you off in the morning. I don't like good-byes. But I do expect to see you again sometime, gel. Enjoyed your company, 'deed I did."

"I'm going to miss you too," Ophelia said. "Are you sure you don't want to come to London with us to enjoy the rest of the Season?"

"Goodness, no! The Season is for young folks. But I'll come for your wedding, once you find the man you want to settle down with."

If that day ever came. But when Ophelia returned to London she wouldn't be shackled with an unwanted engagement or be spending all her time thinking of ways to get out of it, so she could actually concentrate on finding a husband. If there were any good catches left this late in the Season. Although that would hardly matter. She could easily lure any man away . . .

Ophelia stopped the thought abruptly, appalled at herself. Did she really used to think that way? Seeing her past behavior from such a different perspective was quite an illuminating experience. Insensitive, uncaring, self-centered. Did it really matter that she'd felt justified? That she'd merely treated others as they treated her, or at least, as she'd assumed they treated her?

She was going to have to reexamine all of her relationships now, including her relationship with her parents. It might actually be nice not to feel angry at her father all the time. And he would be her greatest test. If she could get through just one conversation with him, without having the bitterness show up . . .

They left Esmerelda's early the next morning. As she'd guessed, the ride was a bit uncomfortable now without the buffer of Rafe's aunt. He seemed to be deep in thought for most of the day, so while she tried a few times to strike up a conversation with him, she soon gave up.

They were pulling up in front of Summers Glade before she realized that was their destination. Sadie had been sleeping, and when she woke up and saw where they were, she said what Ophelia was too surprised to utter: "What the devil are we doing here again?"

Rafe chuckled at both of their expressions. "Merely dropping me off. I figure the happy couple will be getting married anytime now, so I'm saving myself a trip back here from London."

"You could have mentioned that was your intention," Ophelia chided lightly.

"Sorry, thought I did," he replied with a shrug. "But come to think of it, this would be a good time to put what you've learned to the test, don't you think? Would you like to stay for the wedding?"

She didn't have to think about it. Her answer was immediate. "No, those two aren't going to believe that I've changed. And I don't want to put a damper on their happy event. I'll be fine getting home by myself."

"Very well, then. I'll see you in London, probably in a few days."

Another surprise, this one even more unexpected, but much more pleasant. "Will you?"

"Certainly. I have no doubt we'll be attending the same parties."

That wasn't what she thought he'd meant, but she managed to keep her disappointment to herself. Their time together was over. She'd gotten much more than she'd bargained for from his outlandish plan—Rafe's success!

But without further ado, he stepped outside and closed the door behind him. Just like that. No further farewell, no admonishments to behave, no . . .

The door opened again, and Rafe, with an annoyed look on his face, leaned in, grabbed her shoulders, and kissed her hard on her mouth. Her desire for him rose up immediately, and she felt a delicious sense of satisfaction when she saw the heat in his eyes as he leaned back. But then just as abruptly he was gone again.

Sadie was staring at her with both her brows arched higher than Ophelia had ever seen them. She didn't blush. She was too pleased to be the least bit embarrassed.

"Don't ask" was all she told her maid, as if that would work.

It didn't. "Since when has he been taking such liberties with you?"

Ophelia still tried to shrug it off. "That was nothing. We had quite a few heated discussions where I insulted him, repeatedly. That was probably just his way of letting me know there were no hard feelings."

Sadie snorted over that answer. "Saying so would have sufficed."

But it wouldn't have been nearly so thrilling, Ophelia thought, grinning to herself.

Chapter Twenty-eight

IT DIDN'T LOOK AS IF it had snowed in London recently. The streets weren't muddy, just typically wet for this time of year. The sun had even come out for the last leg of the journey, though only briefly before it started drizzling again.

Ophelia had decided to spend one more night at an inn, near the city, so she could arrive home the following day close to noon when her father wasn't likely to be at home. His habit was to lunch with his friends at his club, and she wanted to have a chance to get settled in before she had to deal with him and the questions he would ask.

She hadn't heard from him at all, so she didn't even know if he was still angry that she hadn't brought Duncan to the altar, or if the Locke heir's interest in her had mollified him.

The earl's family home was on Berkeley Street, north of Hyde Park. It was a quiet street, not very long. On the west end of it was Portman Square, and just east was the smaller Manchester Square. Ophelia had never played in either park. Playing was considered childish, and she'd never really been allowed to be a child like other children. As far back as she could remember, she'd been treated more like an adult, at least by her father. Her mother had tried to give her some normalcy, but Sherman had always intervened with his own dictates. He'd been grooming her for an elite marriage from the day she was born.

Her mother would be home, of course. Mary rarely left the house these days because she was always too busy planning her parties. Her friends came to her, she didn't call on them. She hadn't even chaperoned Ophelia at the start of the Season. Sherman had insisted on doing so. It wasn't pride in her, it was more like gloating as he stood back and watched her success. He'd spared no expense for her come-out wardrobe, but it wasn't for her, it was so she would shine and *he'd* be congratulated on having such an amazing daughter.

The bitterness almost snuck up on her, but she recognized the signs and shoved it away. She had her goal now, and the sooner she accomplished it the better. She was going to marry a rich man so she would have nothing more to do with her father.

"Shall I unpack first, or do you want to rest for the afternoon?" Sadie asked as they entered the large town house Ophelia had grown up in.

"I'm not tired, so go ahead and unpack," Ophelia replied.

Their voices drew Mary Reid from the parlor. "You're home! Goodness, I've missed you!"

Mary Reid had a sweet tooth. She had indulged it over the years, until she was quite plump now. An inch shorter than Ophelia, but three times as wide, she was good-natured, almost too good-natured. The only time Ophelia had ever heard her mother raise her voice was that horrid day all those years ago when Ophelia had found out that she didn't have any real friends, and that her father's only interest in her was how she could improve his social standing.

Ophelia's blond hair and blue eyes came from her mother, who had been a beauty herself in her day. Her father's hair and eyes were brown. She was glad she'd inherited nothing from him.

She hugged her mother and kissed her cheek. "I've missed you too, Mama."

"That was quite a surprise that you got engaged to Duncan again."

"And an even bigger surprise that we broke it off yet again?" Ophelia guessed.

"Well, yes. But look whose eye you've caught instead! The Locke heir. Your father is so pleased!"

Ophelia cringed inwardly. "Rafe and I merely became friends, Mama. Nothing is going to come of it."

"Really?" Mary frowned slightly, her disappointment obvious. "You haven't considered him for a husband a'tall?"

"I might have, but he made it quite clear he isn't ready to take such a big step. And it's rather nice, being friends with a man who hasn't fallen at my feet to worship me."

Mary rolled her eyes. "Well, don't discount him yet. Some men take a while to recognize a good thing when they trip over it. But in the meantime we'll carry on as if you haven't caught the eye of the most eligible bachelor in the realm." Mary grinned. "But you should have let us know you were returning. I would have arranged a party for you."

That statement wasn't the least bit surprising. It wasn't surprising either where Ophelia had gotten the notion that giving the grandest balls London had ever seen would make her happy, when her mother's life revolved around entertaining. That would probably still make her happy—at least, she'd enjoy it—but her new goal held priority: getting out from under her father's thumb.

To please her mother she said, "You can still throw a party.

That will be as good a way as any to let everyone know I'm back in London."

"Indeed, my thoughts exactly. But I do have a pile of invitations as well that I've mostly been ignoring. You might want to go through them to see if any are worth attending for the rest of the week."

"I'll take them up to my room."

"Good, then go rest while I work on a quick guest list. I'm sure I can entice a few people into breaking whatever engagements they had for tonight, to come here instead."

Mary managed to do better than that, Ophelia discovered, when she came down to dinner that night. The house was filled with guests, mostly young gentlemen she already knew, though there were a few she didn't recognize. And at least she was dressed splendidly for the occasion.

It was nice to have her full wardrobe available to her again, rather then the slim choices her trunks had supplied. Sadie had picked out a soft cream silk evening gown with white lace trimming. Pearls dangled at her ears, and an oval pendant hung daintily at her neck. Her hair was coiffed in her usual tight style with just a few ringlets dangling at her temples, but Sadie had dug out some pearl hairpins to give it a little more flare.

Her mother caught her in the hall as she was glancing in the parlor. Ophelia raised a brow at her. Mary understood and said merely, "I didn't expect *all* of them to accept the invitation, but I should have known better. You are so very popular, after all."

"Is father going to make an appearance?"

Mary blushed. "I didn't send him word to let him know you're back. I expected to tell him this afternoon when he returned, but then he sent word he won't be home until late." And then Mary shrugged. "No matter. It isn't necessary for him to be here for us to enjoy the evening."

Ophelia almost laughed. It was easy to read between the lines with her mother. Mary knew well that Ophelia and her father didn't get along well and could easily spark each other's temper. By making no effort to let her husband know that she was entertaining tonight and why, she'd assured that Ophelia could relax her first evening back in town and enjoy the impromptu party.

Mary escorted her into the parlor. They barely got through the door before Ophelia was surrounded by her admirers, who all vied for her attention at once.

"So good to have you back in town, Lady O!"

"And not engaged!"

"You take my breath away with your beauty, Ophelia, as always."

"Lord Hatch," another gentlemen reminded her. "I hope you remember me?"

"Charmed, my lady, as always," Lord Cantle said as he kissed her hand.

"Introduce me, Peter," another of them said impatiently to a friend, and when Peter didn't, "I can't tell you how much I've been looking forward to meeting you, Lady Ophelia. Artemus Billings, at your service."

"A pleasure," she said quickly before another young man tried to gain her notice.

Artemus was rather handsome, and at least he hadn't dropped a title, which usually meant a man took it for granted everyone knew who he was. She might have to find out a little more about him, but that would have to wait until she got her hand back. Every single one of them was determined to kiss it.

Except Hamilton Smithfield, Viscount Moorly. Recently turned twenty-one and come into his title, Hamilton had always been quite bashful when he'd spoken to her. He'd certainly never struck her as a man bold enough to pull her away from the crowd, but he did that now.

He led her across the room, then stopped and quickly told her, "I never got up the nerve to ask you this before. And then I could have cried when I heard you were engaged to MacTavish. But since that didn't pan out, I'm not going to risk missing this opportunity again. I beseech you, Ophelia, to marry me." He gazed at her adoringly.

She'd always been rather terse with her refusals, and this was the sort of proposal she detested because it was coming from a man who hadn't taken the time to get to know her first. But her refusal usually left a stricken look of disappointment on the man's face, and she didn't want to confront that now.

To avoid it, she merely said, "Talk to my father, Viscount Moorly."

"Really?"

He looked elated, seeming to take that as her approval, so she gently corrected, "It's simply not my choice."

She was sure Sherman would turn him down, and therefore she wouldn't have to witness the viscount's disappointment. Rather cowardly of her, but she wasn't used to feeling bad about turning down marriage proposals. She'd been too self-centered for it to bother her in the past. Now, she was faced with dashing these young men's hopes, and feeling sorry about it!

Jane and Edith rescued her from those uncomfortable feelings when they pounced on her and dragged her away yet again, wanting to know all the details about why she hadn't married Duncan MacTavish. She didn't elaborate as she once would have. She merely told them exactly what Duncan's grandfather had announced, that they had amicably agreed they weren't suited.

And then she asked, "You didn't have somewhere else to be tonight?"

"Nothing important enough to miss welcoming you home," Jane replied.

That almost had a ring of truth to it, but Ophelia knew better. Both Jane and Edith were highly skilled in saying exactly what they thought she wanted to hear. Unfortunately, they usually had to lie to do so. Which was her fault, she realized. If she hadn't had such a horrid temper all these years, the girls in her circle might have behaved much differently around her.

"But we came by to find out what delayed your return to town," Edith told her. "Your mother said you were visiting the Lockes. Is that really true?"

"You didn't believe her?"

Edith blushed slightly. Both girls were quite pretty; they just didn't come close to Ophelia's beauty. With lesser titles, they didn't expect to land any prime catch for a husband this Season. Actually, what they expected was to have first picks of Ophelia's discards, so both girls were hoping Ophelia would make her choice sooner rather than later.

"Well, actually, we felt she might be misinformed," Edith said, providing the reason for her blush.

What a diplomatic way to say they thought Mary had lied to them. "Misinformed by me?" Ophelia said.

"Yes," Edith admitted, though she quickly explained, "We knew you and Locke didn't take well to each other. Couldn't imagine why, when he's so handsome, but we saw those sparks fly between you two. So we were sure you would have refused an invitation from his family. We just thought that's where you told your parents you were, when you weren't really there a'tall."

Ah, so they were sure that *she* had lied to her mother. Rafe was so right in that regard. Once you start down the path of lying, you'll always be doubted, and both girls knew she was adept at lying.

Oddly, the time she had spent with Rafe—not the reason— was something she would once have gloated about to these two. Now, she preferred that they not know about it, so this wasn't a subject she wanted to discuss.

And Edith and Jane weren't pushy. She thought she could get by with merely saying, "That was a trying time at Summers Glade when I realized I didn't want to marry MacTavish after all. I was afraid he wouldn't let me beg off. But I finally had a nice talk with him and we both agreed it would be better if we didn't marry. I just needed a little time to recover and think about my options. Besides, I was in no hurry to come home and face my father's wrath over it. You know how much he wanted that match."

There was the distinct possibility that they had spoken to Mavis since then and had the truth of the matter, but the "time to recover" part worked either way. Where she'd spent that time recovering was irrelevant.

So she was surprised to hear Edith ask pointedly, "So you weren't really visiting the Lockes?"

Before she could think of a way to prevaricate further, Jane said, "Well, that answers that."

Ophelia followed her gaze to see Raphael Locke stepping into the parlor. Her pulse picked up immediately at the sight of him. She had no idea why he was there, but she couldn't deny she was thrilled to see him. She certainly hadn't expected to, at least not this soon.

"Why didn't you want to tell us you'd won him over?" Edith asked excitedly.

"Perhaps because I'm not sure how I feel about it myself,"

Ophelia heard herself saying, then groaned inwardly. *Just* what she hadn't wanted to confess.

"Good God, you've fallen in love, haven't you?" Jane gasped out.

"No, absolutely not," Ophelia replied immediately. But she was afraid that was one of the biggest lies she'd ever told.

Chapter Twenty-nine

MARY WAS KEEPING RAFE OCCUPIED and had been since he arrived. Ophelia wasn't surprised that her mother had thought to invite him, but she was surprised that he'd been in London to accept the invitation because she'd left him off at Summers Glade the day before. Duncan and Sabrina couldn't have married that quickly. Or perhaps they'd already married and Rafe had missed the wedding?

She wasn't able to appease her curiosity immediately. She'd been given a few minutes to chat with her friends, but then more of her admirers swarmed around her, so it was quite a while later before she found a chance to speak with Rafe alone.

Too many guests were present for a sitdown dinner, but that was often the case at the Reid parties, and Mary was adept at setting up long buffet tables filled with hors d'oeuvres for picky eaters, and heartier fare for bigger appetites.

Ophelia had to leave the room to gain a moment alone, so when she returned, she was able to head straight for Rafe. He'd just filled a plate high with food and was looking about for an empty chair. There weren't any. Every available seat in the room was already occupied now that most of the guests were eating.

"The dining room just might be empty," she suggested in a conspiratorial whisper as she came up beside him.

His light blue eyes came to rest on her and stayed there. Her breath caught in her throat. He was so handsome. He always seemed to have this effect on her, and he was looking especially handsome tonight in his dark broadcloth jacket which fit his wide shoulders perfectly, and his snowy white cravat tied loosely at his throat. His golden locks shimmered in the candlelight. Being this close to him made her pulse race too. God, she hoped it wasn't obvious what he did to her.

He must not have noticed anything out of the ordinary because he asked, "But are there any chairs left in it, or were they all moved in here?"

Ophelia got her breathing under control. "You'd be surprised at how many chairs my mother keeps on hand. She considers small parties a waste of her talents."

When she glanced at his overfilled plate, he grinned and said, "I missed lunch."

"Shall we check then?"

"Why don't you get your dinner first."

"I'm not hungry."

He raised a brow. "We never did get around to working on your thinness, did we?"

He was teasing—or maybe he wasn't. "Do you *really* think I'm too thin?" she asked as she glanced down at herself with a worried frown.

"You don't really want to know what I think about your figure."

She blushed immediately, probably because she looked back

up to see that his gaze had turned lambent as it moved over her breasts and lower. She quickly grabbed a small sausage wrapped in a thin biscuit crust from one of the many offerings on the table, then showed him the way to the dining room.

It was almost empty, but not quite. Two gentlemen were eating at one end of the long table and having a heated discussion. One of them, Jonathan Canters, had asked her to marry him just fifteen minutes ago. Her second proposal of the night. And he'd been as serious as young Hamilton. Jonathan had asked her at the beginning of the Season as well, before it became known she was already engaged to Duncan.

She smiled at the two men, just a cordial smile, then ignored them, so they'd understand she wasn't interested in joining them. She took a seat at the other end of the dining table and waited for Rafe to sit down next to her. She was amazed she'd been able to contain her curiosity that long.

"*What* are you doing here?" she burst out in a whisper. "You're supposed to be at Summers Glade."

"As it turned out, Duncan and Sabrina aren't getting married for another few weeks. Apparently Sabrina's aunts insisted on a proper wedding with all the grand touches that take so long to work out. And with Duncan barely containing his impatience, since he'd rather *not* wait, I decided it wasn't a good place to wait it out m'self, so I returned to London after all."

"It's too bad you didn't find that out before I drove on."

"Indeed. That's why I missed my lunch, actually. I kept thinking I'd catch up to you this morning, but I couldn't find which inn you were staying at."

"I'm still surprised to see you here, that you would actually accept my mother's invitation. I could have sworn you didn't want your name linked to mine in any way."

"My being here doesn't link our names, m'dear. And I haven't been home yet to receive your mother's invitation. I merely stopped by to make sure you got home all right."

"Well, that was nice of you."

"I do have my moments."

He had more than a few of those, good ones. Of course, he'd had more than a few bad ones too, where he hadn't been so nice, had been quite high-handed, but she'd forgiven him for those. They had ended on a good note, perhaps a little too good. . . .

"Besides," he added as he began to eat, "I have a vested interest now, in seeing that you find happiness with the right man. That was part of the deal, if you'll remember."

She went still. He didn't notice. Was he serious? He was going to play matchmaker for her, after what they'd shared?

"Was it?" she said a little curtly. "I don't recall your mentioning that."

"Didn't think I needed to, when it goes part and parcel with your happiness," he replied in his typical jaunty tone. "You do still intend to marry, correct?"

"Certainly."

"Then you'll be spending the rest of your life with this lucky chap, whoever he is, so we need to assure that you'll be happy with him."

"We? And how can that possibly be determined ahead of time, that *he* will be able to make me happy?"

He gave her a surprised look. "Don't tell me you're still only going to look for a fat purse. Money doesn't buy happiness, Phelia, it just makes misery easier to bear. It won't make you happy in the long run."

She took a bite of the sausage she held in her hand and ground it between her teeth. "And what will?"

"Love, of course."

"I wouldn't have taken you for a romantic."

"Neither would I." He grinned. "I'm just trying to look at it from a female perspective. Based on my sister's thoughts on the matter, which I can't tell you how many times I've been forced to listen to, she's convinced love will make her ecstatically happy. It does seem to go hand in hand, love and happiness, that is."

"It probably does. I wouldn't know from personal experience. But there are other things that can make someone happy."

He sighed. He'd probably noticed by now that she sounded annoyed. "Don't tell me you've reverted to form, that all of our combined efforts—"

"Oh, stop it." She let out a sigh of her own. "I merely have a new goal, to reach a point—soon—where I never have to do my father's bidding again. He makes decisions with his happiness in mind, not mine, and I've quite had enough of that."

"That implies you're going to accept the first proposal that comes along."

He looked so worried, she found herself wanting to reassure him, so she chuckled and said, "At least half the men here tonight have already asked me to marry them, a few in the last hour. I haven't accepted a proposal yet."

"Are there any here that—interest you?" he asked a bit hesitantly. "I might know something about them that you don't."

She shrugged. "Not really." She took a moment to smile at Jonathan again. Both men had stopped their discussion when she'd entered the room and had been stealing glances at her ever since. "I haven't given up on the criteria that I would prefer—yet."

"You never did mention what you were looking for in a man, besides wealth."

"No, I didn't."

"Still keeping that to yourself?"

She sighed. "No, I just didn't want to discuss it with you at the time you asked. I simply don't trust any man who professes to love me instantly. And they've all done just that." She waved a hand to encompass—all of London. "I'm waiting for the man who takes some time to know me first—like you did."

She didn't blush. She shouldn't have said that, but she'd already warned him that he didn't need to worry that she was going to set her cap for him and why.

"To be honest, Phelia, that's an excellent goal now, but it probably would have worked against you—"

"Nonsense," she cut in, aware that he was going to mention her past behavior. "I know you'd like to take full credit for the 'new' me, but in fact, you've merely opened my eyes to a few things and helped me to control some flaws that had gotten out of hand. However, I did have some good qualities prior to that, I just kept them mostly to myself."

"Yes, I did notice that."

"What?"

"That you weren't completely lacking in good qualities. The way you easily won my aunt over was a good example."

"Won her over?" She grinned. "She took to me immediately and you know it."

"Yes, I suppose she did. And now you should get back to your guests. Spending a few minutes with me is one thing, but more'n that and tongues will start wagging."

"I know." She stood up to leave. "And thank you for coming by to check on me. That was rather sweet of you."

His blue eyes flashed. "Good God, never use that word in relation to me. You're going to give me a bad reputation, 'deed you are."

"You'd rather be known as an irredeemable rake?"

"Absolutely!"

She knew very well he was teasing, and in the same vein she said, "Then your secret is safe with me."

She turned to leave. He caught her elbow. She drew in her breath, closed her eyes for a moment. She'd been just fine sitting there, concentrating on their conversation rather than his presence so close to her. But his touch made her remember exactly what they'd shared and how wonderful it had been—and what Jane had said. . . .

"How did your homecoming go with your father?" he asked. Her spirits plunged at his reason for stopping her.

She didn't turn back around, afraid to look at him just now. "He hasn't been home since I got here, so he doesn't even know that I've returned."

"Why don't you wait and see how that goes then, before you make any rash decisions."

"Me? Rash?" She left him with a delicate snort and heard him laughing as she walked away.

Chapter Thirty

EELING DISTRACTED AFTER LEAVING RAFE, Ophelia couldn't have picked a worse time to cross from the dining room to the parlor. She didn't even notice her father at the front door shrugging out of his long coat and handing it to the waiting footman. But he noticed her immediately.

"Pheli? When did you get home?"

No welcoming smile for her. No open arms to offer her a warm hug. He merely looked curious.

Sherman Reid, Earl of Durwich, was in his midforties now. He had a full head of dark hair and sharp brown eyes. He was tall and narrow of frame, and if he stood next to his wife, he might be called skinny. He wasn't a plain-looking man, but he'd never been called handsome, either. Which was perhaps why he'd been so amazed to have produced a daughter of such unsurpassed beauty, and why he'd been determined to exact some benefit from that gift of nature for himself.

"I returned this afternoon. Mother, as you can see, managed a welcome-home party and invited quite a few of my admirers."

He glanced toward the noise coming from the parlor. "Was that necessary?"

Ophelia was given pause. She'd mentioned the admirers because normally her father would have been delighted that she was being shown off and racking up even more marriage proposals—well, it would have before he'd settled on Duncan MacTavish for his son-in-law. Besides, he'd always encouraged Mary to entertain. That was one thing husband and wife were in complete agreement on.

"Necessary, no. But it made Mama happy to do it, so it served a purpose."

"Don't take that tone with me, girl."

She almost laughed. Her tone hadn't changed in the least, if anything it was milder than it had ever been with him. But he was obviously expecting her to get snappish. After all, ever since he'd engaged her to Duncan, nothing but heated arguments had passed between them.

"Adjourn to my study. I'd like a few words with you," he said.

"Can't it wait? We have guests."

"No, it won't wait."

He said no more and passed her, heading down the hall to his study. She took a deep breath and followed him. She wasn't going to let him disturb her newfound peace of mind. Somehow, she'd keep her temper under wraps. She'd never been able to do that with him before, but this would be a good start.

He was already seated behind his desk when she entered the study. She hated this room, where they'd had most of their arguments. It's dark browns and greens, in carpet, in drapes, in furnishings, might have been quite tasteful and suited to a man's study, but she found them depressing. Once, long ago, she used to love coming into this room and finding her father there. . . .

She usually sat across from his desk, but tonight she moved to the one window that caught a corner view of the street out front. The drape hadn't yet been drawn on the evening, though someone had started a fire in the fireplace behind his desk earlier to take the chill off the room. Outside, streetlamps had been lit and coaches lined the curb in front of the house. Surprisingly, it had started to snow lightly. There wasn't enough to cover the street yet, but it looked rather pretty, falling about the lamp-posts, and watching it soothed her mounting tension.

"Did you bring home a proposal from Locke?" Sherman asked as he lit one of the lamps on his desk.

Ophelia closed her eyes before she asked, "Is that what you were hoping?"

"Hoping, no. Expecting, yes. That would be the only thing that would make your broken engagement to MacTavish, *for the second time,* palatable."

He'd raised his voice to stress that. She didn't turn around to face him yet. She used to come in here often, hoping for a crumb of his attention. She'd never noticed that she rarely got it. Odd how children take certain things for granted, such as their parents' love.

"Raphael Locke is a rake," she stated in a tired tone. That should have been sufficient to end the subject, but not with *her* father.

"So?"

As she had thought. That information didn't phase him in the least. Rafe could have had the worst reputation imaginable and her father would still have approved of that visit. The Locke title was the *only* thing that mattered to him.

"So he has no intention of getting married to me or anyone else." She turned finally so she could see her father's reaction. "I believe the way he put it was 'not in this century.' "

"Nonsense. You're capable of changing any man's opinion about that."

That was a compliment—of sorts. She just wished she could take it that way instead of feeling insulted.

She wasn't going to tell him how she'd fought that "invitation" tooth and nail to begin with, that she'd more or less been abducted to the wilds of Northumberland. Not only would he not care, it was no longer an issue for her. She'd gotten more out of that trip than she'd ever dreamed. And that she hadn't lost her temper yet with this man was a prime example of the benefits she'd gained from Rafe's interference in her life.

"Is he at least in love with you like all the others?" Sherman asked.

"No, but we became friends of a sort."

"Are you telling me he didn't compromise you? A known rake and he didn't even try to seduce you?"

She flushed, her anger on the rise. "So you did know he was a rake? And you still gave your permission for me to visit with him and his family?"

"Of course I did. He's the best catch in all of England. So tell me, why didn't you catch him?"

Trying to put him on the defensive didn't work. There had to be a measure of guilt, even just a tiny bit, to cause defensiveness. He had none. And her anger was starting to get out of hand.

"Maybe because I didn't want to."

"Have you taken leave of your senses?"

She marched across the room and put her hands on his desk so she could lean forward and glare at him. "No, I believe I've finally regained them. Would you really like to know why he won't do? Yes, he's incredibly handsome, rich, titled. He's everything I could want in a man. But there's just one thing that makes him unacceptable to me."

"What?"

"*You* want him too much for a son-in-law! After you more or less threw me to the wolves in Yorkshire, I'm no longer inclined to make *you* happy in my marriage. Does that surprise you?"

He stood up, was glaring back at her. "That you're a willful, vindictive daughter? That doesn't surprise me in the least. But you *will* marry him. I don't give a bloody damn how you get him to the altar, just do it! Or I'll take matters into my own hands."

There was no point in trying to make him understand that it was her life they were talking about, not his. She knew that from experience. Furious, she marched out of the room. And too angry to rejoin the guests in the parlor, she found herself going into the dining room instead.

Rafe was still there. He was just standing up, his plate empty now. The other two men had already left the room, though she wasn't sure if their presence would have stopped her or not, since she didn't even think about what she was going to do. She simply walked up to Rafe and kissed him hard.

He handled his surprise well. In fact, he was almost instantly kissing her back, his plate dropped back on the table so he had both hands free to draw her in closer against him. That was all it took for her to feel the anger melt away, leaving passion in its place. And it was quite strong, that passion. It increased as he sucked on her tongue, which she'd boldly thrust in his mouth. It grew even more heated as he cupped her derriere with one hand, pressing her more firmly against his arousal.

God, what this man could make her feel! Anger, passion, tenderness, pleasure, she'd felt it all at his hands, and such excitement! He was her bane and her salvation. How the devil had she let him become so important to her? Was Jane right? Had she fallen in love without knowing it?

He kissed her hungrily, stroking her back, making her shiver deliciously for several more moments—until she realized that she couldn't have picked a worse place to share a moment of intimacy with him. The door was wide-open. Dozens of people were just across the hall. Anyone could have walked by and seen them heatedly embracing.

She stepped back immediately with that alarming thought. Her heart was still pounding though. Her cheeks were flushed. Her lips even felt swollen and probably were. She was afraid she looked as if she'd just been thoroughly kissed. So did he, for that matter. She'd mussed his hair. She quickly straightened it now. She couldn't do anything about the heat that was still in his eyes, though.

He drew in a deep, unsteady breath before he said, "That was unexpected."

It took her a moment to regain her own breath. "I learned from you," she said in reference to that kiss he'd returned to give her in the coach the other day. She gave him a half grin to make light of it.

"Had a fight with your father?"

"How did you guess?" she replied drily.

He ran a finger softly along her cheek. "Want to leave the back door open for me tonight?"

The thought almost paralyzed her with delicious anticipation. "I might," she said breathlessly.

But as she ran upstairs to regain her composure and get the thought of making love to Rafe again out of her mind, she knew she would leave that door open.

dining room had already calmed down. So he probably *had* been joking about it, and she'd let her hopes rise that he wasn't.

She padded to the window to pull back the plush lavender drapery. She caught a whiff of the two fresh roses that had been placed on her writing desk next to the window. Her mother didn't have a conservatory or an enclosed garden, yet she always managed to obtain fresh flowers for the house during the winter months.

Ophelia had a pretty room. Her mother had seen to that. Everything in it was in shades of rose, pink, and lavender, with dark cherrywood in the furnishings: the carpet and drapes, the wallpaper, the thick bedcover on her four-poster, even her vanity had a pink velvet curtain surrounding its base. She even had her own dressing room filled with her extensive wardrobe. Clothes were the one thing her father had never stinted on. She had to be decked out grandly, after all, since she was *his* showpiece.

The view outside showed that it hadn't snowed long at all last night, at least there was no evidence left of it. Her room was in the front of the house. With the windows closed, the street traffic rarely woke her and certainly hadn't today. A horseman passed by, reminding her that she needed to make sure her mare was back in the stable. She thought he looked familiar—it *was* Rafe! He even slowed his trot to glance at her house.

She waved at him, but he didn't look at the upper windows to see her, and then he rode on. And she raced like mad to dress and run down the stairs, hoping now that her horse was still outside. It was, but so was her escort's mount. The footman, Mark, usually rode with her, and hadn't she just passed him at the bottom of the stairs?

He came to the door to tell her, "I'll need a minute to fetch my coat, Lady Ophelia."

"Give me a hand up, first," she replied, adding as soon as she

Chapter Thirty-one

O PHELIA SLEPT THROUGH THE ENTIRE morning. She hadn't intended to, though she had warned Sadie not to wake her. But that had been because she'd thought—hoped—that she'd have company in her bed this morning. Before she retired last night, she'd even asked the footman to have her horse brought around at midmorning so she could enjoy a ride in Hyde Park. During her sojourn in the country she'd missed riding, which she did at least a few times a week.

But she'd overslept. It was too late now to go riding today. Five in the morning was the last time she'd looked at her clock. She'd waited up all night for Rafe to sneak into her house and join her. She'd even spent an hour with her ear to her door, listening for footsteps. What a silly chit she was. He didn't come.

Rafe had probably realized it would simply be too risky. Or maybe he just hadn't thought she was serious when she said she "might" leave the door open for him. She shouldn't have played coy. Then again, he might not have been serious himself. He'd said it in reference to her anger after all, which kissing him in the was in the saddle, "I'll wait for you at the Grosvenor Gate to Hyde Park. Don't be long."

She didn't pause to hear his admonishment that she shouldn't leave without him. That same anticipation that had kept her up all night was present again and set her off at a gallop. If she was lucky, she could catch up to Rafe. If she was really lucky, he might suggest another rendezvous and not be teasing about it this time.

She didn't get lucky. She'd glanced down the few side streets she passed by too, but Rafe had gone on to wherever he was going while she'd had to waste time dressing. And scantily at that too she realized as she waited at the gate to the park for Mark to show up.

She'd spared no time to find one of her riding habits, had grabbed the first dress within reach, one of her thin day dresses that she never left the house in! The neck scarf she'd thought might help, didn't; it was so sheer it didn't even conceal the low cut of her dress. And her coat hadn't been where it was usually hung, so she'd tied on a cloak instead. Nor had she bothered to put her hair up. She'd merely stuffed it quickly under a fur cap.

At least holding the cloak close to her kept some of the chill at bay as she mused over such rash behavior. She should return home immediately. If anyone saw what she was wearing, they'd think she was crazy to be out like that. Or maybe not. It wasn't *that* cold today, with no wind blowing. It could be considered a nice day—for winter. It would have been a perfect time for a ride actually, but she was *not* dressed for riding.

She thought she saw Mark trotting down the street in the distance. There was no point in waiting for him to reach her when she would be heading back that way to return home. She started to nudge her mare to do that when she was approached from behind.

"Going for a ride in the park?"

Where the devil had he come from? was her only thought before she said, "Yes," and turned her mount around to face Rafe.

He was giving her a curious look, possibly because she had one gloveless hand gripping her cloak closed. But the cloak didn't close enough to hide the silk and lace of her skirt peaking out from the lower edges of it.

He didn't remark on that, though, merely said, "Somehow I never imagined you on a horse, Phelia. I must say I'm quite surprised."

"Why? I happen to enjoy the exercise."

"Yes, but—" He paused to chuckle at himself. "I think I must still have this pristine image of you in my mind that never gets mussed up. You know, no hair out of place, ever. No wrinkles in your clothes, ever. And heaven forbid any horsey smell, *ever*."

She shared his amusement with a grin of her own. "That was a false image, quite ancient. Let's see, you've pounded me with snow since then, and quite a lot of it. And I was quite mussed up in the parlor at the . . . Nest."

She ended with a soft gasp, his eyes turned heated so abruptly. Reminding him of what had happened between them in that parlor was most improper, quite thoughtless on her part. And the image was in her mind now too, of him, his hair wild from her passionate caresses, the ardent sensuality of his expression—like now.

Good God, this was no place to have her passions aroused. Perhaps a ride was a good idea after all.

"I'll race you," she said impulsively.

Mark had just reached them. He heard her say it and started to protest, but she galloped away into the park. She'd just taken complete advantage of Rafe too, since his thoughts were still in that parlor! So he didn't respond immediately. But she spared a quick glance back to see that he was starting after her, and she laughed at the wide gap of her lead. She lost her cap doing so, the wind catching it from behind and sending it to the ground. She wasn't about to stop to go back for it. A race was a race, and she was competitive enough to want to win it.

Her cloak flew open when she had to grip the reins with both hands. She barely felt the bite of the wind on her chest as her blood was pumping now from the excitement of the race. Her neck scarf started to unwind and one end of it was now flapping behind her. She grabbed the other end in her fist so she didn't lose the scarf too. Her cloak, scarf, and hair were all flapping in the wind now. She didn't care. She dug in her heels, urging her mare to greater speed.

She'd headed down the northern horse path, but since the park was almost deserted, she rashly cut across toward The Serpentine. The north trail made a circuit of the park and passed by the large lake before it turned north again to finish the circuit. It was a much longer ride than the southern trail, which she rarely used. Rafe was gaining on her, but had not nearly yet caught up to her. And she could see the boathouse in the distance now. There might even be some ice-skaters out on such a fine winter day—

She didn't land too hard on the ground. It could have been much worse. Her mare could have come to a dead stop when the garden snake crossed her path and Ophelia would have flown over her head. Instead the mare reared up in her fright and just deposited Ophelia behind her on the ground. Damned horse as big as it was should *not* have been afraid of little, harmless snakes, but she was.

She merely lost a few breaths and was already leaning up on her elbows when Rafe leapt off his horse beside her. He dropped to his knees so fast they probably skidded at least an inch in the dead grass.

"Good God, you scared the life out of me!" he exclaimed rather furiously.

"I'm not hurt," she assured him.

"Damned lucky you're not. Your father should be shot for buying you a skittish mount."

"He didn't pick her out, I did. I merely had to nag him for several months to meet her price. That's how he and I do things. I nag, he gives in just to be done with it. I don't think he's ever even seen her."

"Regardless—"

"Really, I'm fine. If you'll just help me up . . . ? "

He yanked her to her feet, and suddenly he was kissing her, hotly and insistently as his hands moved down to her derrieve and gently rubbed the sports where she was sore from her fall. She moaned with pleasure, her belly flipping over from the hot sensations his slow, sensual caresses and deep kisses were sparking. She felt breathless again, but she didn't miss his intense gaze as he leaned back.

He released her so fast she almost lost her balance. And he turned around to get his eyes off her as she began to dust off her clothes and close her cloak again.

"I hope you don't always dress like that for riding," he chided as he moved away to gather the reins of their horses.

"No, of course I don't."

He was composed again, enough to glance at her. "Then why today?"

"Well, I was in a—that is to say—" She paused, giving up trying to think of an excuse without admitting she'd chased after him. So she finally said, "No, I don't think I care to mention why."

"Suit yourself." He shrugged. "But I'd suggest you go straight home."

"I intend to."

He helped her back into the saddle. He could have put his hands all over her to do so, but he managed not to touch her again, merely to offer his cupped fingers for her to step on for the boost up. He was behaving rather impersonally now, too impersonally. Of course they were in a public park. But there were only a few other people in the area, and they were quite a distance away.

She wanted to ask why he hadn't shown up last night. He obviously wasn't going to say anything about it. But that would be a bit too bold of her. And besides, Mark finally reached them. He'd been left so far behind—which was usually the case—that he wouldn't have seen that she'd fallen. Occasionally she kept to a sedate pace for him since he wasn't a good horseman. Nor did his mount have a chance of keeping up with her Thoroughbred. But more typically she'd have a good gallop, then just wait for him to catch up.

"Thank you for the race," she told Rafe, then added with a grin, "I enjoy winning."

"So do I," he replied with a roguish grin of his own. "Someday we might do this properly and you won't stand a chance in hell of beating me."

She laughed. "I wouldn't count on it. Why do you think it took me two months to get this mare? Her sire is a champion racer. She didn't come cheap!"

"Made sure you'd win any race you entered did you?"

"Of course!"

"Then I might just have to buy her sire."

For some reason, that conversation made her smile all the way home.

Chapter Thirty-two

RAPHAEL RETURNED TO HIS HOME on Grosvenor Street, which was east of the square of the same name. He lived quite a few blocks south of Ophelia's house and he'd had no reason to ride past her residence today, other than that he was distracted from his usual daily routine—by her.

He was so deep in thought when he entered the house that he didn't notice the visitor leaning casually against his parlor door. The images of Ophelia simply wouldn't leave his head, and now he had new ones to add to his collection. Her laughing back at him as her cap flew off her head in the park. Her hair spilled around her on the ground as she leaned up on her elbows, no more than a chagrined look on her face for having tumbled off her horse. The delighted way she'd responded to his tending to her sore spots.

And from last night, her sensual expression after she'd kissed him in the dining room—no, he couldn't think of that, nor how tempted he'd been to sneak into her house after the last light was extinguished. He'd actually stood behind her house in the cold debating the pros and cons and finally convinced himself not to even attempt to see if the door was open. Then he got furious with himself once he was home and in his own bed, for not even trying.

But while he'd like nothing more than to make love to her again, it simply wasn't a good idea, now that she was home. She had to find a husband. The whole point of his experiment in taming her was for her to live happily ever after—with someone else. It was a moot point that the thought of her doing so was starting to irritate him.

The throat-clearing made him glance toward his parlor, and then he exclaimed when he saw the tall man there wearing a Scottish Kilt. "Duncan! Why the deuce didn't you let me know you were coming to town? We could have ridden in together."

"Because I didna know I was," his friend replied. "Sabrina's aunts insisted on the trip for some special lace they want for her wedding veil that they couldna find at home."

"You escorted them?"

Duncan snorted. "It would've been the perfect time tae have the lass tae m'self for a few days, but nae, they had tae be dragging her along wi' them, and I wasna aboot tae let Sabrina come tae this wicked town wi'out me."

"Not that I agree the town is wicked—well, at least not all wicked," Raphael amended with a grin. "But I doubt I would have let my fiancée come alone either—if I had one."

Duncan raised a brow. "Thinking o' getting one?"

"Whatever gave you that idea?"

Duncan chuckled. "Probably because you just said—"

"I was merely agreeing with you. Now confirm for me if you will—this is your first time to the big city, isn't it?"

"First, and hopefully last."

"And how long are you staying?"

"The ladies have already found what they came for, so they've returned tae the hotel. We'll be heading home first thing in the morn."

"That soon? You have to at least see something of London before you hie back to the country. Let me take you out on the town tonight. A mourning, as it were, of your last few days of bachelorhood."

Duncan laughed. "That's a celebration, mon, no' a mourning. I dinna think there was e'er a mon more eager than I tae get his lass tae the altar. Three bluidy weeks they're making me wait! But nae, I willna be going out wi'out the lass."

Raphael sighed. "I suppose I can find some party or other, less wild entertainment that she'll enjoy as well. Actually—" He paused to call out for the footman he'd sent out this morning to nose about the Reid household. "Simon, have you returned?"

Simon poked his head out from a door at the end of the hall. "Yes, m'lord."

"What did you find out?"

"They've made no decision yet about this evening."

"Then get back there and try again. There's no way she'll let a night go by without attending some event."

"Who?" Duncan asked.

"Ophelia—and you owe me one hundred pounds," Raphael added with a grin.

"The devil I do," Duncan retorted. "The bet was that she'd change, and I know verra well she—"

"Did," Raphael cut in. "But you don't have to take my word for it. My man is going to find out where she'll be tonight, and I'll make sure we have invitations, enough to include Sabrina's aunts too."

"You're serious? What makes you think that shrew is any different than she was?"

"Because I just spent the last week with her."

"Did you now?" Duncan replied skeptically.

"No, really. Once you take the time to get to know her, she's quite wonderful."

Duncan started to laugh. "Now I know you're pulling m'leg. What'd you do, abduct her and beat her tae meekness?"

"Something like that," Raphael said cryptically with an abashed grin. "But you'll be able to see for yourself that I'm not joking about this. Talk with her tonight, you'll be amazed. She *might* even apologize to you, though that would be pushing it, since she doesn't feel she did you any harm, which in fact is true. But I'll wager she'll apologize to Sabrina if you can get her to come along. Phelia does have regrets about the way she's treated her."

"Verra well, this I have tae see. And I'd like tae be knowing how you managed this miracle wi'out beating the shrewishness out o' her."

"Well, there's beating, and there's browbeating, and there's simply opening her eyes for her to see how others perceive her actions. Two out of three worked, and it was all on the up-and-up, under the chaperonage of my aunt Esme. So return to your hotel and let your ladies know so they have time to prepare themselves. I'll send word what time I'll pick you all up as soon as I know where we're going."

Chapter Thirty-three

Mary knocked on Ophelia's door, then opened it and poked her head around it. "Did you decide yet, dear?"

Ophelia was sitting at her short writing desk. She'd been staring off into space, deep in thought, rather than sifting through the pile of invitations that her mother had brought her as soon as she'd returned from her ride. Five of the invitations had come in just that morning. Word had spread quickly after the party last night that she was back in town, and quite a few hostesses wanted to take advantage of her popularity. Her presence tended to guarantee a party's success.

She'd read a few of the invitations before getting distracted thinking about Rafe and had decided which one she wanted to accept. "I think Lady Wilcotts's ball sounds like fun. I've been invited last minute. It's tonight."

"I'll let your father know."

"No, don't. I'd rather you go with me. Would you mind terribly?"

"Not at all, dear. I was rather looking forward to attending some of these events with you this Season, but your father discouraged me from going before. He said I'd be too much of a distraction for him, that he needed to keep an eye on you."

Ophelia kept her incredulous reaction to herself. How "kind" of him to make his not wanting his wife along sound like a compliment.

"I thought you simply didn't want to go," Ophelia said. "I know you prefer entertaining at home."

"I just never had a good enough reason to get your father to attend any parties with me. He actually doesn't like social gatherings—unless he's the host."

"I understand. Shall we not mention it to him then? You can leave him a note."

Mary actually chuckled. "That's an interesting thought. It probably won't work without him throwing a tantrum about it later, but it might be worth it to spend an evening out, just the two of us. Goodness, I'm actually looking forward to this!"

Ophelia smiled after her mother left. She was looking forward to it now too. She hadn't gone out with her mother since they went shopping on Bond Street before the Season began, and it had been months before that that they'd gone to the theater together.

There was another reason why a certain excitement built up within her that evening as Sadie helped her dress for the ball. It had nothing to do with how pretty she looked, though she fairly glowed in the powder blue ball gown. It was her favorite color, with good reason: it flattered her light blond hair, her fair complexion, and her blue eyes. She had quite a few gowns in the same shade, but with different trims. This one was trimmed in silver gilt cording. A thin silver chain with small sapphires circled her throat and made her blue eyes appear a shade darker.

But her eyes were filled with an excitement she could barely contain, because she had a feeling Rafe would be there tonight, which wasn't realistic at all, because he wasn't likely to pick such a grand affair if he was going out for the evening. He wasn't wife-shopping, after all. And he'd mentioned to his aunt over dinner one night at the Nest that he was done with escorting Amanda to parties. So a gala ball was quite possibly the very last place that she might see him. And yet she had the feeling that he'd be at the Wilcottses' tonight.

Because of that feeling, she watched for him constantly. Arriving at the Wilcott residence, she'd brought the large ballroom to silence with her entrance. She used to love doing that. She barely noticed it tonight, her attention on only one thing, trying to find Rafe in the crowd. As tall as he was, it only took a few moments to see that he wasn't there—yet. But she was still sure that he'd show up.

"I can honestly say I wish you'd waited to return to London until after I was married."

Ophelia turned around to find that Amanda Locke had followed her across the room. Rafe's sister looked beautiful tonight in her finery, despite her annoyed expression. The necklace of rubies that went well with her pink ball gown was probably a family heirloom that she'd been allowed to use for her come-out. Ophelia might supposedly have been off visiting the Lockes, but she actually wished she'd been able to meet the rest of Rafe's family.

"Hello, Amanda," Ophelia said with a smile. "Did your brother come with you?"

"No," Amanda mumbled. "I know he came home last night, but I didn't search him out. As it happens, I'm still not talking to him."

"Don't be mad at him. A man likes to keep some things private. Surely you've kept a few secrets from him as well?"

"No—well, maybe," Amanda replied with a slight blush, then grumbled, "Oh, very well, I see your point."

"Good. And don't be jealous of me, Amanda. If you'd like to tell me which man you've set your cap for, I'll be sure to snub him most rudely."

"Why would you do that for me?"

"Why not? You might find this hard to believe, but I really don't want every man in town falling at my feet. That gets quite messy, you know. And besides, I can't marry them all!"

Amanda gave her an odd look before she said, "You mean that, don't you?"

"Certainly."

"But it didn't seem that way at the start of the Season when you *did* have them all piled up at your feet."

"I encouraged that, but it was mostly for my father's benefit. I was rubbing his nose in it, as it were, that I could have had any man in town and that he didn't have to engage me to a man I hadn't even met."

Amanda winced. "I don't know how you managed to get through that, well, before you met MacTavish and found out he wasn't an ugly ogre. I would have been furious at my parents— and terrified."

"Thank you. It's nice to know I wasn't unique in having those feelings."

"Actually, you still weren't happy with MacTavish even after you met him, were you?"

Ophelia shook her head. "I suppose some couples just aren't suited to each other no matter what. Fortunately, we realized that before it was too late."

It was only a small lie and not even her lie, so Ophelia didn't feel bad saying it. Amazingly, she and Amanda talked for another twenty minutes. The gentlemen started interrupting, but mostly to sign their dance cards. And Amanda finally admitted that she hadn't set her cap for any one man yet, that she was having too much difficulty making up her mind.

"I'm not sure I can advise you there, other than to wait for love to settle the matter for you. Rafe mentioned that you put a good deal of stock in love going hand in hand with happiness."

"Yes, I probably chewed his ear off about it more'n once. Is that what you're doing? Waiting for love?"

"My situation is a little different, I fear. Unless I can find a husband rather quickly, I'm afraid my father will intervene again and do the choosing for me."

"That is so, so—antiquated!"

The girl was getting irritated on her behalf, and Ophelia didn't doubt for a moment that she was sincere! She was incredulous. What an amazing difference it made to treat people kindly and have that kindness returned! Good God, had she gone through her entire life under a false set of assumptions, deliberately alienating people who might have become her friends?

"Oh, my, how pleasant!" Amanda said, suddenly glancing behind Ophelia. "Sabrina has come to town. Shall we go greet her?"

Ophelia turned to see the Lamberts, aunts and niece, stepping into the ballroom. She barely recognized Sabrina she looked so lovely tonight, and she wasn't even wearing a ball gown, merely a sedate pale green evening gown. But she shone nonetheless. The little brown-haired wren from Yorkshire had turned into a butterfly. Did love do that?

But Ophelia started to feel distinctly uncomfortable as she followed Amanda across the room. Rafe had made her see just how shabbily she'd treated the girl. Jealousy was no excuse. And a tight sensation of regret was forming in her chest. By the time they reached Sabrina, Ophelia was nearly in tears! Good God, she wasn't going to cry in the middle of a ballroom, was she?

She held back while Amanda made her greetings. Sabrina had been smiling while she said a few words to Rafe's sister, but her smile faltered when she glanced at Ophelia. Mary had shown up to greet Sabrina's aunts, who were her old friends as well, distracting Amanda for a moment.

Ophelia took that opportunity to hug Sabrina and whisper by her ear, "I took advantage of your kindness. I'm sorry—" the tears did start! "Sorry for that. But mostly I'm sorry for lying to you about Duncan. I assumed so many things that weren't true, and I was so jealous of you, more than once. I just wanted you to know I regret all of it."

She didn't wait for a reply. Mortified that tears were running down her cheeks, she quickly left the room before anyone noticed.

Chapter Thirty-four

"WHAT ARE YOU SCOWLING ABOOT, lass?" Duncan asked as he finally entered the ballroom and came up beside his fiancée. "Still annoyed wi' me for dragging you here when you didna have a ball gown tae wear?"

Sabrina leaned up to pat his cheek. "No, I'm never annoyed with you. It was Ophelia. She just apologized to me for lying about you before, but I know she didn't mean it, so why did she bother?"

He shrugged his wide shoulders. "Perhaps she's wanting Rafe tae win the bet?"

"Ah, yes, that bet you mentioned, of course!" Sabrina agreed, but then her frown deepened. "No, she'd never demean herself to help someone else. That just isn't *her*."

"Then why did you doubt her sincerity?"

"Because she said she'd been jealous of me."

"And?"

"Isn't that enough? How could *she* be jealous of *me*?"

Duncan started to laugh. "Verra easily, Brina. You dinna ken how wonderful you are? Besides, there's nae rhyme or reason tae jealousy. Just because she's so bluidy beautiful doesna mean she has nae doubts or insecurities o' her own."

"You're sticking up for her?" Sabrina asked incredulously.

"Nae, I'm just wondering if Rafe was right and she really did turn o'er a new leaf."

"So he thinks he's won the bet?"

"Aye, and I'm here tae see for m'self if that's so. So where is she?"

Sabrina's expression turned thoughtful now. "She *did* sound a bit emotional. I assumed it was theatrics. She's good at that. But I suppose she could have left the room to compose herself—in either case."

*   *   *

Raphael and Duncan had gotten detained in the hall by an old friend of Raphael's father's. Duncan had managed to slip away sooner to enter the ballroom, but Raphael couldn't manage a polite way to extricate himself from the conversation for nearly ten minutes. So when he did finally step inside the ballroom he had to do some searching to locate his friends. He didn't even realize he was looking for a blond head as well.

But a hush fell on the room. He'd forgotten that his presence might cause a stir, since he hadn't been to a London ball in several years. He was immediately set upon by more acquaintances who hadn't seen him since his return to England and wanted to welcome him back. And—bloody hell, the mamas again.

When he saw two grand dames staunchly stomping their way toward him, dragging their daughters behind them, he thought about making a hasty retreat, all the way home. But he managed to persevere, put on his most aloof demeanor for their benefit, and declined to dance when they tried to thrust that on him too. He was about to become quite rude when his sister rescued him, pulling him away without a by-your-leave—only Amanda could get away with that, as flighty and overexuberant as she sometimes pretended to be.

She dragged him all the way to the refreshment table, where row after row of glasses were lined up and kept filled with an assortment of beverages, from champagne to weak tea, with a servant on duty to replace the glasses as needed. Raphael took a glass of the champagne. Amanda knew better than to do the same, at least with him watching, and picked up a glass from the other end of the table that would contain no alcohol.

"You could have told me you were coming," she complained as she took a sip from her glass. "Then I wouldn't have had to drag Aunt Julie here, when she didn't really want to come. And before I forget, I was talking to Ophelia earlier. You're not going to believe this, but she was actually nice to me! Nearly bowled me—oh, never mind, I forgot I'm still not talking to *you*."

She flounced off, leaving Raphael chuckling. He could almost pity the man his sister settled on. The poor chap would never have a moment's peace.

He did finally spot Duncan and Sabrina, but merely as they twirled past him on the dance floor. But he had no trouble at all catching sight of Ophelia as she tried to slip unnoticed back into the room. She was like a magnet for his eyes, and as usual her beauty simply took his breath away.

Her powder blue ball gown edged in silver cording would have been appropriate when she was the ice queen, but there was nothing icy about her now. She used to move with an unmistakable haughtiness, which was also missing. Actually, her confidence seemed to be gone.

He went cold at the thought. What had he done? If he'd turned her into a timid little mouse, he might just shoot himself.

He started toward her immediately. He had to hurry. Out of the corner of his eye he could see a half dozen other men heading her way as well. Damned if it didn't feel like a race by the time he reached her! He won, but only by a hair, and because the others were about to converge upon Ophelia, he simply took her hand and pulled her along to the dance floor.

Halfway there he thought to ask, "A dance, m'dear?"

"I'd love to," she replied. "Though if we get interrupted, it will be because I've already promised this dance to someone else."

"I'll take my chances." He whisked her onto the floor.

The moment he placed both hands on her for the waltz, he was beset with an odd sort of possessiveness. Which was ridiculous. He might have had a hand in changing her, or taming the shrew as it were, but she was not his creation. He'd merely helped her to bring out the better qualities she'd already possessed that had been lying dormant.

But there were different types of possessiveness, and he didn't even want to think of the more common form, which had no place in his sphere of emotions. He couldn't deny, though, that he was missing having her to himself in the relaxed atmosphere of the Nest. Extremely so. In a setting such as this or any other public event, he couldn't spend much time alone with her. One dance at the most tonight to keep the tongues from wagging. And yet he wanted to spend more time with her, to see her laugh again, to enjoy her spontaneous wit.

He'd let her go too soon, but he'd had to. He'd been spending all his time thinking about bedding her instead of finishing what they'd started. Thankfully they had finished. But while he couldn't monopolize her time anymore, he'd convinced himself that he did need to keep an eye on her, and now he wanted to make sure he hadn't pushed her demeanor too far in the opposite direction.

She was fine when she was with him, or she seemed to be. Was that merely because she felt relaxed with him after everything they had shared? Did she feel they were friends of a sort now? But he'd yet to see how she behaved with others. And that cowed, embarrassed look she'd worn as she reentered the ballroom worried him.

"It's difficult to touch you without tasting you." Good God, did he say that aloud? He must have. She was blushing now.

He quickly added, "No, don't blush. You're too damn beautiful when you do that." Her blush darkened. "Much better," he said with a grin. "Splotches really do become you. I've thought that more'n once."

She laughed. "You're a terrible tease."

"No, I'm a *good* tease. Unparalleled, if you must know. Quite the best tease in London."

"Oh, stop!"

"Feeling better?"

She glanced at him curiously. "I wasn't aware I was feeling bad."

He shrugged. "You seemed not quite yourself when you just came in."

"Oh, that. I spoke to Sabrina. It was a little disturbing is all."

"It went badly?"

"Well, no, if you *must* know, I apologized to her."

"Not for my benefit I hope."

"No, actually, I feel quite good about it, almost as if a weight has been lifted from my shoulders. I'd probably feel even better if she'd forgiven me."

He frowned, hearing that. "She didn't? That doesn't sound like her."

"No, you misunderstand. She might have, I just didn't

stay to find out if she would or not. I'm afraid I got a little—embarrassed."

"Embarrassed, eh?" he said with a knowing look. "It's all right to admit you cried, you know."

"Don't assume—"

"Don't start lying again," he interrupted in a light, if scolding, tone.

"Oh, shut up. If I want to call crying by another name I will—or do you want to see me blush again?"

He choked out a laugh. "By all means, call it anything you want."

Chapter Thirty-five

S HE WAS IN HIS ARMS again, but it just wasn't the same with dozens of eyes trained on them. And it was difficult for Ophelia, juggling her emotions, and her behavior, when she had Rafe's full attention. She had to temper her smiles—too many people were watching. She had to keep her own eyes away from his, or at least she tried to, because it was too easy to get lost in his blue eyes and forget where they were.

He was too handsome by far in his formal togs. Every woman in the room was probably wishing she were in her shoes, but for once, not for the usual reason! Rafe in black tails and snowy white cravat was devastating.

And he got rakish! God, she couldn't believe he'd mentioned tasting her. Her knees had almost buckled! After all their time together, for him to turn on the sensual charm now with such blatant sexual innuendos, when they could no longer do any-thing about it. She would like to think that he simply couldn't help himself, but it was more likely that he merely felt safe doing so now, when she couldn't respond as she would like, and neither could he.

The dance ended sooner than Ophelia would have liked, which was just as well. She couldn't be that close to Rafe and not want to touch him more intimately than just clasping his hand for the dance.

"I knew you would be here," she said shyly as he led her off the dance floor.

"Caught my man spying, did you?"

"Your man?"

He rolled his eyes. "Never mind. How did you know?"

"I just had a rather strong feeling. Probably because you've intimated that you intend to help me through the choosing of a husband."

She was actually hoping he'd correct that assumption, but all he said was "Ah, and are we going to give this careful consideration now? Not going to rush through it just to get out from under your father's thumb? How did that reunion go, by the by, other than to make you angry?"

"It went exactly as I expected. But considering our past yelling matches, I must say I wasn't nearly as angry as I usually get with him, so in that regard, it went rather well."

And then Rafe had completely defused that anger in the dining room, but she didn't mention that. Recalling that kiss brought a little more color to her cheeks though.

She continued, "But I don't think I'm going to be able to take my time looking for a husband. He's determined to have it settled and done with, and he still pulls the strings."

"I've a mind to have a talk with him."

"Don't do that! That will only encourage him, if he thinks you have a concern for me."

"Bloody hell, what's *his* rush then?"

"Can't you guess? He's waited my entire life to marry me off so he can reap the social benefits. He thought the matter was settled with Duncan and was so happy with that match. Having that fall through, he's decidedly *un*happy. Actually, he's quite furious to be back at square one again. So don't be surprised that he's now setting his cap for you."

"Sorry, but he's not my type."

He said it with such a straight face, she burst out laughing. But she still felt compelled to warn him, "You can make light of it, but he's quite serious. He's single-mindedly set on you for a son-in-law now."

Rafe winced. "I'm afraid I might have encouraged that notion in my original missive to him. Insinuation is a powerful tool open to all sorts of interpretation."

He'd woven their way through the crowd on the edges of the dance floor until he found her mother, with whom he no doubt intended to leave her. Unfortunately, Mary was still chatting with Sabrina and her aunt Hilary. Duncan was there as well, standing behind Sabrina with his hands on her shoulders.

Who would ever have thought that those two would have taken to each other? They were so mismatched, the handsome, brawny Scot and the sweet country wren, who was by no means a beauty. But then Sabrina's gift for finding humor in any situation and sharing it with others was probably what had won Duncan over. They had become friends first, then love had blossomed from that, and Ophelia wished she had seen it sooner instead of letting her colossal conceit convince her Duncan was just trying to make *her* jealous.

She supposed she owed him an apology as well, for all of her false assumptions and putting him through an emotional hell when he'd thought he'd be stuck with her as his wife. But oddly, that whole unhappy time for both of them might have played out quite differently if her eyes had been opened sooner, before she'd met him.

They might actually have fallen in love themselves—what an amazing thought! And yet it could have happened, if she hadn't been so self-centered and dead set on getting out of her engagement to him, and if he hadn't been put off by her insults and haughty airs. So to apologize to him for turning him against her was in essence saying she was sorry he'd found true love with Sabrina instead of her. No, she didn't think that would go over too well.

Sabrina smiled at her this time. Pleased and relieved, Ophelia returned it. But then she caught Duncan's wary gaze and tried to put him at ease.

"Hello, Duncan," she said almost shyly. "I'm surprised to see you and Sabrina in town, so close to your wedding."

" 'Tis nae more'n a shopping trip for a few things m'ladies couldna find at home."

Hilary Lambert beamed at being included in his "m' ladies" remark, though she went right on conversing with Mary. Those two old friends never failed to reminisce about their younger days when they got together.

"Congratulations on the impending nuptials," Ophelia added to Duncan. "I'm very happy for you both."

"I'll be damned," Duncan said a bit incredulously. "You mean that, dinna you."

It wasn't really a question, but she replied, "You and I might have done fine if we hadn't been 'forced' to meet each other, but I have no doubt that Sabrina is the better choice for you. She will make you a much better wife than I ever could."

Duncan turned his incredulous look on Rafe. "I give up, mon. I dinna need tae hear more'n that tae ken that she's turned aboot and verra nicely. That's one bet I'm rather pleased tae be losing tae you."

Ophelia frowned, but what her ex-fiancé, twice removed, was implying didn't sink in immediately. Until she saw Rafe cringe.

"That was a compliment on your success, Phelia," he tried to tell her.

But as if he hadn't spoken, she said, "A bet? It was all about a bet? You put me through hell for a bloody bet?"

"It wasn't like that a'tall."

"Wasn't it?"

"No," Rafe assured her. "I knew you could change, anyone can. The bet was merely my reaction to Duncan's skepticism."

She glanced at Duncan to see him cringing now. Sabrina looked embarrassed. For her fiancé? Or because Ophelia was causing a scene with her raised voice? People *were* turning their way. Mary and Hilary had stopped talking and nearly asked in unison what was wrong.

Ophelia didn't reply. All she could think of was Rafe and Duncan laughing together about her when they'd made their bet, having fun at her expense! Everything she'd thought, everything Rafe had told her, all of it lies?

The look she turned on Rafe was half-stricken, half-murderous. "For my happiness, you said? When all along it was simply because you had money riding on the outcome—on me! My God, you're such a liar!"

"Phelia, I promise you it—"

Ophelia didn't hear any more of his explanation. She was already running out of the room, her mother following her.

"What happened?" Mary asked, slightly out of breath from trying to keep up with her daughter.

They hadn't even retrieved their cloaks, and Ophelia wasn't waiting for their coach to be brought forward either. She had simply rushed out the door to find it herself. With their coach parked on the curb not far down the street, they were on their way home within moments of getting into it.

"What happened?" her mother asked again.

Ophelia didn't answer. She wouldn't have been able to get any words past the lump in her throat anyway. But the tears streaming down her cheeks were answer enough for Mary. She was soon absorbing her daughter's heartrending sobs on her shoulder.

Raphael stood in the doorway watching Ophelia's coach disappear down the street. He'd only been a few moments behind her, having paused only long enough to snarl at Duncan, "Thanks much, old chap."

"She didna know aboot the bet?" Duncan said.

"Hell, no, she didn't know. Do you see *idiot* branded on my forehead? No? Well, give it a moment, it will no doubt appear now."

"What should she care if we made a bet? She changed. She's nae longer a shrew oout o' hell."

"She changed for the right reasons. And now she'll think she changed for the wrong ones. Which could bloody well undo all of my efforts."

"Then go after her mon and explain. Dinna be leaving me wi' this shoe in m'mouth."

Chapter Thirty-six

RAPHAEL ARRIVED AT THE REID town house at the earliest hour that could be considered decent for visiting. He wasn't admitted. The ladies, mother and daughter, weren't receiving today and the earl wasn't at home. He returned in the afternoon and was given the same message. He waited around outside on that second visit to witness others being turned away as well, which was somewhat of a relief. At least it wasn't just him.

His man, Simon, had no luck either in finding out the ladies' agenda for the day and evening. He was in fact given the boot when one of the scullery maids pointed out to the butler that he did not belong to the household. But he already had his orders for that contingency. He waited in his rented coach down the street so he could follow the ladies when they did leave. They never left.

Raphael discovered that anxiety was a distinctly unpleasant feeling. He should have followed Ophelia home last night and, no matter the hour, insisted upon seeing her. Then he wouldn't have gone to bed with his gut churning, a feeling that hadn't left him yet. The thought of her being hurt by what she'd learned was the worst. He'd much prefer her anger. He was an old hand at dealing with that.

It was almost a relief when his father's missive arrived requesting his presence at Norford Hall. He wasn't surprised to receive it. If anything, he was surprised it hadn't come sooner. He hadn't visited for long with his family after his return to England. His father had probably patiently been waiting for him to return to Norford Hall and that patience had finally run out. But even though he didn't think there was anything out of the ordinary in that summons, it wasn't something he could ignore merely because the timing wasn't ideal.

He spent the night writing a long letter to Ophelia, then tore it up. An explanation on paper simply didn't suffice and might even make matters worse depending on her current state of mind. Her emotions could be so volatile that he needed to be present to gauge her response to his explanation. And what could he really say to her other than that a bet might have set his plan in motion, but it had had nothing to do with it in the end.

He left the next morning for Norford Hall. After spending most of the night awake working on that letter to Ophelia, he was too tired even to ask why Amanda chose to join him for the short day trip. He spent most of the morning catching up on lost sleep.

But when he did finally wake close to noon and noticed his sister sitting across from him, trying to read a book between the bounce and jostles of the coach, he said, "Come along to protect me, did you?"

Amanda peeked over the edge of her book. "It occurred to me you might need some protection."

He'd been joking. It didn't sound as if she was. "Why? I've done nothing to be called on the carpet for. Father is probably just annoyed that I'm spending the entire Season away from home."

"Or he heard about you hiding away in the country with Ophelia. I might point out, you *still* haven't told me what that was all about."

Raphael narrowed his eyes. "You didn't tell him about that, did you?"

Amanda took on a hurt look. "Do you really think I'd do something like that?"

"I recall when you were ten and went running to father about the new fort I made."

"You butchered the maze with that fort, cutting a new exit halfway in at the most confusing intersection, and I'd only *just* figured out that maze. I was so proud of that, but you had to go and make it too easy . . . besides, I was a child then."

"You're still a child."

"How dare you . . ."

They bickered mildly for the rest of the trip, which wasn't all that long, and certainly wasn't unusual with Raphael's propensity to tease. But a subdued, anticipatory silence struck them both as they approached Norford Hall. The ducal mansion was spread out so widely that they could both see a good portion of it from either side of the coach. Home. Family, servants they'd grown up with who were like family. A wealth of memories were associated with the old mansion, and it never failed to fill Raphael with a warm sense of peace and well-being.

*   *   *

Ophelia didn't leave her room for two days. She was afraid she'd burst into tears if someone even looked at her askance, then she was afraid she'd shoot someone. She wavered back and forth between experiencing the oddest pain in her chest, which released a flood of tears, and such anger she was sure she could kill someone—well, not just anyone—him.

She was furious at herself as well for being so gullible. She'd thought Rafe had really wanted to help her, when all he'd wanted was to win a bet. And bed her. He'd pretended he didn't want to make love to her, but that too had probably been on his agenda from the start. He was just so practiced at seduction she hadn't even known she'd been seduced! And she couldn't get out of her mind the image of the two friends laughing at her expense!

Sadie couldn't get her to talk about it. For once, her old silence tactics didn't work on Ophelia. Another flaw gone for good? Her mother couldn't get her to talk about it either. She wasn't going to let anyone know just how big a fool she'd been. But Mary was tenacious. She wasn't going to give up until Ophelia was back to herself, so the next time she knocked on her door, Ophelia made an effort to put her mother's mind at ease.

"Feeling better yet?" Mary stuck her head around the door to ask.

"It's all right, Mama, you don't have to tiptoe around me. I'm fine now."

She wasn't, but she didn't like her mother worrying about her. And that look of concern was still on Mary's face as she came farther into the room.

"Would you like to talk about it now?"

"I'd rather not. I just assumed some things that turned out to not be true."

"But you're over it?"

"Yes, of course. I made more of it than I should have, is all. It wasn't really important."

Ophelia broke out a smile, felt it crack, and turned aside quickly so Mary wouldn't notice. "I'm surprised Father hasn't pounded on my door," Ophelia continued. "My having missed two days of husband hunting has probably had him gnashing his teeth."

"Actually, I've rarely seen him in such a good mood." Mary frowned thoughtfully. "He didn't even blister my ears about you and me going out the other night without letting him know about it. But the last time I saw him with so many smiles, he'd doubled his money on one of his investments. That's probably all it is this time."

"He doesn't just tell you when something like that occurs?"

"Goodness, no. He thinks matters of money would be quite beyond my comprehension."

Ophelia laughed. It was the first time she'd felt like laughing since the night of the Wilcotts ball. "You could probably teach him a thing or two—"

"Shh." Mary grinned at her. "I'd prefer he not know that. I'll let him keep his illusions, or delusions, as the case may be."

The moment of levity faded. Not for the first time, Ophelia had to resist making a derogatory remark about her father. And then she wondered why she bothered. It wasn't as if her mother didn't know how she felt about her father.

She gave into the urge and said, "You know, Mama, I wish you'd make a confession, that you'd had an affair before I was born, that Father isn't really my father."

Mary sighed. "Darling, sometimes I too wish I could make that confession, but only for your sake. I know you and he don't get along well together, and that's such a shame. But I do love him, you know. He's a good man, he can just become so bloody single-minded at times," Mary ended in exasperation.

"Where I'm concerned."

"Yes. But don't fret about it, dear. You'll look back on this someday and smile. I'm sure of it."

Highly doubtful, Ophelia thought, but didn't say so. She

moved over to her desk where yet another pile of invitations had been stacked, these all for tonight.

"You can throw these away, Mama. I still don't feel like going out tonight. However, you can accept one for tomorrow night. You choose. I like surprises."

Mary nodded, then paused on her way out of the room. "Will you at least come down to dinner tonight?"

"I'd rather not. But I promise I'll stop frowning. Really, I'm fine. I just haven't been sleeping well and am going to make up for it tonight."

Chapter Thirty-seven

THE DUKE'S HOUSEHOLD QUICKLY KNEW that Amanda and Raphael had arrived thanks to Amanda's squealing and shouting her greetings, and hugging everyone who appeared. Even their grandmother was drawn out of her room by the noise and, from the top of the stairs, shouted down, "Is that you, Julie?"

"It's me, Grandma. Mandy."

"Come give us a hug, Julie."

Amanda rolled her eyes and bounded up the stairs to greet Agatha Locke and help her back to her room. Agatha had been mistaking family members for several years now, and it did no good to correct her. She'd think you were just playing tricks on her and get annoyed. So if she thought you were someone else, it was better just to go along with it.

"Mama has been calling me by your name lately," Preston Locke, the tenth Duke of Norford, said as he gave Raphael a bear hug, their typical greeting. "I'm hoping when she sees us together I can get back to being me."

Raphael grinned. His father was a big man. They were the

same height, even shared the same hair and eye color, though Preston was starting to get a few gray strands mixed in with his blond, barely noticeable yet, but he'd grouched about it the last time Raphael had visited. And Preston had widened a bit over the years as well. He was quite solid. He'd just gotten—bigger.

"That—er, isn't why you sent for me, is it?" Raphael asked.

He wasn't really serious. He knew his father better than that. And the duke snorted to confirm it.

"Come along," Preston said, starting toward the parlor. But then he changed his direction. "Let's go to my study instead where we won't be interrupted."

Raphael frowned as he followed his father down the hall. "Won't be interrupted" didn't bode well for him as he related the duke's study to punishments. Old habit, since he and Amanda always knew that if they got summoned to the study, they were in trouble.

It was a huge room, nearly as big as the parlor, and the parlor was oversize. But it was an odd room by most standards. Raphael's mother had redecorated most of the old mansion over the years, quite tastefully, but she wasn't allowed to touch the study. The oddity of the room was its white walls. Every other room in the house was either paneled or wallpapered. Not this one. The white background made the paintings, and there were dozens of them, stand out more boldly. Raphael actually liked the brightness of the room—when he wasn't being called on the carpet for some misdeed.

"I understand congratulations are in order," Preston said as he sat down behind his desk.

His father's tone, not quite scolding, raised Raphael's defenses even higher. "They are? But you don't sound too happy about it."

"Because it would have been nice if I had been the first to

know, instead of hearing about it secondhand. Sit down. You're going to tell me all about it."

"Certainly. It might help, though, if I knew what the congratulations were for."

Preston raised a golden brow. "You've accomplished more'n one feat lately?"

Raphael was frowning now. "Actually, the only thing I'm rather proud of wouldn't be common knowledge. So what exactly are we talking about?"

"Your engagement, of course."

Raphael had only just started to sit down, but that shot him back to his feet. "I'm . . . not . . . engaged," he said precisely.

"I think you better be, considering what's making the rounds."

Raphael closed his eyes. Good God, what had Ophelia done? Not for a moment did he think his father was talking about anyone else.

Preston continued, "My old friend John Forton couldn't wait to slap me on the back with congratulations, rushed out here to do so, but of course he assumed as the father of the groom that I—"

"I am *not a groom*!"

"—was fully aware of that news." Preston's look said, *Don't interrupt again.* "He didn't know he was knocking me on my arse with surprise. However, John did assume that the rest that he had to tell me, and he made sure he had all the facts first and then some, would bowl me over. You can imagine my concern."

"I suppose that would depend on which facts you were apprised of."

"There's more'n a few?"

"Probably. Ophelia Reid is quite a controversial female. We *are* talking about Ophelia, correct?" Preston's lips merely tightened, so Raphael went on, "You either love her or hate her. Well, in all fairness, that's how it used to be. Now, she's quite different, or at least she was until a few nights ago when she received a shock that either devastated her or sent her on the warpath. I have no idea which."

"Sit down, Rafe."

He did, raking a hand through his hair in frustration. "I don't know why I'm surprised at this turn of events. She was a rumormonger, after all. That would have been her first line of offense."

Preston sighed in exasperation now. "Stop talking to yourself and talk to me. What I was told doesn't sound as if it came from a female, unless she doesn't mind running her own name through the mud."

"Just what were you told?"

"You were spotted leaving Summers Glade with her. That was the start of it, and that neither of you were seen again for the next week. I don't need to tell you what sort of speculation that produced. But during that week, her father let it be known that she'd been invited here. Seems he was quite busting-at-the-britches proud of that coup, but that's understandable. We don't usually invite strangers to Norford Hall."

Raphael winced as he explained, "That was my fault. I told him that I was taking her under my wing and that she'd be visiting my family."

"So you lied to him?"

"No, I just wasn't specific about which family members we'd visit. Our family is spread out all over England, and in fact, we did visit your sister Esmeralda and took her with us to the Nest as a chaperone."

Preston shot to his feet now. "You took a virginal debutante to Alder's Nest? Good God, Rafe, what were you thinking?"

"Well, certainly that it wouldn't be common knowledge and it's not. Is it?"

"No, thank God," Preston replied. "But the very fact that you took her to meet 'the family' as it were leads to only one conclusion."

"The devil it does."

"It does when you're seen kissing her in her own house, with both parents under roof, on her very first day back in London."

Raphael slumped down in his chair somewhat. "*That* wasn't my fault, she did the kissing."

"Does it matter who kissed whom?"

Raphael sighed. "Anything else?"

"Claiming the first dance with her at the Wilcotts ball her second night back."

"Bloody hell, was it the first dance?"

"Apparently."

"*Who* keeps track of these things?"

"The old dames who've got nothing better to do. But that's neither here nor there. The consensus is that you're already engaged to her and just haven't made the official announcement yet. Do you know how bloody hard it is to break a consensus once it's been made?"

"Not in this case. I merely have to deny it."

"You'd think it would be that easy, wouldn't you?" Preston waxed philosophical. "Except for one little hitch in this case. Because you hied off with her in her own coach without a proper chaperone—"

"Her maid was with her—"

"Without a *proper* chaperone," Preston repeated with slightly narrowed eyes. "And because you kissed her—no, don't interrupt again. She might have started it, but you participated. Given just those two damning pieces of the rumor, you know bloody well the girl will be ruined if you aren't engaged to her. So, I suppose my question now would be, are you engaged to her—yet?"

Raphael didn't need to be hit over the head to figure out that his father had just ordered him to get married. He slumped even farther down in his chair.

"Did Forton happen to tell you anything about this girl you now want me to bring into the family?"

Preston shrugged. "You mean that she's quite likely the most beautiful chit to ever show up in London?"

"Well, there is that."

"And a bit haughty because of it."

"She was."

"And a bit of a shrew."

"Not anymore."

"Really? Well, damn, I'm feeling better about this unasked-for match already."

"I wouldn't be. She's also probably going to be after my blood when she finds out that we *have* to marry, if she wasn't already after it. Actually, she could refuse and be damned to the consequences."

"Nonsense."

"You just don't know how destructive she can be when her temper shows up."

"I didn't raise fools, and you, my boy, are quite the charmer when you want to be. I have no doubt you'll talk her around."

Chapter Thirty-eight

RAPHAEL SPENT AN EXTRA DAY VISITING with his family. Ophelia's name didn't come up again, but she was never far from his thoughts. She wasn't mentioned again because he'd spent several more hours in his father's study after their initial discussion, explaining practically everything that he'd done concerning her, and why. It didn't alter Preston's opinion that Raphael was going to have to wed her, but he was sure his father wouldn't be too disappointed now if he could find a way out of it without any damaging repercussions.

The only thing he didn't discuss, and hoped he'd never have to, was that he'd made love to her. His father was old school. That information would have Raphael leg-shackled to Ophelia so quickly, it would be done before he'd noticed. But from what his father had been told by his friend, it didn't really sound as if Ophelia was behind any of the rumors that were circulating through the ton. In fact, if she was furious with him about the bet, and she'd given every indication that night at the ball that she was, these rumors would just amplify that.

He would have swallowed his medicine and offered her marriage if she had cried foul and insisted she was compromised. He didn't make a habit of seducing earls' virginal daughters after all, stayed well away from virgins as a matter of course, had kept his affairs to experienced women only—until now. But he *had* compromised this particular virgin. She'd done just the opposite, though, assuring him that she'd keep it to herself, that she didn't want to marry him. She'd been adamant about not settling on a husband whose social position would delight her father.

And now? Was she still determined to spite her father by not marrying Raphael, or was she angry enough now to spite him instead by making sure they did marry? He had no way of knowing and wouldn't, until he talked to her. If she'd talk to him. If she didn't try to kill him first.

He was going back to London to make sure it didn't happen, and yet he couldn't get the notion out of his mind. Marriage to Ophelia. It just wouldn't do, of course. He wasn't nearly ready to settle down. He had yet to enjoy his bachelorhood to the fullest. But incredibly, the thought of being with other women now was the farthest thing from his mind.

Bloody hell. He *knew* it would be a mistake bedding her. She was the best, the most exquisite, the wittiest, the most beautiful, the most passionate woman he'd ever come across. Every other female would come up short now and be a disappointment. After all, what could you aspire to after having the best?

Marriage to Ophelia. It could be hell. It could be heaven.

"I'd be after your head m'self," Amanda said as if she'd been reading his mind.

She was returning to London with him. They were a good hour into the journey and she hadn't said two words to him. He'd almost forgotten she was in the coach, he'd been so deep in thought. Until now.

"Where, pray tell, did that thought come from?" he asked, raising a brow at her.

"The bet. Yes, I listened at the door to the study. Well, what did you expect when you refused to tell me what you were doing at the Nest with Ophelia? I was dying with curiosity to know."

"How much did you hear?"

"Everything." She grinned at him triumphantly. "I came right back downstairs after I took grandmother to her room. All I wanted to know was why you'd been summoned home. Didn't expect to hear your secrets as well. You wouldn't believe how many scolding looks I got from the servants who passed me in the hall. I was so enthralled I didn't even try to pretend I wasn't eavesdropping."

He scowled at her. "Not a word of that goes beyond here, Mandy."

She gave him a hurt look. "Stop doubting my loyalty. It wasn't necessary to say that."

"Sorry." He sighed. "I'm just rather undone at the moment."

"I'm not surprised. Getting married when you weren't planning on it is quite a milestone for you."

"I'm not getting married."

"But father said—"

"Pay attention, m'dear. One, Phelia probably won't have me. Two, you were more'n likely correct in your first assumption. I have little doubt she'll be after my head."

"I'd rather *not* be right, you know." Then she sighed as well. "But that doesn't surprise me. How could you do that to her, try to change her life as a silly bet?"

"I thought you said you heard it all?"

"Well, grandmother did come back to the top of the stairs to find out what was keeping me. I'd told her I'd be right back. So I to hide for a few minutes. You mean I missed something really important?"

"My bet with Duncan only set the whole thing in motion. It was a rather noble endeavor, if I do say so m'self, but there were many reasons to attempt what I did, including her own happiness. You know how she was before. And you've seen how she is now. Quite the difference, isn't it?"

"Indeed. I'm just amazed that she agreed to accept your tutelage—actually, she didn't, did she? You only told Father you had her parents' permission. Oh my God, Rafe, you absconded with her, didn't you?"

He tsked. "What an appalling word. But she only ranted and raved for a few days. She quickly realized that I was sincere in trying to help her. And she showed me a side of her that few people, if any, see. She can be witty and charming when she sets the bitterness aside. And obviously she *wanted* to change. She was cooperating fully before we returned to London."

"She told you why she spread all those rumors?"

"We discussed everything, Mandy."

"You got to know her pretty well, then?" She gave him a thoughtful look. "Are you sure you don't want to marry her?"

Bloody hell, no, he wasn't sure at all.

Chapter Thirty-nine

"ARE YOU RUNNING OUT OF ball gowns?" Mary asked from the bottom of the stairs when Ophelia came down to join her in the entry hall.

"No, not quite, though I may need one or two more before the Season ends," Ophelia answered. "Why?"

"You're only wearing an evening gown," Mary said, pointing out the obvious. "Quite lovely. That shade of blue definitely becomes you. But we're going to a ball tonight. I don't want you to feel out of place."

Ophelia chuckled. "It wouldn't be the first time I haven't dressed for the occasion, or overdressed. But the ball is tomorrow night, Mama. Tonight is Lady Cade's musical soiree and dinner."

"Oh my, then *I'm* overdressed." Mary shrugged out of her cloak to reveal the ball gown she was wearing. "I'm afraid we accepted too many invitations all at once. I'm going to have to make a list to keep track of them. Give me a few moments to change. Really, I won't be long a'tall."

Mary rushed upstairs. Ophelia smiled to herself. Her mother

simply wasn't used to leaving the house or accepting invitations during a Season. Her forte was sending out invitations!

Ophelia moved into the parlor to sit while she waited, but wished she hadn't. Her father was there, reading a book. He glanced at her with something of a smirk.

"You wouldn't have to wait if I were escorting you," he said, apparently having heard Mary. "That was a ridiculous excuse you came up with anyway, to go with your mother instead of me."

"It wasn't anything of the sort. How do you expect me to concentrate on finding a husband if I'm so furious that I scare all the prospects away?"

He ground his teeth together, his smirk gone. "You and I don't *have* to fight, you know."

"You don't *have* to control my life either, but when did that stop you from doing so?"

"Enough," he grumbled. "We don't need to get into this again. By the by, that color really does become you. You should wear it more often."

A compliment? From him? She thought about pinching her arm, to make sure she was awake. She thought about telling him she did wear powder blue and assorted shades in that hue often, that he was too wrapped up in his own agenda to notice.

Instead she asked with a frown, "Did I miss something? Just this morning you railed at me because I couldn't tell you when Raphael would be back in town."

"Yes, yes, and you railed back that you didn't give a bloody damn if he ever came back," Sherman complained. "Not exactly the right attitude to take where your future husband is concerned. He's the only prospect you need to concentrate on, and since half of London already thinks you're engaged to him, you only need to—"

"Those ridiculous rumors bear no substance."

"You were *seen* kissing him just the other night. I can't tell you how delighted I was that for *once* you followed my directions."

"I've been kissed dozens of times, does that mean I have as many fiancés?"

"Stolen kisses that aren't viewed by other people are irrelevant; ones that are witnessed damn well are."

Ophelia took a deep breath and tried to calm herself. Those damning rumors had been quite unanticipated. She was sure there was a way to put them to rest, but she just hadn't thought of one yet. However, she was *not* going to get into this discussion with her father again.

While they still didn't see eye to eye on anything, he hadn't been nearly as tyrannical these last few days that she'd stayed at home. No doubt because of those rumors about her and Rafe had put him in such a good mood. Her father had assumed the rumors closed the lid on her marriage to the next Duke of Norford. He didn't like hearing her disagree with that notion.

"Is this a new strategy of yours?" she said in a much calmer tone. "Making me so angry I don't want to even leave the house?"

He sighed now, even leaned his head against the back of the sofa he was sitting on. "No. I really don't know why you and I can't have a normal conversation anymore."

Anymore? When had they ever? But her mother returned, so she didn't feel it necessary to answer her father. And what could she have said, anyway, that wouldn't have set him off again?

"There," Mary announced, standing in the doorway. "I told you it wouldn't take me long."

Ophelia moved over to tuck a loose underseam on Mary's evening gown back under her neckline where it belonged. "You look wonderful, Mama. But let's be off immediately. I don't want to be late for the dinner when we haven't eaten yet."

Mary, in her typical motherly fashion, replied, "Are you sure you don't want to eat something here before we go? It's quite fashionable to just pick at your food at a social gathering, you know."

More than just fashionable. Some hostesses didn't even supply enough food because of it! But if they delayed leaving any longer, Ophelia would change her mind about going. She still didn't feel up to social chitchat yet, and it didn't take much to set off the tears again. But she hadn't cried since yesterday. Anger had taken a firmer hold on her after she'd heard about those rumors. And she still had a husband to find. And hopefully Raphael Locke would stay the hell out of London until she was really engaged and not just assumed to be engaged.

Chapter Forty

"Not one word, d'you hear?" Ophelia hissed at her dinner partner as he sat down next to her.

Rafe had shown up at the Cades' home just as the guests were sitting down to dinner. They would have been at opposite ends of the table, since the only chair left was quite a distance from Ophelia's, but their hostess did some last-minute rearranging to seat them next to each other. Those damn rumors again.

No one had actually asked her to confirm them. It would be her third engagement of the Season after all, likely a record, so someone should have asked. But apparently the assumption was set in stone already, so no one felt a need to get it confirmed.

It was a long table, extremely long, long enough to seat twenty-four people, which was all that had been invited to the small gathering. And which was why she was not surprised that with her on Lady Cade's guest list, Rafe would also be invited. The rumors again.

At least Mary sat on her other side, and she turned to her

mother to quickly say, "Talk to me, Mama. Say anything. Pretend we're deep in conversation."

"Certainly, dear. But it's all right if you talk to him in public, you know. He is practically a member of the family already."

Ophelia was incredulous. Her mother too? But that was no doubt her father's doing. He'd obviously convinced his wife it was a foregone conclusion that Ophelia would be marrying the viscount.

Rafe put his arm behind her chair and leaned closer to her, as if the three of them were conversing. "You're not exactly whispering, Phelia," he said in a teasing tone.

She turned back to him, gave him a smile for the benefit of the many people watching them, but gritted out, "I thought I told you not to talk to me."

He sighed. "I don't know why you're so angry—well, I do, but if you'd just think about it, you know very well my effort to help you was sincere. That silly bet was only the motivation for it. And ignoring me isn't going to get us out of this mess."

"Ignoring you is my only option," she whispered angrily, "unless you want to be part of a scene that will embarrass you into the next century."

"I'll pass on the scandal, thank you." He turned to the chap on his other side and struck up a conversation with him.

She stared at the back of his head in disbelief, her mouth open. He was giving up at the mere threat of a scandal? He wasn't going to say anything else in his defense or convince her that he and Duncan hadn't been amusing themselves at her expense? He'd turned her life upside down for a stupid wager, and there was nothing really that he could say to make that more palatable.

Her old shell settled about her shoulders. It had served her well for many years. It didn't keep her bitterness inside, though, and never had. It didn't contain her anger either. Nothing could at the moment.

She had a mind to accept the next proposal that came her way, but then she realized there wouldn't be any more proposals, not as long as everyone in town thought she was engaged to that devil sitting beside her. How utterly infuriating! She couldn't even rub his nose in the fact that she'd prefer *any* man over him. Well, then, she'd marry him instead and make him regret, in a thousand different ways, that he'd tampered with her life.

It wasn't the first time she'd had that thought since she'd heard about his bet with Duncan. And it had stayed in the back of her mind despite her bouts of tears. And that wasn't even the worst of her vengeful thoughts. She wanted him to think that he'd failed utterly, that he hadn't won his bloody bet at all, that her becoming a nicer person was just a ruse she'd come up with to get herself back to London.

Thoughts weren't actions, however. She wouldn't really do any of that. The old Ophelia might have, but she . . . God, why didn't he even try to assuage the hurt and the anger he was causing her?

Her mother nudged her arm. "Your food has been sitting there untouched for five minutes. I could have sworn you said you didn't want to miss it. Are you all right?"

"I'm fine." Ophelia picked up her fork. "I was just a little distracted."

"Or plotting my demise?" Rafe said from her other side, proving he was still listening to her every word.

She turned to glare at him. "How did you guess? Dense men aren't usually so perceptive."

"Going to regress to insults, are we?"

"Who is regressing? You don't really think you won that silly bet, do you?"

So much for thinking she could keep that vengeful scenario in the realm of fantasy. Appalled at herself for what she'd just implied, she was still gratified to see that she'd scored a perfect hit. He stiffened. A muscle ticked in his cheek. And the expression in his eyes was no longer cordial.

"You started these rumors about us?" he said in a low, menacing tone.

"Not so dense after all, are you?" she shot back, and even managed a smirk for icing.

"To what purpose? You don't really want to marry me, do you?"

"To make you pay, yes, I'd do even that. Mark my words, taking away your precious bachelorhood will be just the start."

His response was to stand up, grab her hand, and drag her out of the room, leaving nothing but shocked silence behind them. Horrified that he'd just caused the scene she'd threatened *him* with, she was speechless. Until he led her into Lord Cade's study and closed the door behind them.

She jerked her hand from his and whirled around at him. "Are you positively mad?"

"Yes, furiously so."

"I meant insane."

"I'm close to that too."

"You've just added to those bloody rumors. You do realize that, don't you?"

"No, I've just given us an out from them. Lovers tiff, et cetera, too enraged to reconcile, et cetera."

"With what excuse? Because I chose to break with fashion and eat the food put before me?"

He stared at her blankly for a moment, almost cracked a smile, but then growled, "Dammit, Phelia, how could you!"

"What? Fool you into thinking you'd won your bet? Very

easily. I should have been an actress. No, really. I think I've missed my calling."

He stared at her hard. She almost backed down, felt a distinct unease. If she weren't so angry, she would probably have ended the ruse right then and there. But the anger was still with her and she gave him a tight little smile instead.

"How does it feel, being pushed into the proverbial corner with no avenue for escape? Not very pleasant, is it?" she taunted. "It's what you did to me, you bastard! And for what? Just so you could win a stupid wager?"

Someone knocked on the door, probably her mother. Or possibly Lord Cade objecting to their use of his study. Rafe just leaned his weight back against the closed door so it couldn't be shoved open and growled, "In a moment!" The knocking stopped.

"I'm going to ask you to think this through." He even managed a calm tone. "Marrying for the wrong reason, especially for spite, is going to be more detrimental than you've possibly realized. I know you're capable of it. You refused to marry me before just to spite your father. Now you've turned that spite on me, but consider this. Vengeance is fleeting, but you're talking about the rest of our lives, Phelia."

"I don't care!"

"You're not going to even think about it?"

"The only thing I'll be thinking about is how to make you suffer!"

"Very well, then I see no reason to wait."

He didn't give her a chance to ask what he meant. He grabbed her hand again and pulled her back to the dining room where he announced to the guests, "Ophelia and I have decided to speak our vows tonight. If any of you would like to come along to bear witness, you'll be welcome."

Chapter Forty-one

Iᴛ ᴡᴀs ᴛʜᴇ ᴋɪɴᴅ ᴏғ bad behavior Ophelia had indulged in when she was growing up—speaking words hastily, being too stubborn or too hurt to take them back before it was too late, and suffering the regret afterward that never went away. There was more than just regret this time, however. Much more.

She was married to Raphael Locke, Viscount Lynnfield, in the narrow foyer of a magistrate's house, the special license his father had given him to use at his discretion making their marriage possible, with only Lady Cade and Mary Reid there to witness it. The rest of the Cade guests had been too shocked to come along, but Lady Cade had jumped at the chance. It would be the icing on the cake, the premier event of the Season, and she'd be able to tell it all, right down to the *I do*'s.

It certainly wasn't how Ophelia had imagined her wedding. She'd fantasized many times walking down the aisle in a grand church, wearing a magnificent wedding gown, the seats filled with smiling ladies glad to see her exit the marriage mart, and frowning gentlemen, her many admirers bemoaning that they hadn't won her. It was in fact quite tawdry, a rushed civil service, nothing grand about it. The magistrate's mother was even snoring in the next room! Which was the reason why they weren't invited into the parlor to speak their vows. If they *were* vows.

Maybe they were only promising to get married at a later date. She was so dazed that she couldn't think coherently or focus for long on what was really being said. But if it was quite final, the only bright side to it that Ophelia could grasp to her bosom was that her father wasn't there to gloat because he was getting exactly what *he* wanted.

Nervous and confused, Mary chatted nonstop about nothing pertinent to the situation while they drove Lady Cade back to her home. The newlyweds said not a word to each other, though as if they were on their way to some minor affair, they did join in the conversation, but strictly for Lady Cade's benefit. At least Rafe did. Ophelia had to be nudged to contribute, just as she'd had to be prompted for each word during the ceremony. Somewhere in the mire of her shock she grasped that it was necessary for her to play along. Putting on a good show, as it were. When the news broke in the morning, Lady Cade would be able to say the ceremony had been rushed, yes, and certainly wasn't suited to a duke's son, but how romantic that the couple couldn't wait. Such impatience!

Silence prevailed after they'd returned Lady Cade to her residence. But it was only a few short blocks to the Reid household. However, Rafe wasn't just dropping Mary off there. He also ushered Ophelia out of his coach.

"Now you live with it," he said tersely before he slammed the door and his coach drove away.

There was no snow or ice on the walkway, but Ophelia was

frozen in place nonetheless. One shock after another, but this last one was too much. Having married her, why had Rafe returned her to her parents? Or were they married? She hadn't really listened to anything the magistrate had said.

Mary put an arm around her waist as they both stood there watching the viscount's coach disappear into the distance. "I don't understand what just happened," Mary said in her own confusion. "If your father hadn't assured me you would be marrying that man, I never would have let him rush you off to that magistrate's house. What could you have been thinking, Pheli, to agree to that?"

Agree? Had she? By goading Rafe into it and taking the credit for rumors she hadn't started, yes, she supposed that could have been unspoken agreement. By promising him she'd take his bachelorhood away to make him suffer, yes, that too was an obvious sign of compliance. But she certainly hadn't counted on such immediate results or this particular reaction from him. Actually, she hadn't simply thought any further than trying to hurt him just as he'd hurt her.

"Am I really married, Mama?" she asked in a small voice, still staring in a daze down the empty street. "Or was that just a preliminary process of some sort that we needed to take care of before an actual wedding could take place? Like an official promise to get married that required witnesses and putting it in writing?"

"I've never heard of anything like that." Mary frowned.

"Maybe only duke's sons are required—?"

"Let's get out of the cold." Mary turned Ophelia toward the house. "And, no, there was nothing preliminary about what happened tonight. The only oddity was that you were married the same day the marriage was decided upon, but then I'm not surprised the Lockes would have a special license lying around for emergencies. You know, it's the little things like that, the special privileges of the very highest echelon of society that have always annoyed your father so much, because he doesn't have the connections to acquire the same."

"Then he should have married into that echelon himself, instead of pushing me up the social ladder," Ophelia mumbled to herself.

Mary heard her and smiled. "That *was* his intention, dear—until he fell in love with me."

She glanced at her mother. She'd never actually heard that about her father before. He gave up his own aspirations for Mary? That would have been quite romantic of him—except he hadn't really given them up, he'd just switched them to his daughter instead.

Mary sighed as they removed their wraps in the foyer. "So much for the grand wedding I've always dreamed of arranging for you. When it really sinks in, I'm going to be quite disappointed I'm sure."

Guilt now for that, added to everything else Ophelia was feeling. But entertaining was Mary's forte, her sole purpose, as it were, and the wedding for her only daughter could have been her crowning achievement. But not now. She'd had no part in it other than to be present.

"I'm sorry," Ophelia said.

"Don't be, dear. It certainly wasn't your fault that your young man was so impatient. I could see it on your face, that you were as surprised as the rest of us. If anything, I blame the special license. If you have something like that sitting in your pocket, you're tempted to use it."

The guilt got worse, forcing the words out of Ophelia. "You

have the wrong impression about what occurred, Mama. There was nothing romantic about it."

Mary's frown returned. "What are you saying?"

"You haven't wondered yet why he left me here with you, instead of taking me home with him?"

"Well, of course I have. I did sense some anger from him, which he was trying admirably to hide. But I'm sure there's a good reason."

"Oh, there is, a very good reason. It's because he didn't want to marry me at all, any more than I wanted to marry him. My anger goaded him into it, though that wouldn't have done it alone, not without the rumors circulating about us."

All Mary heard and addressed was "You really didn't want to marry him?"

"Well, I would have wanted to if Papa hadn't been insisting on it, and if Rafe and I had found the right reasons to. We came close to finding them, but—it just wasn't meant to be, I guess."

"But do you love him?"

There was that question again, and all she could say was "I really don't know. I've never felt so comfortable with a man before, where I don't feel I have to guard my every word, nor have I gotten so angry with a man before for that matter, or—it's all extremes, what he makes me feel. I've had some wonderful experiences with him that I'll never forget. He brings out the child in me, and the girl, and the woman. He certainly taps all of my emotions, not just a few of them."

"Oh my" was all Mary said, as if Ophelia had given her a definitive yes or no, rather than a complicated jumble of thoughts.

"Why are you two home so early?" Sherman asked, appearing at the top of the stairs. "And standing there chitchatting in the foyer?"

"Oh, good God," Mary whispered to Ophelia. "It's only just dawned on me that Sherman missed your wedding. He's going to be furious!"

That's one bright note out of a disastrous day, Ophelia thought.

Chapter Forty-two

Raphael turned off the lamp beside the reading chair in his bedroom, leaving only the dim orange glow from the dying fire to flicker about the room. The bottle of rum was close at hand. He would have preferred brandy, but his study was dark when he'd gone in there to grab an armful of bottles, and he had encountered only two. One he knocked on the floor and couldn't find, the other he'd taken up to his room. He'd take a light with him when he went down later to find out what had happened to the rest of the liquor in his well-stocked bar. One, even two bottles, just wasn't going to be enough tonight.

He'd married Ophelia Reid—good God, she was Ophelia Locke now. He was out of his bloody mind.

He could have gotten out of it, had only needed to make it publicly known that they were at unreconcilable odds. Would anyone who knew her doubt it? Hell no. But at the back of his mind had been the ridiculous notion that marriage to her could be good, so good he'd think he was the luckiest man alive. But it had been a foolish notion. What it could be like wasn't going to be a reality. What it would be like was going to be his worst nightmare.

He thought about telling his housekeeper to prepare for a lady of the house, then took another drink instead. He'd be damned if he'd bring that shrew into his home. She was *not* going to know that he still wanted her. She was *not* going to know that he had to fight to keep his hands off her. If he didn't see her, he could keep those urges to himself. And where was it written, after all, that he had to live with the wife he'd married? If her parents wouldn't keep her, he'd find somewhere else to deposit her, but it wouldn't be with him.

He'd never lacked for coin. The title that had come to him that was usually passed along to the firstborn early came with a large estate, and many entailed properties that earned a steady income. To teach responsibility early was the family tradition. So before he was a man, he was his own man.

The London town house was one of those properties. He hadn't had to buy it, but he'd spared no expense decorating it to his taste. It was a man's house, made comfortable for a bachelor. It wasn't suitable for a woman, especially that woman, who'd no doubt wreck it for spite just as she did everything else for spite. He liked the house. He didn't want it ruined. He downed another glass of rum.

He was vaguely aware that his thoughts were beginning to turn incoherent. He'd been hoping the alcohol would give him a little peace before he had to face the realities of the morning, but it wasn't working yet. He downed another glass of rum.

His marriage was going to be on every tongue come morning. News of that sort would travel fast. He had no idea how he was going to deal with congratulations—or condolences, for that matter. He should jot off a note to his father, but he was afraid it would be illegible now. Tomorrow.

He began to feel bad about leaving Ophelia with her parents, though. That sort of spite was foreign to him. But it had been such a perfect payback. Force them to marry for spite, would she? Then he could deny her the one thing she *really* wanted, to get out from under her father's thumb. Priceless—but a little too spiteful for him.

He wouldn't make her stay there, not for long. But he wasn't going to bring her to his home. Hell no. He'd find her some place where she could practice her spiteful ways to her heart's content and he wouldn't have to know about it. They were *not* going to live under the same roof when he couldn't trust a single word out of her mouth.

God, he couldn't believe how adept she was at deception. He'd really believed she'd changed, that her regrets were real, that she'd told the truth. He'd even thought she'd conquered her worst tendencies, but it was all lies. And there was no way he could continually live with that, when he wouldn't be able to trust a single word she ever said.

"I ran home the moment I heard. Congratulations!"

He glanced up to see his sister grinning as she poked her head around the door. "Don't do that."

"What?"

"Congratulate me. You can mourn with me if you like. Just don't look so bloody cheerful, thank you."

"You're foxed." She walked into the room.

"Good guess! Two points for you!"

"*Really* foxed. Why? And where is she?" Amanda looked in particular toward his bed.

"You won't find her in there," he mumbled. "But if you thought she was in here, why the deuce didn't you knock before barging in?"

"I never barge in," she disagreed in a huff.

"You just did."

"No, I didn't. I knocked and knocked and knocked first, and when you didn't answer, I figured you must be sleeping, but on the chance you weren't, I just had to know so I could share my delight with . . . you . . ." She slowed down because of his scowl. "I shouldn't be delighted?"

"No, you shouldn't."

"But I *like* her."

"You didn't before."

"That was before she and I had such a nice talk."

He snorted. "Don't believe a word she says, Mandy. She's a consummate liar, a practiced deceiver, a superb actress. She'll have you believing the sun is shining when you know bloody well it isn't. And how the devil did you find out so soon?"

"Some chap burst into the main room of the party I was attending and simply shouted it into the room. Then he was bombarded with questions and admitted he had been at the Cades' where you announced you were leaving immediately to get leg-shackled to Ophelia, and that even Lady Cade went along to witness it. Of course everyone then turned their eyes accusingly on me because I hadn't even dropped a hint that it was to happen soon. Quite embarrassing, you know, but I forgive you because I was so delighted to . . . very well, not delighted a'tall. There. Happy?"

"Do I look happy?"

She was frowning now as she sat on the arm of his chair. "What happened? Did something prevent you from marrying her?"

"No," he said in self-disgust. "I could have prevented it if I wasn't so furious, but I was, and I didn't." He knew that sounded odd, started to clarify what he meant, but lost the train of his thoughts and gave up. Instead he said, "A word of warning, m'dear. Don't ever ever make a monumental decision about your life when you're in a rage."

"I thought you liked her. You raved about the 'new' her. I even met the 'new' her and had to agree with you. She was more than just changed, it was like she was a completely new person."

"Lies. The woman I liked doesn't even exist. She was a fraud."

Amanda raised a brow at him. "You're sure about that? We're talking about the woman who found out about the bet, remember? The one who would want your head for it. You just called her a superb actress, didn't you? Maybe this woman is the fraud."

Chapter Forty-three

"You don't understand, Sherman," Mary said. "She cried herself to sleep. She's not the least bit happy with this turn of events."

"And I am?"

They were in the dining room working their way through a breakfast neither of them was paying much attention to. Mary had explained to her husband last night what had occurred, as much as she understood of it anyway, and she'd been accurate in her prediction. He'd been furious and his mood hadn't improved much this morning. She didn't usually react to his moods in a like manner, but in this case, she was just as upset, but for different reasons.

"She could have had the grandest wedding of the century," Sherman continued. "Royalty might even have attended. Do you realize the lost opportunities—"

"For *once* will you think about your daughter and not your damned 'opportunities'!"

Mary rarely ever shouted at her husband. Unlike her daughter, it just wasn't in her nature to lose her temper or have emotional outbursts. On the rare occasions it did happen, Sherman usually took quick note of it, which is what he did right now. He slumped down in his chair. The heat went out of his expression. And he eyed his wife warily.

"Take her shopping," he mumbled. "That always cheers you women up."

"That's callous, Sherman."

He flushed. "But it works, doesn't it?"

"For minor upsets, perhaps, but this disaster can hardly be called minor. And this isn't even the first time she's cried this week. She wasn't sick those few days she stayed in her room, you know. She'd heard something that quite undid her."

"What?"

"I have no idea. She wasn't willing to discuss it with me, tried to pretend it was nothing. But I've never seen her quite so angry, or despondent—well, other than when you engaged her to Mac-Tavish."

He flushed again. "Let's please not rehash that again, m'dear. That could have been a grand match if she had just given it a chance."

"That's neither here nor there. The point is, she's currently devastated because she's married to a man who obviously doesn't want her."

He sat up, angry now on Ophelia's behalf. "I will not for a moment believe that *any* man could *not* want that angel."

Mary raised a brow at him. "Angel in looks, certainly, but you know very well that the unusual childhood you put her through not only made her haughty and abrasive, but had her distrusting everyone she met."

"Must I be blamed for everything?"

"When you *are* to blame, yes. I warned you countless times to stop treating her like a bauble you were compelled to show off. You treated her like an adult when she was still a child. You marched an endless stream of bachelors through here to enlist offers for her long before she was ready for them."

"If you must know, even I got annoyed at the extreme number of those offers."

"Then how do you think she felt? Your shouting matches with her are legendary, you know. The entire block snickers about them."

Once again, he flushed. "She wasn't quite as volatile when she returned from that visit with Locke, did you notice that? I almost didn't recognize her."

She rolled her eyes at him. "Because *you* never saw her mellow side for the simple reason that her reaction to you has always been explosive. But, yes, I did notice a remarkable difference in her when she returned home. She was softer. It was as if the brambles had been removed."

"Think the Lockes overwhelmed and humbled her with their superiority?" he wondered aloud.

She tsked at him. "I don't think anything of the sort. And we've never met them, other than the viscount and his sister. Do not presume things about that family that could be far from the mark."

He shrugged. "Then what could have changed her? Surely she mentioned something to you?"

"I'm her mother, Sherman, not her best friend. Though I wish it were otherwise, she rarely confides in me."

But Mary, having said her piece, was still confronted with the same sorry situation, which was worth crying over. In fact, she became quite choked up when she added, "She hasn't had a happy life, Sherman. Do you realize that? She's the most beautiful daughter anyone could ask for, but she's also the most unhappy."

"What can I do?"

"Besides make her angry? I'm sorry, that was uncalled for. But you must admit, that does seem to be the only way she reacts to you. And I'm not sure anything can be done to help this situation. The odd thing is, I think she loves him. She didn't say so exactly, but you see a glow in her eyes when she talks about him. Which doesn't explain why she's here with us and he's gone his merry way. I think she was right, he really didn't want to get married. He only did so because of those silly rumors, which, I might add, *you* helped to propagate by telling all your cronies that she was visiting the Lockes and you expected her to come home with an engagement."

His face flushed to a deeper shade or red. "I'll pay Locke a visit to see which way the wind blows in his court."

"Don't do that," she admonished quickly. "You could make things even worse." But then she amended with a little heat, "However, if he hasn't come by to collect her in the next few days, I'll go with you to give him a piece of *my* mind. I will not have my daughter made a laughingstock because it will appear that he didn't find her acceptable."

Chapter Forty-four

"Y OU AREN'T UP YET? SADIE said you were."

Ophelia sat up abruptly in bed. She had been awake, knew that it was close to noon. She'd just been unwilling to rise to face what she was sure was going to be a difficult day. And she'd been right. By the looks of Jane and Edith, barely containing their excitement as they marched into her room, they knew she was now Lady Locke.

"My maid thinks I should be up, so telling you I am is her ornery way of making sure I am," Ophelia explained, and even pretended a yawn for their benefit.

"A late night, eh?" Jane snickered.

Jane and Edith went to their usual seats at the little breakfast-tray table. It appeared Sadie had left a tray there on her last attempt to get Ophelia out of bed.

That remark was rather bold for Jane, though, an unrestrained reference to a wedding night. But Ophelia didn't need to respond to it.

Edith couldn't contain her excitement any longer and burst out, "You are *so* lucky!"

And Jane added, "We only just found out you were engaged to him. Can you believe it? No one bothered to mention it to us because they were sure we already knew all about it. And now this!"

"But we certainly didn't expect to find you here," Edith said. "We went to Locke's house this morning to see you. His butler didn't know what we were talking about. When we told him you'd married Lord Locke, he nearly called us liars. Said he hadn't heard about it yet, so it couldn't be true. You'll have to fire that man. I don't care if he was just doing his job, he was quite rude about it."

"So why are you here instead of there?" Jane asked next, quite pointedly.

Ophelia sighed inwardly and prevaricated, "His house isn't ready for me yet." But she should have known her friends wouldn't leave it at that.

"Really?" Edith said with a speculating frown. "But his sister is staying with him."

"Amanda doesn't mind. Rafe thinks I will and wants it to be just right for me. First impressions and all that. Which is fine with me. We had our wedding night."

The blush was immediate and not because of the subject, though both girls would assume that was the case. She blushed because it wasn't true. Why was she resorting to lies again? Because she couldn't tolerate pity and she knew that was what she'd get from these two if they knew the truth?

To change the subject somewhat, she said, "One of you must have been up and about early this morning, to have heard the news so soon."

"You must be joking," Edith replied with a laugh. "We heard about it last night."

"All but a few of the Cade guests must have rushed out to every party they could find," Jane added. "You know how the ton is, everyone wanting to be the first with the latest *on dit*. We actually heard about it twice last night. First that you were on your way to get married."

"And then again," Edith finished, "less than an hour later, that you *were* married. A few of the Cade guests stayed behind till Lady Cade returned with the confirmation that, yes, it really did happen, she'd witnessed it herself. Then they too rushed around to spread the word."

"And you're not going to believe this," Jane went on with even more excitement. "But I got my first proposal last night too, right after the news about your wedding spread. It was from Lord Even. Not that I'm the least bit interested in him, but it's a start!"

"Indeed, two of your former beaux called on me this morning," Edith said. "I was incredulous as you can imagine, but quite delighted. They're taking it rather well, their disappointment, but most of them have realized that now that you're definitely out of the running for them, they still *do* need to get married."

"So Edith and I just might find husbands this Season as well, even though there isn't much time left to decide. But the opportunities are endless now."

Listening to them, seeing how excited they both were about her "leftovers," she had to wonder why they didn't hate her. She'd held them back through no fault of her own other than her infamous beauty. They hadn't even tried to decide ahead of time whom they might want to marry. They'd both decided instead that they simply wouldn't stand a chance until she got married first. It was sad. It shouldn't have been that way. And she'd done nothing to make sure it wasn't that way because she hadn't really been a friend to either of them.

"I can make a few recommendations if you'd like," Ophelia said almost shyly. "Though it might not have seemed like it, I *was* paying attention to most of those gentlemen, and some of them were nicer than others, some were more romantic, some I'm sure would make exemplary fathers. And I know you know why I'd look for that in a man." Both girls chuckled. "But having been engaged, I wasn't really interested in any of them myself, so I wasn't shy about putting them on the spot with pertinent questions to find out more about them."

"Did any have all three qualities?" Jane asked with interest.

"Indeed," Ophelia replied. "For instance, Harry Cragg would likely be perfect for you, Jane. He's not only an avid horseman, he also breeds racers on his estate in Kent. I know how disappointed you were when your parents wouldn't let you ride anymore after you took that one tumble and broke your arm. To be honest, I think Harry was only interested in me because he found out I enjoy riding. That man will expect his wife, when he gets one, to ride with him every day, I don't doubt."

"She's right," Edith agreed. "The one time I spoke with Harry, he only wanted to talk about horses. Quite boring for me, but don't you remember me telling you, Jane, that *you* would have been fascinated?"

"He's quite handsome too, isn't he?" Jane said, beginning to look more than just a little interested. "At least I think so."

"A little too outdoorsy for my tastes," Edith replied with a grin. "Course I *am* a bluestocking."

"Yes, we know you'd rather have your nose in a book than go to a party," Jane teased.

"Come to think of it, Edith, you should probably give Lord Paisley a little attention," Ophelia remarked. "Can't remember his first name, but he was boasting about a personal library of over three thousand books. Said he had to add on to his estate just to make more room for them."

"Are you joking?" Edith asked wide-eyed.

"Not .a'tall. I got the impression that he'd travel halfway across the world if he heard of a book he wanted in some foreign country."

"And he's quite pale enough to suit you, m'dear," Jane chuckled.

"You know, Pheli," Edith began spontaneously without thought, "I never would have—oh, I'm sorry, that just slipped out."

"It's all right," Ophelia assured her. "That old nickname doesn't bother me anymore."

"It doesn't?" Jane said with a thoughtful frown. "You've changed, Ophelia, really changed. Truthfully, I've never felt this—this—"

"Relaxed," Edith finished for her. "Yes, I've felt it too. And at the risk of being thrown out, I have to say I love the change in you. Who would have ever thought you'd make an effort to help us figure out who the best choices might be for us, like a real . . ."

Edith didn't finish, but she was blushing profusely. The unspoken *friend* hovered between them. The same embarrassment overtook Ophelia. Rafe had really called it on the nose. The old bitterness had made her far too self-centered and had kept her from ever getting close to these two. They had always reacted to her reactions. Come to think of it, when she wasn't reacting to something, which had been rarely, they were both nice girls and fun to be around.

God, what she'd missed in life, alienating friends so they wouldn't hurt her, when doing that had actually hurt her the most.

Chapter Forty-five

"Your husband is here to see you," Sadie announced at the door.

The two girls had joined Ophelia on the bed, and sitting cross-legged, they'd worked out a nice list of possible husbands for both girls. The camaraderie was warm among them, the laughter spontaneous. It had been a long time since Ophelia had enjoyed herself so much.

But with Sadie's announcement, all three girls were thinking that the word *husband* had a nice ring to it, well, at least two of them were. The reminder that *husband* didn't exactly mean what it should mean for Ophelia abruptly made her mood plummet. But she tried to put a good face on it as her friends rushed off, neither of them wanting to intrude on her first days of married life.

She took her time dressing, even though Sadie tried to hurry her. Rafe could wait, in her opinion. He could wait all day. He deserved to be kept waiting. God, how easily the anger returned, and she couldn't seem to help it.

"It's a good thing your mother went back to bed," Sadie said as she pushed Ophelia out the door. "I heard she was on the warpath this morning, over this turn of events."

"What nonsense," Ophelia scoffed, pausing at the top of the stairs. "My mother never goes on the warpath."

"She did this time, and your father even backed down, if you can believe it. Jerome was eavesdropping at the door. He swears it's true."

Ophelia didn't believe it. That footman was known to embellish his tales to make them more interesting. But she wasn't going to argue about it because Rafe was waiting for her in the parlor. She didn't doubt he was there to collect her. Married, they were expected to live in the same house whether they wanted to or not. She'd make him apologize first for rudely running off on her last night.

She paused in the doorway to the parlor. She was armed for battle, wearing one of her many powder blue gowns that enhanced the color of her eyes, her coiffure in perfect order. Her "husband" stood at the window that looked out on the street. There wasn't much to see out there. But he looked deep in thought, and she doubted he'd heard her arrive.

He did. Without even turning he said, "Kept an hour waiting. Were you hoping I'd get fed up and leave?"

"Not a'tall," she purred. "I was merely hoping you'd get fed up."

He turned about to catch the smirking smile she shot his way as she crossed to a sofa. There were four to choose from, all identical and comfortably upholstered in silk brocade, the colors predominately gold with assorted earth tones that went well with the solid-brown chairs scattered about the rest of the room. The sofas were positioned around a low table that held a few knickknacks and one of her mother's flower arrangements, but was mainly used for tea trays.

She spread her skirts wide so Rafe wouldn't even think about sitting next to her. He came over to join her and sat on the edge of her skirt! She gritted her teeth as she yanked the material out from under his thigh. He didn't even seem to notice as he turned to face her, resting one arm on the back of the sofa. Perhaps he wasn't being deliberately rude, but she was as she moved farther away from him.

He did notice that and said, "Be still."

"Go to the devil."

He started to reach for her but changed his mind and sighed. "Can we at least have a normal conversation for a few minutes?"

"I doubt it. A few minutes is too long for me to be cordial to you."

Her anger was seething. Every single word out of her mouth seemed to make it worse, as if it were feeding upon itself. And she had no other outlet for this anger, it would just continue to grow and fester. The one other outlet he'd introduced her to was no longer an option. She wasn't about to use him to get rid of anger *he* was responsible for.

"I've come up with an ideal solution for us."

He tossed that out as if it were a gold nugget, expecting her to pounce on it and put aside the sarcasm and rancor for the moment. It didn't work.

"I wasn't aware we needed a solution, but I suppose you might think so." The only thing that came to mind was an annulment, but she wasn't going to let him escape that easily. She was ready with her arguments before she said, "An annulment isn't an option."

"I agree," he surprised her by saying. "We've already had our wedding night, albeit a bit early."

If he thought he could embarrass her by mentioning their lovemaking, it didn't work. In fact, it just reminded her how gullible she'd been, how she'd believed all his lies, how she'd really thought he'd wanted to help her when all along she'd just been a source of amusement for him and Duncan. That he *had* helped her was completely irrelevant when his motives had been purely self-serving.

"I've decided to buy a house. There's one for sale not too far from here, so you'll be able to easily visit your parents whenever you like."

"What's wrong with your house?"

"Nothing. My house is perfect—for me. I'm sure you won't be surprised if I want to keep it that way. What I'm talking about is a house just for you."

That was *not* what she had assumed she'd be hearing, but she managed a tight smile for him. "You actually expect me to wreck your house, don't you?"

"The thought did occur to me. You are an unpredictable woman, Phelia, probably the most unpredictable one I've ever met. I'd as soon not take the chance with a home I'm fond of."

"So your brilliant idea is that we won't just be having separate bedrooms, we'll have separate houses? And what if I don't like that idea?"

"I'm not doing this to please you, m'dear. For all I care, you can stay right here. But that will eventually cause you some embarrassment that might whiplash on my family. But keep in mind that you forced this situation on us when I could have extricated us easily enough."

"I forced nothing! You brought this on yourself when you decided to place wagers on my life!"

He ignored her heated tone and shrugged. "Be that as it may, you will accept what I'm offering. Or perhaps you haven't realized yet that the decisions are now mine to make?"

He sounded entirely too smug in saying that. "I wouldn't count on it."

He stood up, wearing that same angry countenance he'd worn in Summers Glade when he'd given her that verbal setdown. "Don't push me, Ophelia. You've done quite enough of that already. I can and will put a leash on you if I have to. I'd rather not assume that much control over your every action—again—but I will if you get out of hand."

He left her with that warning and the clear indication that he'd deposit her back at Alder's Nest, alone this time, and she'd be just as much a prisoner there as she'd been before. That *was* what he'd implied when he'd stressed the word *again*. But she wasn't going to let him get away with this, and she knew just how to make sure he couldn't.

Chapter Forty-six

"THIS IS A BAD IDEA," Sadie grumbled as she tucked the lap robe more tightly about her lap and continued to stare worriedly out the coach window.

"This is a wonderful idea," Ophelia disagreed.

"You don't just barge in on people like this, and especially not these people."

"He may be a duke," Ophelia said with a shrug, "but he's also my father-in-law. Do you really think he won't give me a warm welcome?"

"That's hardly the point. What if he's already heard that you're estranged from his son?"

"No one knows that yet. *Rafe* doesn't even know that yet. He *thinks* keeping us apart is his idea."

"You should be moving into that house that he bought you, instead of barging in on his family."

Ophelia sighed. Sadie was in top form today as grumbles went. Ophelia was nervous enough as it was about meeting the duke for the first time. Her maid was just making that worse.

"One, I don't barge," Ophelia said. "Two, I have no intention of occupying that house he bought."

"But he bought it just for you."

"Yes, and I'm delighted that he wasted the money. I intend to waste even more of his money when we get back to London. I'm going to go on an extravagant shopping spree and have all of the bills sent to him."

"Denting a man's purse when you aren't on good terms with that man is an even worse idea than hieing off to Norford Hall," Sadie warned.

"Everything is a bad idea to you these days."

"Because you've reverted to the old you. I was just getting used to the new you, and—"

"That's not true and you know it," Ophelia cut in, her tone a little hurt. "I've only regressed where *he's* concerned."

Sadie sighed now and admitted, "That's true. I'm sorry. I just had such high hopes for your marriage, some peace for you away from your father finally, some love from a good man, having babies I could adore . . . are you sure you're not enceinte?"

Ophelia wasn't sure at all, but she said, "Yes, quite, but have the driver pull over, I think I'm going to be sick again."

"You *are* enceinte, aren't you?"

"I'm not, really, and never mind, we don't need to stop. It's passed. It's just all this anger that keeps churning in my gut, and this bouncy ride isn't helping."

"It's all right if you are, you know. You're married."

"I am not having a baby!"

"Fine. But being angry never made you sick to your stomach before."

"I've never been *this* angry before."

Sadie offered a few more grumbles, but Ophelia stopped listening. She wasn't sure what she was going to accomplish with this visit. She hadn't really thought that far ahead. She didn't want to cause a rift between Rafe and his family. But the threat he'd hung over her head worried her. She'd like at least someone on his side to look favorably on her and be there to talk reason into Rafe if he really did try to curtail her freedom and stick her somewhere like Alder's Nest again—alone this time.

It only took a good portion of a day to reach Norford Hall. It was definitely the largest estate Ophelia had ever seen, aside from the royal palace. The size wasn't just intimidating, it was disheartening to have it made so clear that a duke lived there. A real duke. You couldn't get much higher up the proverbial ladder outside of the royal family.

Sadie was even more intimidated as they stepped out of the coach and she stared at the mansion with her mouth hanging open. She only had one final thing to say, and she said it in a whisper: "I hope you know what you're doing."

Ophelia didn't answer. Liveried footmen were showing up en masse, to usher them inside, to take care of the coach, to unload their trunks. She *had* dressed rather grandly for the occasion, which was probably why she was being given admittance without having to identify herself or what she was doing there.

Of course she changed her mind about that when she came up against the solid wall of the Norford Hall butler. *He* wasn't going to let her go any farther without finding out who she was. But Sadie was at her best when dealing with the servant class, wasn't the least bit in awe of servants higher up the ladder than she was, and circumvented any extensive questioning by getting right to the point.

"We'll need two rooms," Sadie told the butler. "One of them quite large, so don't even think about giving my lady a mere guest room for her stay here. She's your lord's new daughter-in-law come to meet her husband's family. And considering how big this place is, I'll take a room near hers, thank you."

That easily they were whisked upstairs. If that butler worked for her, Ophelia would have insisted he get a little more proof than a maid's high manner, but perhaps they were more relaxed out here in the country. And the room she was shown to was so large, a good four times the size of her bedroom at home, she felt positively dwarfed by it. The furnishings were exquisite though, in jade and gold mostly, expensive. But she was used to expensive things, so she wasn't hesitant to use what was there. However, it was no wonder Norford Hall spread out so widely like a city block, with rooms this size.

After being on the road most of the day, she should have rested up, at least until dinner, but she was too nervous even to consider it. If she could get her first meeting with the duke out of the way, then she could relax—if it went well—and maybe even enjoy her stay. So she did no more than change out of her traveling clothes and into her least wrinkled day dress and went back downstairs to "meet" her new family.

Chapter Forty-seven

I T WAS EASY TO GET lost in Norford Hall, Ophelia found as she wandered around on the lower floor, trying to get her bearings. There wasn't just one main hall with rooms off it, there were quite a few. She finally gave up trying to figure out where the main rooms were and requested an audience with the duke. That at least was easy enough to do since there were footmen everywhere it seemed. She'd already discovered that there was more than one parlor. She was shown to what they referred to as the blue room and hoped she wouldn't have to wait long.

The blue parlor, so named because the walls, the floors, the windows, were all covered in pale shades of that color, wasn't empty. A middle-aged woman was lying down on one of the sofas. She actually appeared to be napping there, one arm draped over her eyes to block out the light streaming in through a long bank of windows. But at the sound of footsteps she sat up immediately, took one look at Ophelia, and scowled.

"Who are you? Never mind. This won't do a'tall. Do go away before my son comes downstairs."

Not a normal greeting by any means, Ophelia didn't know whether to laugh or get annoyed. Rafe's mother? She could have sworn she'd heard that his mother had died long ago. Then who? She was a striking woman, with blond hair and blue eyes, and she bore a definite resemblance to Rafe. But she was so gruff and bossy, her manner could almost be called masculine.

"I beg your pardon?" Ophelia said.

"My son, Rupert, is too impressed with beautiful women," the woman took a moment to explain. "*You* are too bloody pretty. He'll be slobbering at your feet if he claps eyes on you. You must go."

Ophelia chose to ignore those remarks entirely and made an effort to start afresh. "Might you be one of my husband's many aunts? I'm Ophelia."

"Don't care who you are, gel, you need to make yourself scarce and quickly—oh, never mind. We'll leave. We can visit my brother another time."

She stood up to do just that, but then made a low growl in her throat because she was too late. The young man under discussion, her son, sauntered casually into the room. His eyes went immediately to Ophelia, which stopped him in his tracks. He stared, hard. Nothing she wasn't used to, but he wasn't rendered speechless as most were.

"My God," he said. "My God, when did angels come down to earth?"

With black hair with flyaway curls and pale blue eyes, he was incredibly handsome, but in an effeminate way. His skin was too smooth, his nose too thin. He wore lace at his cuffs, an excessive amount in his cravat, and a bright lime green satin waistcoat. She was surprised he wasn't wearing dandyish knee breeches. He definitely had a girlish air about him, which was almost funny, because his mother seemed rather mannish.

"You can close your mouth, Rupert," his mother snapped in disgust. "She's married to your cousin Rafe."

"Ah, that would explain it." He didn't sound too disappointed that she was married. "The incomparable Ophelia, no doubt. I knew I should have sought her out when I heard about her, but frankly, I didn't believe a jot of it. No one could be as beautiful as they were claiming she is. Bloody hell, for once I wish I hadn't played know-it-all. But no matter." He gave Ophelia a truly magnificent smile. "Forget about my cousin. You must run away with me. I'll make you deliriously happy."

"Rupert, I raised a fool," his mother admonished.

Rupert wasn't paying the least bit of attention to his mother now. He'd leapt forward and was bending over to kiss Ophelia's hand, nor would he release her fingers, continuing to hold them to his mouth while his blue eyes remained locked to hers. She feared he'd start sucking them in a minute.

They were joined by another man, one of such stature, dignity, and noble bearing, even though he was casually dressed in a rumpled frock coat, there was no doubt he was the Duke of Norford. He was also, undeniably, an older version of Rafe, the same height, the same blond hair and blue eyes, just stockier in girth.

He glanced at the scowling woman and said, "Julie, go home. You've overstayed your welcome."

"I just got here!"

"Exactly."

But he moved farther into the room to hug her, and she snorted before she hugged him back. He was teasing her? A duke was teasing his sister?

Then he turned to Ophelia. "I don't believe I need to ask who you are. The rumors of your beauty don't do you justice. Come along. We'll find somewhere to get acquainted where my nephews aren't drooling over you."

"Oh, I say, I really don't drool," Rupert protested vehemently.

But the Duke of Norford had already left the room, and Ophelia was sure he didn't doubt for a moment that she would follow. She still had to tug her hand away from Rupert first, who didn't want to let go. Finally succeeding, she rushed out of the room.

"Don't be long, love. I'll be waiting right here," Rupert called after her. Then she heard him howl. His mother must have hit him with something.

Ophelia just caught sight of Preston Locke's back disappearing into a room down the hall. She picked up her skirt to run after him, slid a few inches on the marble floor as she stopped, and took a few seconds to compose herself before she entered. She wasn't sure if she was in a library or a study. It was a large room. Filled bookshelves lined nearly every wall. But there was also a desk, twice the size of any she'd ever seen before, placed in front of some windows in a corner. The room was filled with small groupings of comfortable-looking chairs.

"This is a nice—study," she remarked as she joined him by seating herself in one of those comfortable chairs. A tray of tea had been placed on the low table between them.

"My study is utilitarian and a few doors further down this hall," he corrected. "This is where I come to relax and not deal with estate business. Would you like to pour us tea? It was just served."

"Certainly."

His tone gave no indication of his mood. She couldn't tell if he was pleased to meet her or annoyed by her presence in his home. She was amazed the teacups didn't rattle in their china saucers, she was so nervous. She could feel his eyes on her face accessing her.

He finally said, "You really are too beautiful for words, aren't you? I honestly thought people were exaggerating as they tend to do, but not in this case."

"I wish it were otherwise, Your Grace."

"Come now, no formality amongst family. I suppose you can call me Father if you like, though if you feel uncomfortable doing so, Preston will do. Do you really not like being so pretty?"

Her eyes met his as she handed him a teacup. "It has been a blessing and a bane, more so a bane."

"Why is that?"

She was given pause. No one had ever asked her that before, and she saw no reason not to be truthful about it. This was her father-in-law after all.

"Mainly, it has caused my father to treat me as a prized bauble good only for showing off, which has set him and me at complete odds. But there's also the reaction people have to me when they meet me. Your nephew for instance."

The duke actually laughed. "Rupert isn't a good example, m'dear. The boy behaves like that around any skirt he crosses paths with. But I understand how you might see that sort of re-action as a problem."

"It's not just the men. Women flock to me as well, not be-cause they like me, but just to be associated with me. This face has made me quite popular. It's also caused me to distrust people for most of my life. They are so rarely sincere when they're around me. Anyway, that's been my bane."

He stared at her oddly for a moment. "You would think that anyone as incredibly beautiful as you are would have led a charmed life. How unusual that it would seem you've led just the opposite."

She shrugged. "I'm not quite so bitter about it anymore, and that's your son's doing. He helped me to view things from perspectives other than my own. It's made an amazing difference, having a little trust in my life again, when I had absolutely none."

"Yes, he mentioned—working with you."

His pause indicated that Rafe had told his father far too much about their relationship. He might even have mentioned that they'd been intimate. Father and son could be close enough to discuss things like that.

She felt a blush coming on, but it halted when he added, "By the by, where is the groom? I expected him to bring you here for this first visit."

She hesitated only a moment before admitting, "He doesn't know I've come here. Rafe and I aren't talking—or living together."

That produced an instant frown. "You refuse to live with him?"

"On the contrary. He married me and then promptly returned me to my parents' home."

Preston shot immediately to his feet, his face suffused with color. "The devil he did."

She wasn't really surprised that he'd be offended on her behalf, or perhaps it was just his son doing something so out of the ordinary that he objected to. But oddly enough, she found herself defending Rafe.

"He didn't want to marry me. He's quite angry that he feels he was forced to."

He digested that for a moment, then sighed as he sat back down. "I'm afraid that's my doing. I did more or less order him to do right by you. The rumors, you know. Couldn't have them getting out of hand. They could have been quite detrimental to your reputation if you weren't engaged to marry the boy. But I certainly didn't expect it to happen this quickly."

"Neither did he. In fact, he didn't expect it to happen at all.

His intention was to defuse the rumors and avoid marriage entirely. But my own anger got out of hand and I pretty much goaded him into acting hastily, so, no, it wasn't your fault a'tall."

"I could have sworn he said something to the effect that your temper had been tamed."

Her lips tightened. "Did he? Well, yes, in most regards that's true. I can even get through a conversation with my father these days without screaming at him. The one exception is Rafe. I can't seem to control my temper a'tall where he's concerned."

"I see," the duke said thoughtfully.

She wished she did. "At any rate, I'd rather not live alone in the house that he bought me. I'm sure it's a nice house and I probably won't mind living there eventually. But just now while my moods are so turbulent, I think it would better if I remained in the company of other people."

"You're more than welcome to stay here," he said, and appeared to mean it.

"Thank you, but that's not why I've come. My maid, Sadie, thinks I'm with child. I dis—"

"Truly?" he cut in with a brilliant smile. "That's wonderful news! So he didn't desert you immediately after the wedding after all?"

"Oh, he did. But our time together at Alder's Nest was—eventful—in a number of ways." She was glad to see by his expression, mixed with understanding and disapproval, that she didn't need to elaborate further. "But as I was saying, I disagree with Sadie. It's rather soon to know for certain. But on the oft chance that she's correct, I thought this would be a good time to meet Rafe's family. Frankly, I wanted to make sure you aren't all as aggravating as he is."

The Duke of Norford didn't take offense at that remark. In fact, he burst out laughing.

garding their marriage. And he'd been bombarded with questions himself. But he was rather adept at providing answers without really divulging any pertinent information. And his sister, who was also being barraged for some juicy tidbits, had agreed to continue to assert that she was annoyed with him.

Dining with her last night before she'd left for yet another ball, she'd assured him, "They think I'm still not talking to you. It's *so* much easier to just say I don't know."

He finally gave up wondering what Ophelia was up to and early that evening went to find out for himself. He'd staffed the house he'd bought her. It had come fully furnished, tastefully, all in excellent condition, which was in fact what had sold him. Having told Ophelia he was buying her this house, he didn't want her to have to wait for furniture to be delivered before she could move in.

He wouldn't have been surprised if she'd dismissed the staff he'd selected for her, so she could hire people of her own choosing, but she hadn't yet done so. The butler who answered his knock and let him in was the same chap he'd sent over.

"Where is she?" he asked Mr. Collins.

"Who, m'lord?"

"My wife, of course," Raphael said as he handed over his hat and greatcoat. He was already remembering the last time she'd kept him waiting. He might as well get comfortable.

"Lady Locke hasn't taken up residence yet," Mr. Collins informed him, appearing rather embarrassed to impart that information.

Now *that* he wasn't expecting. "It's been nearly a week since I let her know this house was ready for her. Did she at least move her belongings in?"

"We haven't seen the lady yet at all."

Chapter Forty-eight

THE LULL BEFORE THE STORM was driving Raphael crazy. He had fully expected his "wife" to do some outlandish thing to enrage him. She had promised retribution. She had sworn she intended to make him suffer. By mere chance he'd remained apart from her so that she couldn't taunt him into ruining his life any further.

He *had* gone looking for her, he just hadn't been obvious about it. He'd attended quite a few parties, expecting to encounter her at one or more of them. But she was either attending different parties or she was too busy moving into her new house.

Then it occurred to him that she might be staying out of the public eye because she didn't want to answer any questions about them. Smart girl. It would be highly embarrassing to have to admit that her husband didn't want to be her husband. Of course, he couldn't really see her admitting to that a'tall. No, she was more likely to create a completely false scenario that would show him in a bad light.

But he'd heard no rumors to that effect, no rumors period re-

Raphael asked no more questions. He grabbed his coat back, forgot his hat, and was on his way to the Reid household within moments. There he was told where she'd gone and that she'd left two days ago! And that was when he panicked.

The trouble she could cause in his family could be everlasting—for him. And he didn't doubt for a minute that she'd gone to Norford Hall with the express purpose of turning his family against him. And she'd had two days to do so. She was once again the Ophelia he'd first met, the one he didn't like, the one capable of spreading false rumors and backing them up with lies, the one who didn't give a damn about anything other than her own selfish ends. She didn't care whom she hurt on the way to her goal, and her goal was to hurt him.

A few hours later he arrived at Norford Hall. The house was quiet at that time of night, most of the lights extinguished. The footman who manned the front door during the late hours was sleeping in a chair beside it and didn't wake when Raphael slipped inside and went up to his room to get some sleep before he faced Ophelia in the morning.

She was in his bed. He hadn't expected that they would put her in his room. He should have. She was his wife, after all.

He should leave and find another room for the night. Most of them were empty in this wing of the house. He was too tired after racing pell-mell for Norford to deal with her tonight. In the morning, when he was fresh, he would be clearheaded enough to force her to reveal what she was up to. But he didn't move to retrace his steps.

She was in his bed. That kept him riveted to the spot, standing next to the bed, staring down at her sleeping form.

Her hair was glossy white in the moonlight, spread across his pillows. She hadn't closed the drapery. It was a clear night, a bright moon, which is why he'd made such good time getting there. It was still late. She'd probably been asleep for several hours.

She was in his bed. And she was his wife. Wild horses couldn't have pulled him out of there.

Was she a deep sleeper? Would she even notice if he got into bed with her? He quickly stripped off his clothes and did just that. She didn't wake. She didn't move a speck. And he was tired. It had been a stressful day full of unpleasant surprises. He ought to get some sleep. She'd be sure to wake him when she found him there in the morning. That would be soon enough to deal with the raging shrew.

But just now the shrew wasn't present. And there was no way he was going to sleep with her soft, warm body only inches from his. Sex had tamed her anger before, or had that been a lie too, just another part of her ruse to trick him into believing he'd succeeded in changing her? There was one way to find out. . . .

Chapter Forty-nine

IT ONLY TOOK A MOMENT for Ophelia to realize why she felt so good. It only took another moment for her to decide that she wasn't about to deny Rafe the path he seemed intent on taking. She wasn't stupid. She wasn't going to refuse the exquisite pleasure he was capable of giving her, just because the anger he'd ignited in her wouldn't go away.

She knew instinctively that making love with him again wouldn't alleviate that anger, though. It might make her forget it briefly, but that would be all, because she'd been betrayed, maybe not in the typical sense, but that's what it felt like. A broken heart. She'd had all the symptoms of one and still did, which more or less answered the question she'd been avoiding. She *had* fallen in love with this man. And that's why making love with him again wasn't going to mend her broken heart. But it certainly was gratifying to know that he still couldn't resist her.

Her linen nightgown, which she typically raised up above her knees once she was under the covers, had been no hindrance to him and was now bunched up above her hips. He had been stroking the insides of her thighs and now slipped a finger inside her, just deep enough to set all her nerves tingling. The top of her gown, which had been nice and snug when she'd gone to sleep, was now wide open, giving him full access to her breasts. He was suckling one of them, drawing on it deeply, though gently.

She wasn't fighting the hot sensual feelings he was arousing in her, quite the opposite. She luxuriated in every sensation, struggling to keep her breath under control and her sighs of pleasure to herself. She wasn't pretending to still be asleep. She simply didn't want to talk to him, confront him with the many angry questions she knew she should ask him, or . . . distract him from what he was doing to her.

And she watched him. Seeing him take so much enjoyment from the simple act of sucking on her nipple was heady indeed. She gently ran her fingers through his hair, then stopped when she realized what she'd done. She hadn't meant to give him such an obvious clue that she was fully aware of what he was doing to her—and enjoying it. She'd just done it without thinking. It brought his eyes directly to hers.

Don't say a word, not a single word, his gaze seemed to warn her.

She knew that if she spoke, it wouldn't be to say anything nice. If he spoke, the sensual trance he'd lulled her into would be broken.

He leaned up on an elbow, continuing to gaze at her. It seemed like forever. It also seemed as if he was debating whether to say something.

She couldn't remain silent any longer. "You've deliberately avoided my bed. Why are you here now?" she demanded.

"The bed is mine," he replied softly. "And so is the woman in it. We may have a lot to talk about, but now isn't the time to talk."

He kissed her. And, oh, my, what a kiss it was, deep and sweet and intended to change her mind if she had any reservations about making love with him. She didn't have a single one. If the kiss hadn't been enough to sway her, his calling her "his woman" pulled on her heartstrings in a most persuasive way. She fully participated in his sensual exploration, drawing his tongue into her mouth, slipping her own into his to taste him more fully. She put her arms around his neck and held him tightly, to try to keep him there . . . forever.

And then she realized . . . his finger was still inside her. And it was no longer still. He was moving his finger deeper, steadily penetrating her, moving it in and out, changing tempo, exquisitely slow, then a few quick thrusts, then slow again. His knuckles, possibly his thumb, rubbed against the small sensitive bud at the apex of her thighs. She gasped and her body thrust upward in surprise. He continued stroking her that way, again and again, as she writhed on the sheets moaning in pleasure. And all the while he just kissed her harder.

The room had been quite comfortable with the fireplace burning low, just cool enough to make her want to snuggle under the blankets. Now it was far too warm. The cloth of her nightgown was irritating her skin at the few places the linen was still touching her body. Actually, her whole body seemed overly sensitized to the slightest touch!

It was him. She knew it was him, and her body's reaction to him. She wanted him so much! She'd thought she'd never again be able to hold him in her arms like this. She'd thought she'd never again experience the beauty of his lovemaking. And now that it was happening, her body seemed to want to race ahead to the climax and finally experience complete satisfaction, while she wanted to proceed slowly to savor every minute she could, and the two completely different urges just weren't compatible.

He had tossed the blankets off the bed and must have been feeling the heat as well. She ran her hands over his broad shoulders and back; he was very warm to her touch. His breathing was becoming labored as well. She found herself holding her own breath each time it felt as if she were approaching a climax, but then the unbearable pleasure would recede and she'd breathe again, only to have the sensations build back up again. Every one of her nerves was screaming for that release. If she'd had the strength, she'd probably push Rafe on his back and have her way with him.

The thought almost made her laugh. It relieved a little of the tension, but not enough to let her relax. But then as if he'd been reading her thoughts, he finally moved his hips between hers and entered her, in a deep, smooth thrust that took her over the edge.

"God, now this is really coming home," he murmured into her ear.

She exploded with pleasure almost instantly. And held on to him for dear life. And when the haze cleared a little from her mind, the tender feelings she had for him returned to her so abruptly, she was almost moved to tears.

Yes, she loved him. And hated him. And tomorrow would be soon enough to figure out what to do about it. Tonight, right now, he was carefully removing her nightgown to show her again what he'd mentioned to her once before—what it would be like to be in a bed with him, where he could devote the proper time to her and her pleasure.

Chapter Fifty

WHAT A COWARD SHE WAS turning out to be. Ophelia didn't sleep again that night, and unfortunately that led to a lot of deep introspection as she lay in bed next to Rafe. She shed a few silent tears and finally decided not to ruin such a beautiful night with the acrimony that would surely reappear in the morning. So before dawn, while her husband was still sound asleep, she snuck out of the bedroom, fully dressed for travel, and got Sadie and her coach brought around, without waking too many members of the household.

She left a note for Preston Locke, thanking him for his hospitality and asking him not to mention to his son what they had discussed, that if it did come to pass that she was carrying their baby, she wanted to be the one to tell him. She still didn't think she was with child. The few brief bouts of nausea she had experienced had all occurred when she'd been seething with anger, which was a perfectly good reason to be sick to her stomach.

She had only to mention to Sadie that Rafe had arrived for the maid not to ask or complain about their leaving while it was still dark. But after taking two steps out the door toward the waiting coach, she stopped and told Sadie, "I forgot something. I'll only be a moment," and she ran back into Norford Hall.

Rafe was still sleeping, of course, his head half on her pillow, one arm draped over her side of the bed as if he thought he were still holding her. She leaned over and kissed his brow. She couldn't wake him. All of her hurt would come spilling out: it was already spilling down her cheeks. But she wasn't going to leave him without a word. She jotted off another note in the dim light of the dying fire and left it with a footman downstairs before she joined Sadie in the coach.

Hoping to regain better control of her emotions, she caught up on her missed sleep, napping nearly the entire trip home.

She arrived in London just before noon, and in time to share lunch with her mother.

"That was a short trip," her mother said as she directed the staff to bring another plate for Ophelia. "We didn't expect you back so soon. Didn't it go well?"

"It went fine, Mama. The Lockes are very nice people. And Rafe's grandmother, the dowager duchess, is a charming old bird. The entire time I was there, she confused me with her granddaughter Amanda, whom she adores, so we got along splendidly."

"Then why didn't you stay longer?"

"Rafe showed up."

That simple statement said so much and didn't need any further explanation, at least not for Mary. "I was afraid that would happen. Our butler informed me that he came here looking for you. Mr. Nates wasn't aware that he shouldn't have mentioned your direction."

Ophelia shrugged, unaware of how dejected she looked. "It's all right. I got to meet a few of the Lockes under a congenial atmosphere before he showed up. I just didn't want to treat them to one of our verbal skirmishes. I'd as soon they don't know how easily I can still lose my temper—when I'm around him."

Mary abruptly suggested, "We should go shopping tomorrow, after you're rested from your journey. Take your mind off all this unpleasantness for a while."

Ophelia started to agree. She was open to anything that would give her thoughts some peace, however briefly. But then she caught the aroma of the poached fish being served for lunch and her stomach abruptly turned over nauseously. But she loved poached fish! And she wasn't the least bit angry at the moment!

"Let's go this afternoon," she quickly told her mother as she stood up and backed away from the plate that had been set in front of her. "I'm not tired and not hungry. I'll go change while you finish your lunch."

She didn't wait for Mary to agree. She ran out of the room, trying to get as far away as she could from the smell that was making her sick.

*   *   *

Raphael woke so refreshed, his body so relaxed, he was quite certain that had been the best night's sleep he'd had in months. Before he left the bed, he leaned over and smelled the empty pillow next to his and smiled that Ophelia's scent had been left behind. It hadn't been a dream. She wasn't in the room with him now, but her clothes were scattered here and there.

She couldn't still be angry with him. That was the first thing that occurred to him as he pulled himself out of bed. She couldn't make love with him like that and then turn around and still want to hurt him. Something had to have happened here, before he arrived, to expunge most of her anger.

He could probably thank his father for that. Preston had such a calming influence on friend and foe alike. If it could be said that someone had been born to be a diplomat, fingers would point at Preston Locke. He didn't argue his points, he got them across in a reasonable manner, and if he was proven wrong, he'd merely laugh about it and go on from there. The only exception was how he dealt with his siblings. Where his sisters were concerned, he enjoyed pulling their cords.

Raphael dressed quickly and went in search of his wife and his father, in that order. Considering the early hour, he checked the breakfast room first. Ophelia wasn't there, but Preston was.

"You still know how to work miracles, don't you?" Raphael, entering the room, said cheerfully to his father. "Took the steam right out of her, didn't you?"

"I'm not wearing a halo this week, and you look entirely too exuberant for this time of day. Sit down and explain yourself."

"I'm talking about Ophelia, of course." Raphael thanked the servant who added a few more platters of food to the table for him to pick from. "How did you manage to defuse her anger?"

Preston shook his head. "She didn't come here angry, so there was nothing to defuse."

"She didn't try to stir up trouble while she was here? Didn't dump all the blame at my door?"

"On the contrary, I found her to be quite charming, straightforward, and willing to accept responsibility if the errors were in her court. She even admitted that in anger she'd prodded you into marrying her, but my question is, why did you let her? You could have merely announced your engagement officially and married her properly within a reasonable time. You don't think she would have wanted a nice wedding with all her friends and family present? All of *your* friends and family present as well?"

Raphael flushed slightly at the topic, as well as his father's admonishing tone. He'd known he'd have to answer for excluding his entire family from his wedding. If it had been a joyful wedding, he'd really be feeling guilty, but it wasn't, and this embarrassment was bad enough.

"I'll tell you honestly, Father. If it didn't happen as it did, it would never have happened."

Preston raised a disapproving brow. "Despite the rumors? Are you actually saying you would have let her be thrown to the wolves?"

"Of course not. I could have defused all that. It was merely one bloody kiss that was seen!"

"It was much more than that. You were seen going off with her and you both didn't reappear for nearly a week."

"Visiting my family," Raphael corrected. "You were the one who pointed out to me when I was here before that her father even boasted about it."

"Yes, he boasted that you'd brought his daughter here specifically to Norford Hall. What I didn't mention was that I had a number of visitors that week who asked after you and were told you *weren't* here. It doesn't take much to add that up, Rafe. And we've already had this conversation more or less, so let me ask you this. If there had been no rumors, would you have stood by and let her marry someone else? And keep in mind, I've met her."

"Forget for a moment that she's the most beautiful woman you've ever come across. What if she were nothing but blackened ice inside, malicious, spiteful—"

"Are we talking about the same woman?"

Raphael sighed. "All right, to be honest, I was having a few regrets about turning her loose on London again. I'd grown fond of her during our brief time together, perhaps a little too fond of her. But I thought she had changed, that the shrew was gone for good. I might even have asked her to marry me—if I had continued to think that."

"I saw no evidence of this shrew."

"Because she's very good at keeping her temper and viper's tongue under wraps when she wants to. And she had me convinced, one hundred percent, that the shrew was gone. I really believed I'd helped her to change for the better. But she admitted it was all a ruse, just a pretense so I'd send her back to London sooner."

"Are you sure about that?"

"What do you mean?"

"Maybe it wasn't a lie that she'd changed. Maybe the lie is that she didn't."

Chapter Fifty-one

CHARMING? STRAIGHTFORWARD? WILLING TO ACCEPT responsibility for her actions? That sounded like the new Ophelia, not the old one whom Raphael believed he had been dealing with ever since she'd found out about that damn bet. Was he the only one who got to see the shrew?

He wasn't going to think about it anymore. He was simply going to confront her. Either way, she'd fooled him completely. He was tired of being fooled. But he had to return to London to do that.

She'd left Norford Hall before he even woke, snuck off was how it appeared, since she didn't even pack her clothes. Doing so would probably have woken him, and obviously she didn't want to discuss what had happened between them last night. Or maybe she did. . . .

The footman handed him Ophelia's note just as he was leaving. It was unexpected and gave him a little hope: *That wasn't a homecoming, that was merely a truce. If you want a real homecom-*

ing, you need to make me understand why you tampered with my life on a whim.

Hadn't she listened to anything he'd said? Or had she simply been too angry to *hear* him? They would discuss it, he vowed to himself, that and a lot more, just as soon as he got back to town.

Arriving back in London, he rode straight to her house, missing her by just thirty minutes. She'd gone shopping with her mother on Bond Street, he was informed. No, they didn't say which shops they were going to visit. He ought to just wait till she returned home. It was highly doubtful he could find her on that crowded street in the middle of the day, when it would be the most congested. He'd have to check every bloody shop!

He rode that way anyway.

*   *   *

Ophelia had never felt so distracted. She wasn't listening to a word her mother was saying as Mary pulled her along from one shop to another. When she actually had to make a decision about buying something, she managed to utter a yes or a no, but she had no idea about what.

She was going to have a baby. She could no longer deny it, not after one of her favorite foods, poached fish, had made her nauseous the entire time she could smell it. As soon as she'd gotten away from that aroma, she was fine!

She was going to have a baby. One single fall from grace and such a miraculous result. A baby. And how odd that the knowledge filled her with joy. How silly she'd been to try to deny it. And how amazing that maternal instincts were already welling up in her. This baby would be raised right. She knew how *not* to raise a child, so it would be a simple matter for her to do it right. This child would be loved and nourished and protected. She would not give in on any decisions about her baby if she disagreed with them. She loved her mother, but she knew Mary had buckled under too many times to Sherman's will. Ophelia wouldn't do that. She'd fight tooth and nail.

She supposed she ought to tell Rafe, but she was in no hurry to do so. In due time. She wanted to savor the knowledge by herself for a while. He had chosen not to live with her, so he didn't warrant the right to know immediately. He could miss the birth of his baby as far as she was concerned—no, that was her anger talking. She was going to have to get rid of that anger before she gave birth. There would be no raised voices around *her* baby.

"Pheli? Pheli, are you all right?"

Ophelia brought her attention back to the present and saw that her mother had just entered a shop that had numerous bolts of lace crowded into its small display window box. She turned around to see who'd spoken to her and was completely surprised to find Mavis Newbolt standing next to her on the busy walkway, her hands stuffed in a fur muff. Her expression was concerned. Mavis? Her one and only enemy concerned about her? Not likely.

What had Mavis said? Oh, yes. "I'm fine," Ophelia answered cautiously in a neutral tone. She hadn't seen Mavis since the parties at Summers Glade, and the two altercations they'd had there hadn't been the least bit pleasant. "Why do you ask?"

Mavis shrugged one shoulder. "You looked like you were in another world."

"Did I? I must have let my thoughts distract me for a moment."

"Well, my coach was driving past and I saw you. I had to stop."

Ophelia was immediately filled with dread. They weren't going to have yet another fight, were they? "Why?" she asked pointedly.

Oddly enough, Mavis suddenly appeared uncomfortable. "I've been meaning to come by and visit you for several days now. Would you like to go for a ride where we can talk? My coach is just across the street."

"Talk? What more can we say to each other that hasn't already been said?"

Mavis stepped aside for a couple passing arm in arm. The walkway was nearly as crowded with pedestrians as the street was crowded with carriages, coaches, and wagons.

"I wanted to congratulate you on your marriage," Mavis said.

"Thank you."

"And wish you—"

"Don't," Ophelia cut in sharply, and instantly regretted her tone.

She quickly controlled her rising anger. She was aware that she *could* control it and felt a bolster of pride in doing so. Mavis was the one person, aside from her father, who was guaranteed to bring out the worst in her, but she was managing to keep the bitterness at bay too.

She finished in a much calmer tone, "No more hurtful remarks."

"I wasn't going to—"

"Please, Mavis, I don't want to fight anymore."

"I don't either."

Ophelia just stared at her ex-friend doubtfully. There was no way that she could believe that statement. Mavis hadn't got her revenge after all, at least not as much as she'd been hoping for. All she'd done at Summers Glade was embarrass Ophelia, at least that's what she thought. Mavis didn't know how much she'd hurt her, or that she'd made her cry because of it. And she'd never know.

"I can see by your expression that you don't believe me, and I can hardly blame you at this point." Mavis actually sounded, *and* looked, regretful. "All this hate I've had for you and it's been so misdirected. I thought you had lied about Lawrence. I knew you lied all the time back then. It was just about minor things, so it never bothered me when we were friends. I just ignored it— until you tried to convince me Lawrence was a bastard just using me to get to you. I really didn't believe you, you know, not even a little. And that's why I hated you so much. And it's made me so miserable all this time, because I didn't really *want* to hate you, I just couldn't help myself."

Mavis's voice had turned so plaintive, Ophelia could feel a lump rising in her own throat. "Why are we rehashing this again, Mavis?"

"I saw Lawrence just recently. The heiress he married has left him. I'd already heard that, but it had been so long since I'd seen him. He's grown fat, and dissipated, and apparently he's a drunkard now too. He was foxed when I ran into him. He didn't even recognize me. When I reminded him who I was, he laughed."

"I'm sorry," Ophelia said, but her old friend appeared not to hear her.

"Do you know what he said to me? He said, 'Ah, the gullible little chit who thought I'd marry her? Have you smartened up, love?' "

Mavis started to cry. Ophelia, choked, put out a hand, but Mavis backed away from her. "You warned me, and instead of thanking you, I hated you. Oh, God, I'm so sorry! I just wanted you to know that!" Mavis cried before she rushed across the street to her waiting coach.

Ophelia tried to stop her, called her name, but Mavis didn't hear her. She thought about running after her, but there was too much traffic and one coach seemed a bit out of control, veering too close to the other vehicles. She'd go see Mavis tomorrow and assure her that she didn't hold grudges anymore—except where her husband was concerned. She and Mavis might even be able to become friends again!

But she still watched Mavis, wanting to make sure she reached the other side of the street safely. The girl wasn't exactly paying attention, with her head lowered to hide her tears. And then Ophelia frowned. That out-of-control vehicle was heading straight toward Mavis!

She bolted out into the street, didn't even give it another thought. She'd never run so fast. She made it around a slow-moving wagon, dodged a man on a horse. With just a little luck, she'd reach Mavis to yank her back out of the way. But the driver of the runaway coach did have a little control of his wildly frightened horses. He was fighting madly with the reins and screaming at people to get out of the way, and actually slowing down a little. With barely any time left, he veered his horses off to the side to avoid Mavis—and ran right into Ophelia.

It would have been a blessing if she'd been knocked out of the way, but she wasn't. She crumpled beneath the horses. Pain was instant and everywhere, her chest, her shoulder, her face, so much pain that within seconds she could no longer tell where it was coming from. Then the light was blurring from her eyes. And then there was none.

Chapter Fifty-two

R APHAEL VAGUELY TOOK NOTE OF the crowd of people in the street who were surrounding a large coach, which usually indicated an accident. He rode past it.

Accidents happened all too often in London, and not just on busy streets like this one. If no one had been there, he would have stopped to help, but too many people were present and one more wouldn't help, would more likely just add to the confusion.

He was searching the walkways, though, looking for a familiar blond head, hoping he could find Ophelia between her visits to shops, so he wouldn't actually have to enter any. He was hailed by several acquaintances in passing. He merely nodded distractedly and continued on. One chap—Lord Thistle, was it?—came at him on horseback from the opposite direction and blocked his way for a moment.

"Been meaning to look you up, Locke," Thistle said as he yanked his horse about out of the way. "Gad, man, I've been feeling so guilty about this. When I saw you kissing Lady O in her dining room, I was so surprised I didn't even think to keep it to m'self. I hope you weren't forced to marry her because of my loose tongue. Course I can't think of any man who would mind being forced to marry her. But—"

"It's all right," Raphael interrupted the long-winded fellow and assured him by rote, "Think nothing of it."

Raphael rode on quickly, before he could be stopped again. So she'd lied? His father had been right. It was as he'd *first* thought, the rumors weren't her doing at all. She'd merely claimed responsibility so she could slap him in the face with it?

He was even more eager to find her now. Reaching the end of the street with no luck, he headed back down it for another pass. Nearing the accident again, which had attracted even more curious onlookers, it finally dawned on him that his wife might be in that crowd, just as curious as everyone else was to see what had happened. He pulled his horse to the side out of the way of the traffic, which was still moving slowly around the accident, so he could peruse the crowd more thoroughly.

He didn't see Ophelia, but his eyes passed over and then came abruptly back to Mavis Newbolt, who was standing at the center of the crowd, crying her eyes out. He frowned, seeing that, but then the most horrible dread filled him. It was too coincidental that Mavis would be there, crying, when Ophelia was in the vicinity.

He leapt off his horse, pushed his way through to the center of the crowd. And saw the blond head he'd been searching for, on the ground, bloodied.

"What'd you do?" he shouted at Mavis. "Push her in front of this coach?"

The girl seemed to be in shock. All she said was "She was try-ing to save me."

He barely heard her. He was already on his knees next to Ophelia. He was terrified to touch her. She looked so broken lying there, unmoving, barely breathing. One horseshoe, proba-bly with a loose nail, had ripped through her coat and the dress under it. Blood was soaked around the tear and elsewhere. He couldn't tell if it was from the same wound or if there were more along her body, but there was no doubt that she hadn't just taken a fall, she'd actually been trampled. More than one dirty hoof-print was on her coat.

The horses that had done this had been moved back only several feet. They were still maddened, fighting their traces, stamping at the ground. A man, probably the driver of the coach, was standing in front of them, arms spread, trying to keep them back.

He was saying to anyone who would listen, "I tried to stop them. Some boy set off a popper, a child's prank, but they got spooked good. But I tried to stop them!"

"Don't touch 'er, gov," someone else said at Raphael's back.

"There's 'elp coming, be 'ere any minute."

"Someone went to fetch a doctor. Said they know one that lives on the next street over."

"I seen it happen, both them girls running across the street right in front of that runaway coach. It's lucky it is that it didn't take them both down."

"I seen it happen too. Saw her and couldn't take my eyes off her. Like an angel, she looked. And then she just disappeared under those horses. Shoot 'em, I say. You can't never trust a skit-tish horse."

"Such a pity, pretty girl like that."

The voices came from all around him now, not talking to him, just talking about what they'd witnessed. But it was like a roar in his ears. He couldn't just leave her lying there. He couldn't.

Someone tried to stop him from picking her up in his arms. "She's my wife!" he growled, and they left him alone. He didn't know tears were running down his cheeks. He didn't know he looked like a madman.

"God, Phelia, don't you die on me!" he kept repeating, like a mantra, praying she'd hear him somehow.

"I have a coach. I have a coach! Please, Locke, you can't carry her on your horse!"

It was Mavis shouting at him and yanking at his jacket. He was at a dead stop, standing in front of his horse, having come to the horrible realization that he couldn't get on it and still hold Ophelia gently.

"Lord Locke?"

He finally glanced down at Mavis. "Where?"

"Follow me. It's not far."

The crowd hadn't dispersed yet. They actually held back the traffic on the street for him, so he could cross it with Ophelia in his arms. Mavis didn't get into the coach with him when they reached it, she was afraid to after the way he'd looked at her. But she shouted up the address for her driver. The Reid house. He would have preferred to take her to his own house.

"I'll bring your horse, and a doctor!" he thought he heard Mavis shouting as the coach drove away.

It was the longest ride of his life, even though it only took a few minutes with the driver moving the coach quickly but carefully through the congested streets. He couldn't take his eyes off

Ophelia's bloodied face. One cheek was swollen terribly. He couldn't see through the blood where the cut was, but with that much blood, it would probably have to be stitched and would leave a scar. That was the least of his concerns. At the moment, he wasn't even sure if she would live.

Chapter Fifty-three

THE PAIN WAS ALL-CONSUMING. OPHELIA floated in and out of it. It seemed endless. She had no way of knowing how much time was passing. And she couldn't seem to fight her way up to real consciousness. Each time she tried, she could hear voices, she just wasn't sure if she was replying to them with other than gibberish, or if it was all just part of the ongoing nightmare she was mired in. But the more she tried to concentrate, the more she hurt, so she never tried for long.

"Don't you dare give up, Phelia. Don't even think about dying to avoid me. I won't allow it. Wake up so I can tell you!"

She knew that voice well. He couldn't tell she was awake? Why wouldn't her eyes open so she could see him? Was she really in danger of dying?

Voices continued to drift in and out of her head, but it hurt so bad to try to concentrate on them, she gave up. Would she remember them when she did wake up? Why couldn't she wake up?

"The wounds will heal but the scars will be permanent. I'm sorry."

She didn't know that voice. What scars? And why was a woman crying? The sound faded away.

"The doctor has suggested that you try to sleep through most of the pain. This will help, dear."

She knew that voice. Her mother. And the warm liquid running down her throat was beginning to taste familiar. She was being drugged? No wonder she couldn't seem to wake fully or get any words out. And once again, she passed into blissful oblivion.

It hurt when the bandages were changed. The side of her head, her cheek, her shoulder. It hurt enough to make her run away from it to the deep, dark nothingness again, so she never stayed conscious long enough to know just how many bandages were spread across her body. Her head hurt the worst. The dull throbbing never stopped. It continued even in her dreams, an endless reminder that something was dreadfully wrong with her. Did she really want to wake up to find out what that was?

"Stop crying. Dammit, Mary, you're not helping with those tears. What's a little scar or two. It's not the bloody end of the world."

She knew that voice too and wished it would go away. She didn't mind her mother's soft sobs. It was actually a soothing sound. She couldn't manage any tears herself. Her mother was crying for her. She did mind her father's grating voice though.

"Go away."

Did she manage to say it aloud, or did she only think it? But she went away instead, back to her blissful nothingness that held the pain at bay.

The one time she did get her eyes open, it was to see she was in her own room. Her father was sitting in a chair by her bed. He was holding her hand to his cheek. His tears were wetting her fingers.

"Why are you crying?" she asked him. "Did I die?"

He glanced at her immediately, so she must have gotten the words out this time. His expression filled with delight. She didn't think she'd ever seen Sherman Reid look happy like that before.

"No, angel, you're going to be—"

Angel? An endearment from him? "Never mind," she cut in. "I must be dreaming." And she promptly drifted off again.

But her brief spans of consciousness started to get longer after that. The throbbing pain wasn't continuous anymore, either. She actually had moments where she felt no pain—as long as she didn't try to move.

And then she woke one morning and stayed awake. Sadie was flitting about the room as she usually did, adding wood to the fireplace, dusting the tables, the vanity, the . . .

Oh, God, they'd put a cover over her vanity mirror. The wound on her face was so grotesque? They were afraid for her to see it? In horror, she brought her hands to her face, but all she could feel was the cloth bandages. They seemed to be wrapped tightly around her entire head and across her cheeks and chin.

She was afraid to tear the bandages off, afraid she'd damage herself even more by doing so. Unable to feel them for herself, she started to ask Sadie how bad the scars were, but the words lodged in her throat. She was afraid to find out. And the tears started. She closed her eyes, hoping Sadie would leave without noticing.

The irony was incredible. All her life she'd hated the face she was born with, and now that it was deformed, all she could do was cry about it.

And she cried, for hours. She cried herself dry. By the time Sadie returned around noon, she was just lying there staring at the ceiling. She wasn't exactly resigned to her deformity, but she knew there was nothing she could do about it. She'd get used to it. Somehow. She hated self-pity, especially her own.

"Thank God you're awake and can eat now," Sadie said when she came near enough to see that her eyes were open. "This broth we've been trickling down your throat isn't enough to feed a rabbit! You were getting close to wasting away to nothing!"

Sadie said that too cheerfully for it to be true. "How long has it been?"

"Nigh a week now."

"That long? Really?"

"You obviously needed the rest, so don't be fretting that. How is your head?"

"Which part of it?" Ophelia asked drily. "It's been one big throb."

"You took a bad bump on the side of your head. That wound bled the most. The doctor had the nerve to suggest you might not wake up from it. Your papa told him to get the hell out and sent for a different doctor."

"He did?"

"Oh, yes. He was furious with the fellow. The new chap was more optimistic and rightly so. Look at you! Now that you're awake, you're going to be just fine. And I'll be taking this broth back to the kitchen for something more substantial for you!"

"Poached fish," Ophelia said, suddenly filled with the most horrible dread.

"Poached fish it will be," Sadie said, still sounding overly cheerful. "Even if I have to run to market myself to fetch a fresh one."

Sadie didn't return anytime soon. She must actually have gone to market. But before she left, she'd let the household know that Ophelia was awake. Her father was the next to arrive, the one person who *could* get her mind off the possibility that she'd lost her baby.

She wasn't his pretty bauble anymore, was she? Had she really woken during her nightmare to see him crying? If so, that was no doubt why.

"You're finally coming out of it?" he asked. "I had to see for myself before I go wake your mother to give her the good news. She's been sitting up with you most every night, so she's still abed."

"Did I really need so much bandaging about my head?" she asked as he pulled up the chair next to her bed and sat down.

"Well, yes, but it was twofold. Some of it was to hold down the cold compresses your mother insisted on for your cheek, which was quite swollen. But most of it is to keep the bandage on tight for that lump on your head. The alternative would have been to stitch your cut there and shave your hair back for it, and your mother had a fit about you losing even one strand of hair. So you were just bandaged up more tightly around that area, and as it happens, the cut did seal well enough without stitches. Those bandages can probably be removed when the doctor comes round later today."

"How many stitches did I receive—elsewhere?"

He sighed. "A few."

It was a lie. He should practice not blushing when he lies, she thought. And actually, she didn't really want to know. She'd see for herself eventually—when she got up the nerve to pull that cover off her vanity mirror.

He still seemed quite uncomfortable as he continued, "I never doubted for a minute that you would recover, but—it could have been much worse, and coming close to losing you like that has given me some insight that I'm not proud of. I am not a demonstrative man. I'm set in my ways, I'm gruff, I'm—"

She cut in, "You're not telling me anything I don't already know, Papa, but why are you mentioning it?"

"It occurred to me that, well, that is to say . . . bloody hell," he ended in frustration.

"What? Just say it."

He sighed again. He even took her hand in his and held it lightly, staring down at it. "You and I fought so much over the years, it became a habit. And once habits form, we lose sight of other things. It occurred to me that you might not think that I love you. There, I've said it. I do love you, you know."

He glanced up to see her reaction. She stared at him incredulously. She didn't really know what to say or if she could even say anything with the lump that was rising in her throat. Was that moisture gathering in her eyes?

"I'm going to tell you something that your mother doesn't even know," he continued. "I didn't have an easy childhood. The schools I was sent to were the best, filled with the elite upper crust. I could have wished they weren't. Boys can be cruel. It was rubbed in my face constantly that I wasn't in their league. Can you believe that? An earl's son, not in their league."

He appeared to be looking back, caught up in old, unpleasant memories. Amazingly, she vaguely understood why he was telling her this.

"You weren't on the street looking in, Papa. Your title has always been as good as any."

"I know. I even came to suspect it was mere jealousy, because my family was quite rich, while many of those boys with loftier titles weren't. But that made no difference to the driving goal I had to prove that I was as good as they were, to fit in, as it were. And that drive never left me, even when I had no way to accomplish that goal—until you were born, and you grew prettier and prettier every year. *You* were my proof. So, yes, I showed you off—too much. The amazement you caused, the claps on the back, the congratulations, I couldn't get enough of it. It made up for all those years that I felt inferior. But I realize now how selfish it was of me, that I pushed you into social situations you weren't ready for. I was just so damn proud of you, Pheli."

"You weren't proud of me, Papa," she said in a small voice. "You were proud of yourself for siring me. There is no comparison of the two."

He bowed his head. "You're right. It took almost losing you for me to open my eyes and see just how many regrets I really have where you're concerned. Your mother always tried to tell me. It was the only time she and I ever argued. I just never listened. I was too caught up in that misplaced pride. I wish I could do it all over. I know I can't. But it's not too late to correct my most recent blunder."

"What do you mean?"

"I know you aren't happy with this marriage I forced on you."

"You didn't force that, Papa."

"Of course I did. I ordered you to marry Locke. I made sure everyone expected it to happen."

She gave him a sad smile. "When did I ever follow your orders without scheming to do just the opposite? It was my temper that pushed Rafe into dragging us to the altar. It was nothing you did."

He cleared his throat with a slightly raised brow. "Be that as it may, you don't need to remain in this marriage. Your husband hasn't exactly behaved as a husband should, so I don't believe you'll have any difficulty in getting it annulled with my help."

She was amazed. "You'd give up a dukedom in the family without a fight?"

"Pheli, I've come to the realization that I want *you* to be happy. The title wasn't just for me, you know. Your mother and I do talk about you without arguing occasionally. I know that you aspired to be like her but on a higher level, that you hoped to be the grandest hostess in all of London. The loftier title would have helped you in that goal."

She sighed. How little importance that held for her now. *Right* now, all she wanted was for poached fish to still make her nauseous.

She could feel those tears coming on again and fought to keep them back. "You're probably right. Rafe and I just weren't meant to be. He won't fight an annulment. But—" She started to say she wasn't sure if one was possible now. That would tell her father that she and Rafe had been intimate, and she'd rather not do that when she would know soon enough whether she was still with child. In fact, if she'd miscarried, the doctor might already have told her parents and they were just protecting her from the sad truth.

She sighed, adding, "Thank you for making the offer. Let me think about it before we decide."

"Of course. Recover first. When you're feeling up to scratch will be soon enough to give it some thought."

He hugged her before he left. A real hug. Gently, afraid she might break, but a *real* hug.

She cried the moment the door closed behind him. After all these years, to feel reconciled with her father, to feel as if she finally had a father, a real one, one who cared. That was going to take some getting used to.

But then the poached fish arrived and she cried much, much harder because she didn't feel nauseous. There really would be nothing to prevent her from putting Rafe out of her life with an annulment. Oh, God, the scars she would have to live with were nothing in comparison to losing her baby—and Rafe with it.

Chapter Fifty-four

"Only a little dented," the doctor said as he held Ophelia's chin and studied her face with all the bandages removed from it. Her immediate blanch had him quickly amending, "Good God, girl, I was joking." Then he sighed. "My wife nags me constantly about my bedside manner. I should listen to her. You're going to be just fine. The scars will fade. Before you know it, you won't even notice them."

He was being kind. He was a nice man. They should have found him sooner to serve as their family doctor, not that anyone in the family got sick very often. And having upset her, he said they should wait a few more days before they removed the bandages from the rest of her body.

Mary, who was standing on the other side of her bed, assured her, "The doctor is right, you know. We were so worried about that crushed cheekbone, but it's such a little imperfection, barely noticeable. When I think how much worse it could have been . . . but goodness, your dimples are deeper!"

Her mother wasn't helping. Dimples didn't sit at the top of a cheekbone. "Adds character if you ask me," Sadie remarked from the foot of the bed. "You're still the most beautiful girl I've ever seen, so don't give it another thought, dear."

They continued to try to cheer her up. But nothing could. Her perfect face was no longer perfect.

She left her bed to dress as soon as Mary escorted the doctor out of the room. "He didn't say you could get up and gallivant about," Sadie objected.

"He didn't say I couldn't either. But I'm not leaving the room, I'm just leaving the damned bed. A robe will do."

Her wounds didn't hurt as long as she didn't stretch the skin around them. The pain was inside her now, and all she'd been doing in that bed was crying. She'd had enough of that.

Sadie left her alone with a few more admonishments to continue resting. She stood for a long while in front of her fireplace, just staring at the fire. The bed really had nothing to do with her tears. She could still feel them just below the surface, ready to well up on her if she even got close to thinking about the things that were tearing at her heart. So she tried not to think of anything. She really tried . . .

"Got tired of lazing about in bed, did you?"

She swung about—and winced. She couldn't move quickly like that yet. Rafe stood in her open doorway, leaning against the frame, his hands in his pockets. Her eyes devoured him. God, it was good to see him. But then she remembered her face and quickly turned back toward the fire. And winced again.

"Who let you in?"

"The chap who usually opens the door." He sounded too jaunty for her present mood.

"Why are you here? I don't want to fight with you anymore. Go away."

"We're not fighting. And I'm not leaving." He shut the door behind him, loudly, to reinforce that statement.

She didn't want to deal with him yet. She could feel a panic coming on. If she cried in front of him, she'd never forgive herself. And she couldn't bear for him to see her disfigured face.

"What are you *doing* here?" she repeated, her tone rising.

"Where else would I be but at my wife's bedside in her hour of need."

"What rubbish."

"No, really. I've been here quite often, you know. Every day actually. Your father was quite rude not to offer me a room, I spent so much time here."

She didn't believe a word of it. And the panic was getting worse. She kept her face averted from him. If she detected even a little pity . . .

She couldn't face him without knowing what he would see when he looked at her. She went over to her vanity and yanked the cover off the mirror, then stared in surprise. The mirror wasn't there, just the empty frame that had held it. The dent on her face was that bad then? Enough to remove the mirror from her room?

"I was in a rage because I couldn't do anything to help you," Rafe said from across the room. "I broke your bloody mirror. Sorry. I just didn't want you to catch sight of yourself looking like a mummy, they had you so wrapped up. The sight frightened me enough, I knew it would surely terrify you."

She could hear the smile in his voice. Making a joke about her condition? That was so unkind.

Then softly, right behind her: "Does it still hurt?"

God, yes, it hurt, deep inside it hurt, and all she wanted to do was turn into his arms and cry her heart out. But she couldn't do that. He might be her husband, but he wasn't hers. She claimed no part of his heart as he did hers. But he wasn't going to know. She wasn't going to saddle him with a deformed wife. Her father had given her the means to see to that. And she should make it easy for him to accept that and be glad of such an easy solution. She could do that by continuing the charade.

"I'll be fine. You probably feel this is just desserts, the ice queen brought down to earth. But don't think for a moment that I won't overcome this."

"What are you talking about?"

"My deformed face!"

He suddenly grabbed her arm, pulled her out of her room and down the corridor, where he stopped to poke his head into every room he passed until he found a mirror. And he shoved her in front of it. She closed her eyes. She couldn't bear it.

But he was persistent. "You see? The top layer of skin was scraped off your cheek a bit on top of the bruise, but you lose that much skin yourself after a few face scrubbings. The redness will be gone in another week, the bruise probably before that. And I have a feeling the little dent that will be left behind is going to enhance your beauty. Leave it to you to figure out a way to make yourself even more pretty."

The teasing in his tone . . . her eyes flew open to stare at her face. He wasn't lying. There was a red patch there, which alarmed her at first glance, but it wasn't even deep enough to form a scab. An ugly bruise still covered most of her cheek. And under it all, high on her cheekbone, was an indentation. She leaned closer to the mirror to inspect the damage. It was an obvious imperfection, she acknowledged as she swallowed back tears, but it wasn't nearly as deep as she'd feared. People would notice it, but it was a small price to pay for coming away from that accident alive.

"Scars were mentioned," she said. "Where are they?"

"You didn't see for yourself, even without a mirror?"

"No, I don't make a habit of looking at my naked body."

"You should. It's absolutely gorgeous."

She turned about to face him. "That isn't funny."

He cupped her face in his hands. "Phelia, I was here when you were sewn up. You'll have a small scar on your shoulder, another on your side, and one on your hip, all of which will fade in time. By the grace of God, not a single bone was broken, just a severe amount of bruises that are almost gone. The only wound that worried us was the one to your head, but that's mending as well, I'm told."

It took her a moment to assimilate it all. Half of her tears had been for nothing? But not the other half.

She pushed away from him and headed back to her room. He followed her. He even closed the door again. Why didn't he go away? She should tell him about the annulment. *That* would send him away—happy.

She tried to formulate the words in her mind, but he was too much of a distraction. Gazing at her tenderly. Oh, God!

"It wasn't really a bet that I accepted, it was the challenge," he began.

"Don't!"

"You're going to hear this if I have to tie you down. Duncan was positive you'd never change. I disagreed with that notion. Anyone can change, even you, was my contention. And you did. Beautifully. And since you obviously weren't a very happy woman—happy women don't stir up trouble everywhere they go—I wanted to change that too. I didn't collect on that wager. Helping you was a sincere effort to *help* you."

"Your motives were a lie!"

"No, they weren't, I just failed to mention what started them."

"Ah, yes, you're good at failing to mention something and thinking that isn't lying, aren't you?"

"I could say the same thing about you. Or are you going to still try and maintain you started those rumors about us, when I know now that you didn't."

"I would have!"

He laughed. "No, you wouldn't have, Phelia. Give it up. You know you're not that woman anymore. And you should be grateful for that bet, not mad about it. It helped us to find each other."

She went very still. Was he implying what it sounded like? It couldn't be, and yet, the look in his eyes, filled with such warmth, confirmed it.

Her breathless silence gave him the opportunity to pull her close to him. "There's something else I failed to mention that I should have, long before now."

She was almost afraid to ask. "What?"

"I love you," he said with poignant tenderness. "I love every part of you. I'm even fond of your temper, so don't feel you have to hide that from me—all the time. I love how you look. I love how you feel. I love how you've found the courage to be you."

Telling her every single thing she wanted to hear. God, she wasn't still dreaming, was she? Making this up in her mind because it's what she'd wanted so badly?

"You didn't want to marry. I forced your hand with my damn temper."

He was shaking his head at her. "Do you really think you could goad me into something like that if I didn't want to marry you?"

"Then why did you bring me back to my parents' home that night?"

"Because I *was* angry. You know how to pull my strings very well."

He was smiling as he said it. She only blushed a little.

"That's why you wasted money on a home for me? It was just your anger?"

"And yours. It seemed like a good, temporary measure. But buying property is never a waste. It's actually a large house, bigger than mine. And it has a ballroom."

He remembered her old goal? That was so sweet, but those old goals seemed so trivial now when she was filled with such joy. She needed nothing other than his love to complete her.

"Mainly," he continued, "it was because I know how much you wanted to be out from under your father's thumb, and since you weren't ready to live with me yet—"

"I get the idea," she cut in softly.

"Do you? Are you sure we don't have anything else to fight about?"

She grinned. "I don't think so."

"Then I'm taking you home, where I should have taken you to begin with. My home, where you belong."

Epilogue

"Your first ball can't be too grand. If you're going to be the premier hostess every Season, you don't want to start at the top because how will you be able to work your way up from there? You'd be leaving yourself no room for improvement."

Ophelia glanced at her husband. They were snuggled on a sofa, his arm around her shoulders, she curled against his side. He was such an affectionate man. He couldn't be near her without touching her somewhere or kissing her or just hugging her. She loved that about him, that and, well, she didn't think there was anything she *didn't* love about this man.

"A ball, eh?" she asked.

"One per Season. I draw the line at more'n that."

"I hate to disappoint you, love, but I think I'm going to be too busy raising our daughter to even think about giving balls for a while."

"She is a handful, isn't she?"

The golden-haired child was sitting on a fluffy blanket on the floor in front of them, examining the toys around her, unable to make up her mind which one to pounce on. She'd discovered how to crawl only a few weeks ago and quite excelled at it already, and, oh, my, it was amazing that she was sitting still for even a few minutes.

Ophelia hadn't lost her child as she'd thought. Her relief and joy, when that nasty nausea returned and lasted for several bloody months, had been tremendous. The trauma of the accident had merely given her a brief reprieve from it.

Rafe had been delighted when she'd told him. He didn't want too many children. Just a handful, he'd told her! But she was in complete agreement. Having borne her first, and being in awe of this child, she was quite ready for more.

They had settled down in London and had moved into the bigger house that Rafe had bought for Ophelia. Slowly, she had redecorated it. She entertained, but not often. There had been one grand party though, to belatedly celebrate their marriage. It had been Rafe's idea, and he'd asked her mother to arrange it. Even Mavis had been invited, but then it hadn't taken long for the two old friends to become close again—closer than ever. Jealousies had no place in Ophelia's life now.

Rafe kissed the top of her brow, then her imperfect cheek. She moved a little so he could reach her lips. He didn't need more of an invitation than that. It was a tender kiss, filled with all the love they shared. If they had been in any other room in the house, that kiss would quite quickly have progressed to something else. But not in the nursery!

The squeal drew their eyes back to their daughter, who was crawling toward them for her share of attention, a big grin on her cherubic face. She wasn't going to be the most beautiful girl ever to grace a London Season. Oh, no. She was going to be the most beautiful girl in the world, the smartest girl in the world, and the sweetest girl in the world. Her doting parents had no doubt.